I0730730

Tinsel TEMPTATION

MELODY TYDEN

Chapter One

CHRISTMAS ON THE FARM

~Olivia~

The day I'd been waiting for had finally arrived. As my roommate came bounding into our shared dorm room with a Santa hat on her head, I knew what she was going to say before the words were out of her mouth.

"Liv, your hot dad is here!"

Alright, I didn't expect her to say *exactly* that. "Please, Tessa, I just ate. I don't want to think about my dad like that."

Her lips pressed into a pretend pout as she flopped down on my bed despite her bed being only six feet away. "You can ignore the facts if you want to, but I swear he's going to be mobbed by half the dorm if you don't get down there soon. The sharks with daddy issues are already circling."

Luckily, I'd been packed for hours already. I'd been counting down to that day for months, ever since my mom told me we were going to spend Christmas with the Stamers up at Aunt Isabel's farm.

Technically, Isabel wasn't my aunt, but 'my dad's best friend's sister' sounded more complicated than it needed to be. Basically, my dad, Jackson, was best friends with the man I called Uncle Cole, while their two wives - my mom, Holly, and Cole's wife, Gemma - were also best friends. Because they were all so close, our two families had grown up together. Gemma and Cole also had two kids close in age to my sister and I. In fact, my sister, Noelle, had been born on the very same day as Eve Stamer, and they had always been best friends too.

The prospect of spending time with all of them excited me, but one person in particular stood out as the one I *really* couldn't wait to see. The one who made my stomach flutter whenever he crossed my mind: Noah Stamer.

Two and a half years older than me, Noah was absolutely perfect in my eyes, and I'd been in love with him for as long as I could remember. From the first moment I realized that I could pick the person I got to marry, I wanted to pick Noah.

It took a little while longer for me to realize that he got to have some say in the matter too.

We were very close as kids; not quite siblings, but closer than friends. Even as we got older, we still had fun together, but I suspected that deep down, he still saw me as the little girl who used to chase after him and force him to play with me and my dolls. Meanwhile, I'd begun to think about him in very different ways.

That distance between us only got worse when he went to college. The few things we had in common seemed to disappear as he got a whole new set of friends and new interests. When he came home to visit, I would try to talk to him, but everything I had to say sounded childish, even to me. I didn't know how to connect with him anymore, and when I suggested that we keep in touch by text, he blew me off. He did it nicely, to be fair, but it stung all the same.

For two years, I'd suffered, but that year, things were different. Having started at college too, halfway through my first year, I had my own stories about campus parties and midterms and everything else that made up college life. Finally, we were on a level playing field again and I couldn't wait to hang out with him that Christmas. It would be the first time we'd seen each other since the summer, and I simply knew that the time had come for us to make a real connection.

Whether he realized it yet or not, Noah was finally going to notice me.

Giving Tessa a big hug and wishing her a merry Christmas, I ran down the stairs to where my dad waited. Tessa had been exaggerating a little bit about the girls circling, but not by much. Quite a few kept glancing over at him, pretending not to be, and if I wanted to be completely honest and objective, I could see why.

Although he was approaching fifty, my dad was still in great shape. His slightly curly brown hair had a sprinkling of grey but his warm eyes and his kind smile made him look younger than his age. Dressed in a well-cut winter coat with a scarf around his neck, he looked like he'd stepped off the pages of a gentleman's magazine, and if he weren't my dad, I would have to agree he *was* kinda hot.

He also looked completely oblivious to the attention he was receiving. My dad only had eyes for my mom; they were ridiculously in love even after more than twenty years together, which, as a teenager, kind of grossed me out. I found their public displays of affection embarrassing, but with a few more years behind me, I had to admit they were pretty sweet together.

If I could find someone who looked at me the way my dad looked at my mom, I would be pretty damn lucky, and if Noah Stamer ever looked at me that way, I could die a happy woman.

"You ready to go, Livy?" My dad's face lit up as he saw me and he reached out to take the bag from my hand.

"I can't wait." That was the truth, though he didn't need to know exactly why.

He had come on his own to pick me up while my mom and Noelle travelled with Aunt Gemma, Uncle Cole and Eve up from the city. Noah would be driving himself and arriving a little later.

As we drove the few hours up to the farm, there was hardly a moment's silence. My dad wanted to know everything about my classes and my friends and I told him about all of it in detail. We had the same sense of humour and we'd always gotten along well. He'd always been the one I ran to when things went wrong. Though I loved my mom too, I couldn't really argue with anyone who said I was a total daddy's girl.

He asked about men and I could be honest with him there too: I'd been on some dates but I hadn't found anyone special yet. Tessa claimed my single status was because my standards were impossibly high, and maybe she had a point. After all, I wanted someone like Noah, but no one could compare to Noah besides Noah himself. He was truly one-of-a-kind.

So, although I went out with other guys and made out with some of them, it never turned into anything serious. I hadn't slept with any of them either, though I didn't share *that* particular piece of information with my dad. We had a 'don't ask, don't tell' policy when it came to my sex life and his, although at least he actually had one.

I was still waiting for the right moment to lose my virginity, a moment I hoped with all my might would happen in the next few days.

Finally, we pulled onto the snow-covered drive up to Isabel's gorgeous house, fully decked out for Christmas, as always. Fresh pine garlands draped between the columns of the porch, the outside trees were covered in lights and weather-proof decorations, and a large wreath hung on the front door. By the time we got out of the car, the porch had filled up with people waiting for us.

"There she is!" My mom's British accent rang out above the general cries of greeting and I quickly found myself swallowed up in hugs from her, Isabel, Gemma, Noelle, Eve and Isabel's daughter, Jennifer. Meanwhile, Cole hung back, watching the whole scene with a hint of bemusement as he said hello to my dad.

"Merry Christmas, Olivia," Cole said to me when I finally got myself disentangled from the others. "Are you ready to come work for me yet?"

We had a long-standing joke about how I would follow my dad into the hotel business and be Noah's right-hand-woman, just like my dad was Cole's second-in-command. To be honest, I didn't really care that much about hotels, but the idea of working with Noah definitely carried some appeal, so I hadn't completely ruled it out either.

"Not quite yet, Uncle Cole," I replied with a smile as we stepped inside. The pine scent was even stronger than it had been outside, coming from the gorgeous eight-foot tree that dominated the hall, and Christmas music played in the background, lending the whole scene an extra bit of festive ambiance. Isabel had gone all out. "I've only written my first exams, there's still a long way to go."

"A formality," he assured me as he headed towards the kitchen, the social centre of the house.

I hurried to keep up with him, my socks sliding on the polished hardwood floors as I kept my voice low so the others wouldn't hear. "Do you know when Noah's getting here?"

His lips tightened, which was about as much emotion as he ever displayed. "Actually, I just heard from him. He won't be arriving until tomorrow. I told him if he misses Christmas Eve, he'll break his mother's heart and I'll kick his ass, so let's hope he listens to that, at least."

Gemma might be disappointed, but she wasn't the only one; my heart sank too. I had to wait another whole day? That felt like a lifetime when I had been so ready for that night. Apparently, I wore my best underwear for nothing.

What could be so important to keep Noah at school an extra day? Hopefully, whatever had come up would be taken care of by early the next day and we could still have most of Christmas Eve together. As far as I was concerned, he couldn't arrive a moment too soon.

~Noah~

The sun shone brightly on Christmas Eve morning as I threw my bags in my car, ready for the drive up to my aunt's farm.

"Have a good time," Tate called out from the porch of the house we shared. "Though how you're going to go ten days without getting laid, I have no idea."

His exaggeration made me roll my eyes. "I have done it before, you know."

"What, when you were six?" he shot back with a laugh. His disbelief wasn't entirely unreasonable; since we'd moved into the house we shared, I certainly hadn't gone that long and neither had he.

"Last night should keep me satisfied for a while," I replied, laughing as his eyes lit up at the memory.

My dad had been pissed off at me when I delayed my trip home, but how could I refuse? Twins had been on the fuckit list Tate and I shared since we became friends and realized we were into the same kind of things, and while we were out the day before doing some last-minute shopping, we met an amazing pair of twins who were *very* willing to help us cross that particular item off our list. I couldn't pass up the opportunity.

The fuckit list – essentially a bucket list for all the kinky shit we wanted to do before we had to grow up and be professional – had been Tate's idea and he took it very seriously. He even had it written down, though that seemed dangerous to me. As the future CEO of Stamer Hotels, I didn't need all my college antics getting out in the open, but he swore the file was unhackable, and reluctantly, I let it go. My dad had taught me the value of discretion, one of many lessons I'd learned from him that I took very seriously.

Just like how I always used protection since my dad liked to remind me that I was the product of his own forgetfulness. He meant it as a joke and I took it that way; he and my mom loved me, I'd never had any doubt about that, and I knew they never regretted having me. However, I also knew he wasn't kidding: he really had forgotten just one time and ended up with a kid out of it, and I had no intention of letting that happen to me.

I couldn't imagine being tied to any one woman that way, at least not at that point in my life. Eventually, I would have to be, I supposed, if I wanted to have an heir to take over the family business, but that all seemed far in the future. Up to that point, I'd never met anyone who held my interest both in and out of the bedroom that way.

"You're sure you don't want to come?" I asked Tate as I moved around to the driver's side of the car. I'd already offered to bring him along, partly to keep me company on the drive and partly because I felt bad that he had no family of his own to go home to. Our home lives could hardly be more different. Where I grew up the adored and pampered eldest child of a wealthy, successful couple, his dad was in jail for killing his mom during a domestic violence episode that went too far. The story was horrible, and he'd only told me about it one night when he got drunk and lost his filter.

Nobody else would ever guess at that dark history from spending time with him. On the outside, he was cool, confident and laid-back, like the world had never been anything but kind to him. Still, I suspected his past was part of what drew him to the kind of lifestyle we'd both embraced: a need for physical pleasure to distract him from his emotional pain.

That, and the fact that it came with no strings and no attachments. Neither of us dated; we weren't interested in that.

"Nah, I'm good," Tate replied, turning me down once again. "I've got the whole house to myself so maybe I'll call one of the guys over and finally cross number twenty seven off the list. I've been dreaming about it lately."

Since he knew I'd kill him for doing that one without me, he obviously didn't mean it. "Keep dreaming. I'll see you after New Year's."

With a last wave goodbye, I got in the car and headed out of town, out onto the highway that would take me to the farm.

The lack of sex aside, the week actually promised to be a really good one. Both my mom and my aunt were crazy about Christmas and they always made sure we had a great time. My cousins would be there along with my sister, Eve, and the Hanmer girls too. We were all pretty close in age and I always enjoyed getting a chance to kick back with them. There would be lots of snow and we had an ongoing snowball war that had been in progress for at least ten years already. Each Christmas we were together, we simply picked up where we left off, with my team consisting of me, my cousin, Darryn, and Olivia Hanmer.

A smile spread across my face as soon as Olivia crossed my mind. Her fierce competitiveness had made her a natural pick for my team. Every year, she had a new strategy on how we were going to overcome our 'enemies', meaning our two sisters and my cousin, Jennifer. It didn't matter to her who they were: if they were in our way, they were going down.

Even as a little kid, Olivia had to be the best at everything, and she usually succeeded. A star volleyball player, she'd earned herself an athletic scholarship to Princeton, though she qualified for an academic one as well. She'd graduated from high school at the top of her class in the spring, somehow managing to be both class president and homecoming queen at the same time. With her long blonde hair and blue eyes, she looked like an angel until you tried to beat her at something and then she'd turn into your worst nightmare.

Once, Tate had caught a glimpse of a picture of her I kept on my phone and his eyes nearly popped out of his head. "Where the fuck have you been hiding her?"

I quickly turned the screen off so he couldn't get a closer look. From experience, I knew that the longer you looked, the more beautiful she seemed. "She's a friend of the family. Off-limits."

Though he groaned in disappointment, he accepted that answer. He knew I never had any problem sharing, so if I said no, it meant no. And the truth was that I didn't think of Olivia like that, like one of the girls I usually hooked up with. She inhabited a completely different part of my life and she knew nothing about my particular proclivities. On the rare occasions I did try to imagine a future where my kids and I were the ones coming up to Isabel's farm at Christmas, my wife usually bore a striking resemblance to Olivia.

However, it wouldn't be Olivia herself, because as much as she was off-limits to Tate, she wasn't an option for me either. Her dad had made that very clear to me.

Usually, Jackson was the friendliest, most easygoing guy I'd ever met, but at Olivia's graduation, he'd caught me staring at her a moment too long, and he laid down the law, his expression more severe than I'd ever seen it before. "I like you, Noah, but I love my daughter a lot more. You're not looking for anything serious right now and that's fine, but if you even think of messing around with Olivia on a whim, I will not only cut your balls off, I'll take Stamer Hotels down from the inside. I've worked there twenty-five years, you know I can do it. Are we clear?"

"Yes, sir." It would be hard not to be, since he hadn't left much to the imagination.

So, even though Olivia hinted at wanting to keep in touch once she went to college, I put her off. Subjecting myself to temptation would be pointless when the stakes were so high.

Still, I had to admit I was looking forward to seeing her that day. Maybe she even had a boyfriend that she'd brought home with her. That would probably be for the best, to help remind me that we were friends and nothing more. That was all a girl like her and a guy like me would ever be. Sweet and innocent, she deserved someone who would appreciate that.

She deserved someone very different than me.

I half-expected a big welcoming committee as I pulled up the drive to the farmhouse, but although the house looked as festive as ever, not a soul was in sight. After I parked and grabbed my bags from the back seat, one bag with my clothes and the other full of presents, I headed inside.

"Hello?" I called out as I walked through the front door. The scent of freshly-baked gingerbread wafted through the air, mingling with the pine of the Christmas tree, but the house was unusually quiet.

"Noah?" My dad was the one who responded, appearing from around the corner with a stern expression. He might be playing tough, but I knew him well enough to know that he was happy to see me. "It's about time."

"You already gave me the lecture," I reminded him as he came over to give me a hug. We were practically the same height; actually, I was pretty sure I was a tiny bit taller, though he'd never admit it.

"Hey, Noah! Glad you could make it." Jackson appeared next, a beer in his hand and he quickly joined us to give me a hug too. "How was the drive?"

"Fine," I assured him, glancing around to see who else might be nearby, but it appeared to be just the two of them. "Where is everyone?"

"They went out for a sleigh ride," he explained. "You just missed them. We volunteered to stay behind and keep an eye on the cookies."

"And the football game," my dad added with a smirk. "Come and join us."

"I will in a minute," I promised. "Let me just run this stuff upstairs. I'm in the green room?"

Aunt Isabel's guest rooms were all colour-coded, like a B&B, and the green room had been mine for years. Once my dad nodded in confirmation, I headed up there with my bags. Everything was clean and fresh as always, and the scattered memories of a dozen past Christmases flitted across my mind. Something about being there always made me feel like a kid again. Maybe it always would.

After putting everything away, I started to head back downstairs, but as I passed by the open door of the room next to mine, something caught my eye: a bit of black lace on top of the white dresser. Taking a quick look around to make sure no one else was there, I ducked into the room to take a closer look.

As I'd suspected from the hall, the fabric was a pair of rather seductive panties. I had seen enough of them in my time to be able to recognize them from a distance. Clothes folded like that on top of the dresser usually meant that Aunt Isabel had done laundry and left it there for whoever was staying in the room. That room usually stayed empty, and having only a single pair of panties cleaned was a little strange, but the thought crossed my mind that they might be my sister's and that quickly made me back out of the room again.

Shaking my head at myself, I headed down the stairs. In that house, nothing remotely kinky should be crossing my mind. The two parts of my life were completely separate and I wanted it to keep it that way.

Nothing good could come from mixing the two together, I knew that for sure.

~Olivia~

The sleigh ride had always been one of my favourite parts of Christmas at Isabel's farm. As we glided along the snowy path, my mom and Aunt Gemma were singing British Christmas pop songs, making us all laugh as they argued over the lyrics. The afternoon was beautifully sunny, not too cold but not warm enough that the snow was melting either, and it would be perfect weather to pick up our snowball fight as soon as Noah arrived.

Although I always enjoyed it, I had been tempted to skip the sleigh ride that day just in case Noah showed up while we were gone, but I couldn't think of a good excuse. My mom would want to know why I didn't want to go, and since I couldn't exactly tell her the truth, in the end, I didn't even try to get out of it.

However, as the horses came back around the front of the house, the silver Mercedes caught my eye, a car that hadn't been there before, and my heart leapt in anticipation. He'd arrived! That initial joy was quickly followed by a wish that I had brought a mirror to double check how I looked before I saw him. Was my hair messed up from the wind? Did my lips look dried out from the cold? I quickly wet them, running my tongue across them, top and bottom. I wanted to look perfect for the first time he saw me, because in my dreams, as soon as he saw me, he would wonder how he had never noticed me that way before.

In my head, the whole encounter had been all planned out, played over in my imagination a hundred times or more. Noah just needed to follow the script.

The men must have been waiting for us because they came out onto the porch as we pulled up outside the house and my heart skipped a beat as I caught sight of Noah at last. How could he possibly have gotten better-looking since I saw him last? He had a lot of his dad in him, the height and build and the dark hair and strong jawline. However, he had his mom's sparkling green eyes which somehow softened his look, making him less imposing than Cole and even more appealing, at least to me.

Those eyes suggested that a playful man lay beneath the hard exterior, and I desperately wanted to find out to what extent that was true.

"Noah!" Gemma cried out in excitement, hopping down from the sleigh to go hug her son. Eve went next and soon, he was surrounded. Meanwhile, I took my time, waiting until everyone else had left and lowering myself slowly from the back of the sleigh, hoping that if he happened to glance my way, he would get a nice view of my ass in the jeans I'd picked out especially for that day.

Everything I'd chosen to wear had been selected with one message in mind: Olivia Hanmer was all grown up.

It seemed to be working, because when I turned around, he had stepped free of the rest of the group and had his eyes fixed on me, a half-smile on his face. "Hey, Liv."

"Hey, yourself." I gave my best confident, flirty smile, the one I'd been practicing in the mirror, hoping I didn't have gingerbread dough on my teeth or anything. "You finally made it."

"Yeah. Sorry I'm late." He swallowed as his eyes scanned me, and I wished once again that I could see what I looked like. "I hope you didn't start the snowball fight without me."

"Of course not. I need to fill you in on this year's plan before we begin."

That made him laugh, his eyes twinkling as he did, which set my stomach fluttering. "I figured you would. Let's go talk strategy, then."

Doing my best to hide my giddy smile, I stepped past him and headed towards the front door. I could have sworn I felt his hand against my back through my bulky winter coat, just for a second, but it quickly disappeared.

Everyone else had already begun to assemble in the kitchen so we headed there too after I'd shed my coat and boots at the door, the melting snow leaving tiny puddles on the floor. Noah was accosted by his cousins as soon as we entered Isabel's huge kitchen, wanting to catch up with him, and I watched in frustration as he sat down with them around the island in the centre of the room. Sure, they were family, but I wanted him to choose to spend time with me first. Instead, my mom, Gemma and Isabel drew me into their conversation, though my gaze continually drifted to Noah's back.

"Everything okay, Livy?" My dad had always been able to read me so I did my best to cover up how I felt with a smile as he walked over to me.

"Yeah, I'm just a little chilled. I think I'm going to go put another layer on."

"Good plan. I think you guys are all getting kicked out soon so the adults can gossip about you."

Leaving the busy kitchen behind, I headed upstairs to the blue room where I was staying that year. Usually, I stayed in the yellow room at the end of the hall but Noah always stayed in the green one, and since I wanted to be as close to him as possible, I'd requested the one next door to him instead. If Isabel thought my request was odd in any way, she didn't mention it.

My underwear on the dresser caught my eye as soon as I walked in, and I quickly swept them into the drawer. Isabel must have left them there; I had put them in the dryer that morning but forgot about them. The last thing I needed was for someone else to catch sight of them, like my dad, for one.

I didn't put them on just yet, figuring I would wait and see how the rest of the afternoon went first. I didn't want to waste them again and end up washing them over and over again, which might start to look suspicious. For the moment, I just needed some warmer pants to wear outside.

"There you are." Noah's deep voice from the doorway sent electricity all through my body as I jumped in surprise. "I thought we were making plans and you disappeared."

As he took a step into my room, my heart began to pound. I had imagined that moment so many times, the two of us alone together in a bedroom, any bedroom, and as he looked around the room curiously, I almost thought his eyes rested a moment on the spot where my panties had previously been sitting. That didn't make any sense, though; I must have imagined it.

"You don't usually stay in this room," he pointed out, his eyes moving back to me in all their startling greenness.

"No, I don't," I agreed, scrambling for a reason I could give him for the change besides the real one. "But it's got a perfect view over the creek where I think we should set up our stronghold this year."

I pointed to the window and, with a smile, he followed me over to it. "Show me."

The two words were simple but full of authority and they sent a shiver down my spine as I imagined him saying them to me in a completely different context. My stomach was going crazy as desire built up even lower, making me glad I hadn't put my best panties back on or they would definitely need to be washed again.

Fuck, I needed to concentrate.

That was a lot easier said than done as he leaned over my shoulder to peer out the window, his firm body giving off heat and his masculine scent flooding my senses.

"Th-there," I stuttered, pointing to the spot I'd chosen. "If they go anywhere between the trees and the house, we'll have a clear shot of them."

He took a deep breath in as he considered it, and I had to fight the urge to lean back against him. Did he feel the magnetism between us? He had to, didn't he? It couldn't all be in my head.

But to my disappointment, he took a step back. "That's a great idea. Let's go get Darryn and get started."

"Sure." I put on a bright smile to cover my true feelings. "I was just going to change my pants."

I could have sworn his pupils dilated a little before his eyes flicked back to the spot on my dresser where my panties had been. "What?"

I gestured down to my jeans. "These will get soaked out in the snow, I'm going to put on something warmer."

He nodded, swallowing again, as if the air were particularly dry. "Right. I'll meet you downstairs, then."

He left the room, closing the door behind him, and I quickly changed into the ski pants I had brought along for just that occasion. When I got back downstairs, everyone else had their winter gear on too; all the younger generation, at least. Our parents had opened some wine and were pretending to be too busy with dinner preparation to join us, but we all knew they just wanted an excuse to talk, as my dad had said.

We must have been outside for hours but it felt like mere minutes with me and Noah working together and laughing together as we tried to take down our opponents. Even when it got dark, we didn't stop, using the Christmas lights from the house as our only illumination. By the time Isabel called us all in to eat, I was exhausted in the best possible way.

Well, maybe the *second*-best possible way. Hopefully, I would be able to make the comparison for myself very soon.

As we peeled off our winter layers at the back door, Noah grinned at me. "We nearly had them surrounded out there. After all these years, I thought it might finally happen."

His smile filled my whole body with warmth. "There's still the rest of the week."

"The whole week," he repeated, his eyes seeming to fill with a heat of their own before he quickly looked away. "I'm going to change into something dry."

That was a good idea, so I followed him up the stairs, each of us going into our own rooms. That time, I *did* put my black lace panties back on. Why the hell not? I might as well think positive. I also put my skinny jeans back on with a form-fitting Christmas sweater my mom had picked out for me; a jumper, as she called it, still holding onto some of her British terms despite having lived in the USA for more than twenty years. After giving my hair a brush, I gave myself a nod of satisfaction in the mirror. Noah would *have* to notice me looking like that.

When I got back into the hall, Noah's door stood open, and a flash of disappointment ran through me that he hadn't waited for me to go back downstairs. It only lasted a second though, until I heard a drawer close and realized he must still be inside. Smoothing down my hair once more, I stepped into the open doorway, and my jaw nearly hit the floor.

He was standing there with his shirt off, a new one in his hands, about to pull it over his head.

It had been a few years since I'd seen him without a shirt on, not since the last beach vacation we all took together, and he had definitely filled out since then. With muscles like that, he must be using the gym on campus nearly every day. His chest and abs were fit and firm and *perfect*, and I very nearly literally began to drool.

Forcing my mouth shut, I knocked on the door so I wouldn't startle him. He looked up in surprise anyway before quickly pulling his shirt over his head. "That was quick."

I shrugged at him. "I already knew what I was going to wear. I'm very decisive."

He smiled again, almost to himself. "I bet you are."

Clearing his throat, he stepped towards me as my heart began to beat faster. His eyes were fixed on me as he drew closer, so close that I could feel his body heat once again. Along with the memory of that chest beneath his sweater, it had me aching in all the right places.

"Liv?"

He said my name softly, his face only inches from mine.

"Yeah?" I resisted the very strong urge to lick my lips even though they were incredibly dry. I didn't want to look *too* obvious.

"You're in the way."

I blinked at him in confusion for a second before I realized what he meant: I was completely blocking the door.

"Sorry," I mumbled, taking a step back, and he walked past me, throwing a smirk over his shoulder.

"Let's go, they'll all be waiting for us."

Right. Dinner. Family. That was what we were there for.

"I'm coming."

Those two words nearly made him trip over his feet, grabbing hold of the banister at the top of the staircase just before he fell down the stairs. When he glanced back at me, his expression almost looked pained, but he didn't say anything. He simply stared at me for a moment before turning and continuing down the stairs.

Chapter Two

MAKING A MOVE

~Noah~

She had to be doing it on purpose.

That thought kept running through my head as I made my way back downstairs and into the dining room where dinner was being brought out. From the view Olivia had given me as she climbed out of the sleigh, to talking about changing her pants when I knew exactly what kind of underwear she liked to wear, to standing in the door of my room like some kind of beautiful siren, tempting me to pull her inside, she *must* know what she was doing to me.

Not to mention her sweet voice telling me she was coming. *Fuck.* I grimaced again as I tried not to imagine what it would be like to hear her saying those words under completely different circumstances.

Was she *trying* to drive me crazy, or was she really so completely innocent that she had no idea what it sounded like?

When I first saw her outside by the sleigh that afternoon, she nearly took my breath away. She had always been pretty, but that day, with her blonde hair beneath her woolly white hat, her bright blue eyes and her cheeks pink from the cold, she had never looked more angelic, nor more downright sinful at the same time.

If Tate could see her, he wouldn't be doing nearly as good a job of holding himself in check as I'd managed to. As far as I was concerned, at that point in time, I was a fucking saint.

"Do you need any help?" I asked my mom, partly to make myself useful and partly because it would keep me away from Olivia and my increasingly dirty thoughts.

She led me back to the kitchen where she loaded my hands with food. When I got back to the dining room, Olivia had taken a seat next to her dad, giving me another good reminder of exactly why I needed to keep myself under control. I hadn't forgotten his words to me, and I knew my dad would also kill me if I messed things up between our two families. He considered the Hanmers as practically family, though I certainly didn't think of Olivia as a sister. As soon as I set the food down, I spun around and returned to the kitchen again, still needing a minute.

By the time I brought the last dishes out, most of the chairs were already taken, but one empty one remained next to Olivia. She smiled at me and waved me over as I looked around the table indecisively. *Shit.* So much for keeping my distance.

Along with being Christmas Eve, that night was also Noelle's and Eve's joint birthday, so we all drank a toast to them before digging in. The conversation over dinner was loud and boisterous as we all got caught up on what everyone had been up to. A couple of times, Olivia's hand brushed against mine as we both reached for our glasses, or her leg touched mine beneath the table, sending an unwelcome rush of blood to the area. Was she doing it on purpose? I really couldn't tell.

"What about you two?" my aunt asked, looking over at Olivia and me once my cousin had finished telling us all about her new boyfriend. "Anyone special in your lives yet?"

Olivia and I glanced at each other at the same time, and I quickly looked away, answering first. "I'm in no hurry. I'm only at school for another 18 months so it doesn't make much sense to get involved in anything serious. Life could take a lot of turns after that."

Nobody argued with me there, and all eyes around the table moved to Olivia next. Part of me hoped she would say she *did* have a boyfriend, which would be just one more reason for me to temper my thoughts. The other part of me, the much darker part, really hoped she didn't.

"No, not yet," she replied, and I internally groaned and celebrated at the same time. "Like Noah said: what's the rush? There's still a lot I need to learn about myself first."

Jackson beamed with pride at that answer, but I had a feeling he had interpreted it in a completely different way than I had. All I could imagine was her touching herself, figuring out all the things that turned her on. Would she be doing that in her room later, right next door to me?

That was the last thing I needed to be thinking about, I reminded myself, as I adjusted my pants beneath the table. Getting to sleep that night already seemed impossible.

"Who wants some eggnog?" my mom asked when dinner was over, and I quickly volunteered to help her bring it out so I could get away from the table. Pouring mine out first, I made it two-thirds rum, hoping it would help to take the edge off.

"That looks good." Olivia's voice came from beside me as she took the glass from my hand and brought it to her lips.

"Wait, no, that's not for..." My protests were too late as she took a large gulp of it, her eyes widening as the alcohol hit her throat, and I winced. "...you."

To my surprise, once the shock had passed, she just gave me a smile. "Perfect." Still holding onto the glass, she walked away, her hips swaying slightly as she went.

Damn it. Now I had to worry about getting in trouble for getting her drunk too. When I poured myself a new glass, I made it almost entirely rum, needing all the help I could get.

Everyone had moved into the large living room with the sparkling Christmas tree in front of the window at one end of the room and the roaring fireplace along the opposite wall. The smell of the fresh pine filled the air, along with the happy chatter and laughter of everyone assembled. Olivia had already taken a seat next to her parents so I went as far away as I could, finding a spot near Darryn instead.

"Are you really not seeing anyone?" he asked me curiously as I got settled and took a mouthful of my drink, grateful for the burning sensation it made on the way down. Anything to distract me from my lustful thoughts would be welcome at that point.

Three years older than me, Darryn had just gotten engaged, but his fiancée's family lived on the other side of the country so they were spending the holidays apart that year. The wedding was set for the spring.

"Or was that a lie to keep Mom from digging too deep?" he teased. We both knew how much Isabel liked to know everyone's business.

"I'm seeing lots of people," I replied with a smirk. "Just not more than once."

He rolled his eyes at my boast, which didn't phase me in the least. "I just hope you don't miss out on something good because you're too busy chasing the next thing. I had a friend like that back in college, he had the perfect girl right in front of him but he thought he could always settle down with her later. Now, she's getting married and he's still hitting up campus bars every other night even though he graduated two years ago. It's kind of sad."

It didn't sound that bad to me, especially since I did *not* want to be getting married in two years. I still had way too much fun to have before then.

Besides, the perfect girl for me would be someone just as kinky as I was, at least in private. As nice as the fantasy of the sweet and wholesome girl was, a girl like the blonde one across the room from me, currently braiding tinsel into her hair along with our sisters, I knew myself too well. The kind of life Olivia was made for wouldn't satisfy me in the long run. I needed more than that.

I always had.

"And there are other people who like that too?" I asked tentatively.

She laughed at my naivete. "Of course! There are people who like *everything*. There are even clubs you can go to where you can have sex in front of other people. It's definitely a thing."

Back in my room, I started looking up information about some of those clubs. There were a few of them in New York, which didn't really surprise me. If something existed, you could find it in New York, but the idea of going to a place like that where I might run into someone I knew – or worse, someone who knew my parents – didn't appeal to me at all.

One of those trips down the Google rabbit hole led me to reviews for The Playground in Vienna, a sex club which sounded insane and intense and fascinating. The website promised you didn't need to speak German to have a good time since there wouldn't be a lot of talking going on. Getting in wasn't easy: you had to fill out an application, submit up-to-date STD tests and pay a ridiculous 'membership fee', but that all made me feel more positive about it. The club wasn't going to be filled with random tourists or people off the street who were merely curious. It had been designed for people serious about the lifestyle, and if I wanted to figure out if I was one of those people, it seemed like the perfect place to do it.

I'd always been a good student, and I took my research seriously.

When I showed Tessa the website and asked if she would consider going with me, her face lit up. "Are you kidding? You couldn't get me out of those bondage rooms... literally!"

I rolled my eyes at her terrible joke, but her words intrigued me. "You like being tied up?"

"You've got your kinks, I've got mine," she told me with a wink.

And that was that. We planned a whole trip abroad around visits to The Playground. We *were* planning on visiting Vienna too and seeing the city at Christmastime, but that all came second to the very particular nightlife I wanted to experience.

The time had come for me to find out just how kinky I actually was, far away from anyone who might ever see me again. I had a fake name ready to use and a few days earlier, I had my naturally blonde hair dyed a deep chestnut brown. It made me look completely different, and I was ready to feel different too. For the next two weeks, the Olivia the rest of the world knew would no longer exist.

As we stepped into the lobby of the hotel, just off the ring road that encircled the historic centre of the city, my plan was clear: we were having a nap before going to the spa to get ready for that night, our first night at the club. We'd already had a wax two days earlier at home, but the hotel's spa had a 'special event' package that promised to make us glow before a big night out. That was just what I wanted.

I must have been so focused on what I had to do that I didn't notice the man in the suit until I ran straight into him.

"I'm so sorry, ma'am," a deep, American voice apologized, even though I was clearly the one who ran into him. "Are you alright?"

My eyes travelled up his firm body, the tailored suit not doing a very good job at hiding just how built he must be beneath it, until they rested on his handsome face and the stunning green eyes that were looking down on me, and my mouth dropped open in disbelief.

"Noah?"

~**Noah**~

The woman caught my eye as soon as she walked in the front door of the hotel. In the middle of a conversation with the front-of-house manager, I couldn't help being distracted by the tall, beautiful, dark-haired woman, laughing with her friend as they pulled their suitcases behind them.

I had seen a lot of beautiful women since arriving in Vienna two weeks earlier, but she still stood out. Something about her felt familiar but new at the same time. She was too far away for me to see her face very well, but her confidence, her exuberance and, let's face it, her incredible body, all combined to draw my attention in a way that almost felt magnetic.

What a shame that the hotel discouraged staff from flirting with guests.

As part of my final year of college, all international business students were expected to do an internship abroad. There really hadn't been any question that I would go to one of my family's hotels; the only tricky part had been deciding which city to spend a month in.

In the end, Tate made the call. Since he was in the same program as me, I offered to hook him up with an internship too so we could do it together, and he quickly got to work researching which cities had the best nightlife.

When he came back with Vienna, I thought he must have been kidding. I'd visited the city with my family as a kid and I only really remembered classical music and dancing horses. It didn't seem very edgy or cool to me then. I had expected him to suggest Amsterdam or Bangkok or somewhere like that.

But when Tate showed me the info for The Playground, I couldn't argue with him: it looked amazing, and I needed something amazing to get myself out of the slump I'd been in.

Ever since the previous Christmas, I found it hard to stay in the moment during sex. I still enjoyed it, unlike when I was young and confused, but lately, instead of the intensity of the other people in the room being what worked best for me, my imagination had started doing most of the heavy lifting.

And what I liked to imagine most of all was Olivia watching me do whatever I was doing, except that in my fantasies, she didn't look shocked and appalled as she had when she actually walked in on me in real life. In my dreams, she enjoyed herself just as much as I did. Her hand down those lacy black panties I'd seen her in before, her cheeks flushed and her body writhing with need, she got as much pleasure from watching me as I got from having her watch me.

I knew the idea was insane. Nothing like that would ever happen; she'd made that clear enough when she ran out of my house the previous December.

"Who was that?" Tate asked curiously from his position on the living room floor as we all heard the front door slam behind Olivia.

"She's an old friend of my family," I explained, not wanting to tell him she was the same one I'd run away from just a few days earlier. I wanted to run *after* her that night and see if she was okay, but by the time I got some clothes on, it would have been too late. She'd have been long gone and I didn't have her number since I had insisted on not taking it. I had no way of tracking her down.

"She knows your parents? Is she going to tell them about this?" the girl on her knees in front of me asked, her eyes wide with horror at the thought.

That idea didn't particularly worry me. My parents wouldn't really care what I did, as long as I kept it all consensual, although they might be upset that Olivia had seen me doing it.

What Olivia must think of me was the thought that really terrified me.

Telling everyone in the room they'd have to finish without me, I went up to my room and lay down on my bed, trying to figure out what to do next. I *could* reach out to her. My parents would give me her number if I asked, and it wouldn't be that hard to just send her a text and say: *Sorry you had to see that, are you ok?*

But deep down, I didn't want to have to apologize. I hadn't intended for her to see it. How could I have known she would ever show up at my door when she never had before?

And what I could barely bring myself to admit, even in the privacy of my room, was that I didn't want to apologize because I wanted her to be okay with it. I wanted her to understand why I enjoyed it.

My dad had told me to find someone who liked the same things I did and somewhere deep in my soul, I wanted Olivia to be that someone.

In the end, I decided not to do anything, to wait and see if she contacted me instead. Clearly, she knew how to track me down if she really wanted to, and for a few weeks, I lived in hope that she would turn up at my door once again, that time with a smile, and we could really talk and get to know each other properly, on a deeper level.

But days went by, and then more of them, without any word from her or from anyone. Obviously, she hadn't told anyone what happened and she didn't want to talk to me about it, which must mean the whole thing disgusted her just as much as I'd been afraid it would. Whenever she crossed my mind, I felt slightly sick at the idea of having lost her even as a friend.

A few months later, I heard she was seeing someone. Jackson mentioned it when we all went to a Yankees game together, Olivia's family and mine, though Olivia herself didn't come.

"He's a good guy," I heard Jackson tell my mom. "I think they might be getting serious."

Of course Olivia would end up with a good guy. That was what good girls did.

And if things were getting serious between them, no matter how 'good' he was, they'd be sleeping together soon, if they weren't already. He'd be teaching her all the things she'd asked me to show her, and I couldn't help groaning out loud at the thought.

My sister gave me a concerned look. "Are you okay, Noah?"

"Fine," I muttered, gesturing vaguely to the ball players in front of us. "That just... should have been a strike."

When I went home that night, my mind seemed determined to torture me with images of Olivia and her unknown boyfriend together. I had no idea what he looked like, but in my head he appeared almost god-like and she was helpless to resist him.

As I let the scenario play out in my head, however, my agony began to turn into something else. I began to get a little turned on.

My hand moved to my dick as I pictured him pushing into her, and with each imaginary thrust, I stroked myself, getting harder and harder by the second. In my mind, her head turned and her eyes met mine. She knew I was there, watching her, and she didn't mind. In fact, she rather liked it.

Our eyes stayed fixed on each other as the other man continued to fuck her. I could see in her face how close she was, so I whispered to her: "You're so fucking gorgeous, Liv."

That pushed her over the edge in my dream, and me too in reality as I spurt out all over myself, alone in my room, shuddering in pleasure and a bit of disbelief.

That was more intense than any orgasm I'd had with a partner in a long time.

Since then, she was often in my thoughts whenever I had sex with anyone. I saw her face on the girls I watched Tate fuck, and I pictured her watching me when I took my turn. I knew my obsession was unusual, but other people pictured a hot celebrity in place of their partner, and it really wasn't all that different. Both scenarios were fantasies, and I knew there was no way it would ever happen for real.

And when it came to fantasies, The Playground was turning out to be everything it had been hyped up to be. Tate and I had spent almost every night there since arriving in town two weeks earlier. They had very strict entry requirements, so everyone there was not only clean but had money and looks too. The selection of partners was incredible and once you were in, there was no kink you couldn't satisfy.

Unless you wanted one specific person. The one thing I truly wanted, no club in the world could provide, but I was enjoying myself anyway, so much so that I hadn't even thought of Olivia in a few days.

At least not until the beautiful brunette I had noticed earlier walked straight into me and looked up at me with Olivia's face.

For a moment, I thought I had actually lost my mind. Whenever I imagined her before, the illusion had been intentional. My mind had never played tricks on me out of the blue like that before.

But when she said my name, I realized I wasn't hallucinating at all. It really *was* Olivia, as impossible as that seemed.

"Liv?" I took a step back from her as my heart raced and my mind tried to make sense of what I was seeing. "What are you doing here?"

"I'm on vacation." She looked just as confused as I felt, which was a hell of a lot. "What are *you* doing here?"

"I'm working here. Temporarily. This is one of my hotels."

She let out a shaky breath. "Of course it is. That's why we're here too. I mean, because it's a Stamer Hotel and my dad recommended it."

That made sense, but her being in Vienna at all was still an unbelievable coincidence. What would have made her choose that city out of all the places in the world to go on vacation?

If I were a more optimistic man, I might think she had chosen it specifically because she knew I'd be there, but the stunned expression on her face made it clear she hadn't expected to come across me. The whole thing was just as big a surprise to her as it was to me.

"Hi, I'm Tessa." The woman next to Olivia stuck her hand out in front of me, a big smile on her face. "I've heard a lot about you, Noah."

Olivia's cheeks turned slightly pink, giving me a good idea exactly what this woman might have heard about me.

"Nice to meet you, Tessa." I gave her a smile as I shook her hand, trying to act normally. Although a very pretty woman, with copper hair and a bright smile, she paled next to Olivia, who I turned back to as soon as I let go of Tessa's hand. "I almost didn't recognize you with the new hair. What brought that on?"

Part of me missed the angelic blonde hair, but I couldn't deny she looked amazing. A little more devilish, which wasn't a bad thing at all.

She shrugged. "I just felt like a change. It's good to try new things, right?"

I couldn't argue with that, nor could I think of anything clever to say in reply. "Well, I hope you enjoy your stay. You must be tired from your flight so I won't keep you, but I'll be around if you need anything. You can always ask the front desk to give me a call, they'll know where to find me."

"We might just take you up on that, Noah," Tessa said, her tone suggesting she might have some particular ideas in mind already.

I said goodbye to them and, my heart still pounding, I headed to the staff room where Tate was already on his break.

"You okay?" he asked as I sat down across from him. "You look like you've seen a ghost."

"The ghost of Christmas past," I muttered under my breath, and he gave me a funny look.

"What?"

I shook my head. "Never mind. Let's just get through the next few hours. I am definitely going to need some stress relief tonight."

We had plans at The Playground that evening. We'd been sticking to the private rooms to that point, but Tate was eager to go for a more public experience and after what had just happened, I felt ready for it too. The thought of the crowd watching me and imagining Olivia among them had already begun to make me hard, even though that was completely ridiculous.

Someone like her would never even know that a place like The Playground existed.

Chapter Five

THINGS IN COMMON

~Olivia~

Keeping myself together while we checked into our hotel room after the encounter with Noah didn't come easily. I didn't know if I wanted to laugh or scream or cry, or all three at the same time. There I was, halfway around the world from home, where I had come specifically so that I wouldn't know anyone, and the man I had spent the last year trying not to think about was staying at the same hotel.

Could it be some kind of karma? Was it a sign that I should call the whole thing off? Out of all the people I knew, Noah was the most likely to go to The Playground himself. What if he went there that night?

The thought immediately sent a shiver of excitement down my spine as months of fantasies rushed through my memory all at once. What if he *was* there? What if my fantasies could literally come true?

Did I really want that, or was it one of those things that should stay in my imagination?

By the time Tessa and I got up to our suite, my hands were shaking, but whether excitement or nerves were to blame, I honestly didn't know.

My friend turned to me the moment we got in the door. "You are not backing out on me!"

"What?" Where had she got that idea? I hadn't said a word.

"I can see the panic in your eyes," she explained, covering my eyes with her hands so I had to close them. "You think he might be there tonight and you're freaking out."

There didn't seem any point in hiding it as I pushed her hands away. "I don't know what to feel, Tessa. There's definitely a chance that he'll be there if he's still into the kind of stuff I saw him doing last year. They have group sex rooms at The Playground."

I'd considered whether I might want to spend some time in one, but it got me less excited than the idea of just being with one person, or two at most, and having other people watch. The research I'd done suggested that group sex and exhibitionism were two separate kinks which sometimes went together, but not always, and for me, being part of a group wasn't such a big turn-on. I liked the idea of being the centre of attention instead.

As far as I knew, Noah was into the group element, so even if we *were* both at the club that evening, we wouldn't necessarily be in the same area. Surely, the kink world was big enough for the both of us without having to be right on top of each other, as it were.

"So, you still want to go?" she confirmed hopefully.

"Definitely." After a month of planning, I wasn't about to let one little coincidence... or even a great big one... hold me back.

Noah looked amazing, I had to admit to myself as we went through all the preparations for our night out. I noticed the way people looked at him as he walked away from us in the lobby. In his suit and with his natural confidence, looking like he owned the place, which he technically did, not a woman in the room could keep her eyes off him. He must have had his pick of women for years, and I felt foolish for not understanding that before, for not seeing just what a catch he must seem like to the outside world. To me, he had always just been Noah, the boy I grew up with, not 'Noah the billionaire' or 'Noah the future CEO'.

Seeing him in his natural element made me realize it had been naïve to think I had ever had a shot with him.

Even so, I wasn't about to let that stop me from enjoying myself that night. The trip was not about Noah.

At least not entirely. Without him and the experience of the previous Christmas, I might not have discovered the kinkier side of myself, so technically, he had a little to do with it. But being there was much more about *me* and finding out what satisfied me. That was my game plan, and so I shoved Noah firmly to the back of my mind, where he belonged.

When we finished at the spa, Tessa and I went back to our suite and got changed into our lingerie for that night. The Playground didn't have a dress code; people could wear as much or as little as they wanted, but since the point of being there was to have sex, it made sense to show people what you had to offer. Tessa and I had gone shopping together in New York to pick out a variety of things to wear during our visits, and for our first night, she settled on a red teddy made mostly of lace while I chose a black bra and panties set with stockings and garter belt. We put other clothes over top for the trip to the club, but once we were inside, everything would come back off.

We were both quiet during the taxi ride to the club, and I had a feeling we were both a little nervous though we didn't want to admit it to each other. For the last month, I had been thinking about and dreaming of that moment, but now that we were actually there, part of me wondered if I had built it up so much that it could never live up to my expectations.

That part quickly fell silent as we pulled up outside the club. From the street, the building looked discreet. The sign above the door had the name of the club and its logo, which at first glance appeared to be a rather innocent-looking slide, the kind you might see at any playground, but a closer look revealed that the length of the slide was actually something else entirely.

At the door, they checked the membership confirmation on my app and our photo IDs before letting us into the elegant reception area beyond. A beautiful woman in a suit sat behind the desk and she looked up as we approached, her demeanour cool and professional. "Guten Abend. Kann ich Ihnen helfen?"

I had studied a few German phrases before we arrived, so I understood she was asking if she could help us, but I definitely didn't know enough to reply to her so I answered in English. "Hi, it's our first time here, so yes, please."

She gave a nod, switching to flawless English with only a slight accent. "Of course. I will call your guide, may I please have your confirmation?"

I handed over my phone again and she pulled up our information on her computer. After tapping the necessary codes into her keyboard, she handed the phone back, and only a few moments later, a door opened on the opposite wall and a very pretty blonde woman came over to us with a big smile, wearing a silk robe and high heels.

"You must be Belle and Tiffany," she greeted us in an American accent not very different from our own, and using the fake names we had entered in our application. We had been told that no one in the club would refer to us by our real names. They took privacy very seriously. "I'm Nina and I'll be showing you around tonight. Welcome to The Playground."

With that, she led us through the door she had just come in. The hallway beyond the lobby was dark with glowing, pulsing red lights, and a low, humming bass sound that seemed to vibrate deep within me.

"Is this meant to look like a vagina?" Tessa whispered to me.

Apparently, she didn't whisper quietly enough because Nina turned back to her with a laugh. "Absolutely. The owners are big on symbolism. First stop is the changing room."

As promised, she took us into a room near the end of the hall that looked like a high-class version of any high school locker room, where we could take off whatever we wanted to leave behind and lock it up in a locker that we could program with our own thumbprint, since there was nowhere on our clothing for us to carry a key.

When we were down to our lingerie, Nina removed her robe too, hanging it on a hook by the door. I was pleased to see she wore something quite similar to me, though her set was blue and silky. At least it meant I should fit in once we got inside.

Opening one of the smaller lockers near the door, Nina pulled out two wristbands. "These are your assistance buttons," she explained as she secured one to my wrist and then moved over to do the same to Tessa. "Everything at The Playground is consensual. If any of the patrons makes you feel uncomfortable in any way, just press against the band and our security will be right with you. If you're being tied up, make sure you can still press it against some kind of surface – a wall, a bedpost, whatever. It just needs a bit of pressure. Our doms all know this and should confirm it with you before they do anything."

I tried my best to absorb everything she said even though I didn't have any intention of being tied up. Since Tessa was thinking about it, she paid extra attention. Either way, knowing the club cared about safety reassured us both.

Nina confirmed it even further with her next words. "Our priority is making sure that everyone here enjoys themselves. I know it's your first time here, but have you been to other clubs like this before?"

Tessa and I both shook our heads. We might as well tell the truth and get as much information as we could.

Nina smiled again. "Well, you picked a great place to start. I might be a little biased, but it's my favourite club in the world. My advice for you both would be to ease into things. Spend some time talking to people before you jump into a scene. Try something small first to make sure you like it and build your way up."

That was good advice, and since we had two weeks there, it made a lot of sense. We didn't need to do everything all in one night.

"Now, let's go see which parts of The Playground are right for you."

With a wink, she opened a door on the opposite side of the room from where we had entered.

"This is the Plaza," Nina explained as she took us into the large room beyond. It looked like a fairly typical high-end bar with booths and tables, and stools along the bar itself. The room was already full of people, many of whom gave us curious and appreciative looks as we watched by. Nina offered us a conspiratorial smile as she led us over to the bar. "A lot of the people who hang out in the Plaza are regulars and they're always looking for a bit of fresh blood. If you hang out here, you'll get a lot of offers, but feel free to be picky if you're just not interested. Rule number one of The Playground is that no means no, so if you turn someone down, they'll leave you alone. If they don't, that's what your wristband is for."

My eyes scanned the room as she spoke. There were indeed several people watching us and making no secret of it. As the eyes of both men and women I had never seen before roamed over my body, examining every curve, my veins began to thrum in anticipation, confirming what I had already expected. This was what I wanted: people looking at me, getting their own pleasure from what they could see. Being there was already a rush, and nothing had even happened yet.

We didn't linger there, though. Nina took us through the rest of the club, pointing out all the different areas we could try. "This room is for animal play," she explained, pointing through one open doorway, and I peered in curiously.

The first thing I saw was an incredibly good-looking, muscular man on his hands and knees, a collar around his neck that had a leash attached, while another man gave him commands, trying to get him to roll over.

"Puppy training," Nina told me, following my gaze. "He'll get his reward when he learns his trick."

I simply nodded, though I had a million more questions, and Nina laughed at the expression on my face.

"You don't need to think it's sexy, but it works for them. There's a common saying in clubs like this: your kink is not my kink but your kink is okay. Nobody judges anyone else. All flavours are good."

The no judgement part definitely sounded good to me. We moved on, through the BDSM area with chains hanging from the ceiling and crosses against the wall. Tessa asked quite a few questions before we moved on to one of the group sex rooms. Of course my mind flashed back to what I had seen the year before at Noah's house and I couldn't help looking around for him when we peered into the room. I couldn't be sure if I felt relieved or disappointed that I didn't see him anywhere.

Finally, we ended up in the exhibition area, where my interest lay.

"There are three 'levels', for lack of a better word," Nina told me. "First are the private rooms where you can invite other people in to watch you. You have full control over who sees you. Second are the viewing rooms."

She took us over to them as she continued her explanation. Four large picture windows took up one long wall of the room, almost like displays at a museum. Two of them were dark, but the other two had people inside, engaged in various sexual activities, while people on our side stood and watched.

"Here, you have more of an audience," she explained. "Anyone can stop and watch, but you have control over what they see since everyone is seeing you from the same angle."

I nodded, the throbbing within my body getting stronger as I watched the couple in the room closest to us. The woman was lying on a table, her back arching in pleasure as her lover thrust powerfully into her, but she wasn't looking at him. She was watching the people watching her and obviously loving it, and a jolt of desire ran through me. Was that really going to be me? The thought both thrilled and scared me at the same time.

"And finally, there's the public stage," Nina said, taking us through one more door into a theatre-style room. A stage had been set up in the middle of the room, with seats all around, enough to hold a few hundred people at capacity. "Here, anyone can come in and watch, and they can watch from wherever they like. It's as open as it can get."

I could see that. At that moment, three women on the stage had formed a daisy chain, each giving and receiving oral sex at the same time, while men and women watched from all angles.

"And, as you can see, if it gets you turned on enough, you can find your satisfaction in the audience too," Nina added, pointing to a couple who were fucking just a few rows in front of us, as they watched the performance.

Part of me could hardly believe all of it was real, but the vibrations of the music, the moans of pleasure and the scent of perfume and sex made it all clear that not only was it really happening, I was about to be part of it.

I couldn't wait to begin.

~Noah~

So far, my plan to blow off some steam that evening had been a miserable failure.

People often described my dad as broody, or even grumpy, but that wasn't usually me. I seemed to have inherited my mom's ability to have a good time in just about any circumstance instead, but that evening was proving to be an exception. I felt irritable and on edge, like a kettle about to reach its boiling point.

As soon as we arrived at The Playground, Tate wanted to go sign up for the main stage. Even mid-week, there was usually a waiting list for it and he wanted to make sure we didn't miss out. But as I took a look around at the women, many of whom I had started to recognize after two weeks there, I couldn't muster any great deal of enthusiasm.

"I don't think I'm in the mood tonight," I told him. "Go ahead if you want to."

Frowning, he led us over to one of the tables in the Plaza instead, using the tablet at the table to order some drinks from the bar. "Are you going to tell me what's going on?"

I wasn't sure I could even if I wanted to. Tate and I didn't usually talk about anything too deep. We talked about school, we talked about our plans for the future, we sure as hell talked about sex, but anything to do with feelings? That was a lot less common.

I tried to deflect again. "Can't I just not be horny for one night?"

That made him laugh. "Not as far as I've ever seen. The only time you ever didn't want to fuck was last Christmas when that girl showed up at our house."

Shit. I hadn't realized he'd been paying that much attention. I had only ever told him the bare minimum about Olivia. He didn't know her name, he still didn't know that the girl who walked in on us last year was the same one I'd come home early to avoid, and he definitely didn't know how much time I spent thinking about her.

On top of that, I also hadn't told him about running into her at the hotel that afternoon. He represented one thing in my life and she symbolized another, and I didn't want the two crossing paths.

Why I should feel that way, I didn't quite understand. Olivia already knew about my kinks, so what harm would it do for her to meet Tate? I wasn't ashamed of him; he was my best friend. My parents had met him and my sister had even met him, though we had a firm talk first about how Eve was definitely off-limits, which he completely respected.

Could I actually be jealous at the idea that Tate and Olivia might hit it off? A little twinge of tightness in my chest suggested I may be on the right track. The idea of them physically being together didn't bother me; in fact, if I stopped to imagine them having sex, with me watching, it didn't upset me at all. It even turned me on.

What did bother me was the idea of her smiling at him or holding his hand, or sitting down next to him at a family dinner. If she actually *liked* him, rather than simply fucking him, that *would* bother me a lot, and I couldn't even explain why.

Tate let out a low whistle, his eyes fixed on something across the room. "Check out those two that just came in with Nina. They must be new. If you need something to get your motor running, that'll do it."

I didn't bother to look. I really wasn't in the mood, and I couldn't remember why I'd even decided to go to the club that evening at all.

"I think I'm going to head back to the hotel. I'll see you tomorrow."

With a shrug, Tate let me go, and I made my way back out into the chilly December night. The Christmas lights hanging in the street above me as I walked back to the hotel reminded me of the nights we used to go touring the lights in New York with the Hanmer family. I could almost picture Olivia's face, her eyes wide with delight, as she looked up at them. Knowing that she was there in Vienna too, that we could be walking under the lights together if things were just a little different, made me feel even more alone.

For a moment, I was tempted to go to her room when I got back to the hotel. I knew which room she was staying in; it only took me two minutes to look it up in the hotel system that afternoon. However, she was probably still tired from her flight and having an early night in, and I didn't want to disturb her.

Besides, what did I really think would happen if I went and knocked? The fundamental issue between us hadn't gone away. When it came to sex, we had nothing in common.

In the end, I simply went back to my own room alone.

~Olivia~

At the end of the tour, Nina took us back to the Plaza and ordered us a couple of drinks on the house to get us started. She explained that sitting at the bar meant you were looking for a hookup, choosing one of the tables meant you were open to being approached, and sitting in a booth meant you were taking a break.

Tessa and I chose one of the tables, figuring we could take our time to talk over everything we'd just seen, but not wanting to put off anyone who might approach us either.

It didn't take long for people to start coming over. As I sipped my martini, three very good-looking men with eastern European accents came up and asked to join us. While most of the women in the club were practically naked, the men wore a bit more. They all had pants on, for a start. Some were shirtless, some had tight, clingy shirts, and some were in a full suit, looking like they were at a business meeting rather than a temple of hedonism.

For some reason, the suits turned me on most of all, and I couldn't stop my mind from summoning the image of Noah in the hotel lobby earlier that day and how good he had looked in *his* suit.

Since that wasn't what I needed to be thinking about, I closed my eyes for a second, pushing the image away so I could focus on the men at the table instead.

"We're from New York," Tessa was telling them. The table was circular and Tessa and I were sitting across from each other, so the men had sat down between us, two on my right side and one to my left. "It's our first night here."

That seemed to please them all. "We would be very happy to show you all the places," the man sitting closest to Tessa said, his eyes wandering across her body with open interest. "We are from Russia, my name is Andrei."

The other two introduced themselves as Alexei and Dimitri. Dimitri was the one immediately to my right. He looked younger than the other two who were probably in their early thirties. Dimitri was closer to 25, with short, blond hair and cool, blue eyes. His hand went to my thigh beneath the table as he asked for my name.

No man had ever been so brazenly forward with me, but that was the point, I reminded myself. They were here for exactly the same reason we were, and as his fingers gently kneaded at my skin just above the top of my stocking, my body reacted to the invitation, desire pooling deep within me. This man I had literally just met wanted me, and though I knew absolutely nothing about him, I wanted him as well.

I had never felt so sexy or desired before.

"I'm Belle," I told him, using my fake name. "What's your favourite part of the club, Dimitri?"

In my roundabout way, I wanted to know what he was into, and he understood that immediately. "Me and my friends, we are all doms and we like to share."

Well, that was to the point. I tried to catch Tessa's eye to see if she'd heard that, but she was caught up in whatever Andrei was whispering in her ear.

Over the throbbing of my libido, the logical part of my brain was trying to get a word in. Nina's advice about being picky and easing ourselves in came back to me. Though these men were certainly attractive, I wasn't looking for a dom, and I wasn't sure about group sex either.

We didn't need to run off with the very first men who came over to us.

Tessa, however, didn't seem to agree. She had already started to get to her feet with Andrei's arm around her waist. Her eyes gleamed with excitement as she looked over at me. "Are you coming, Li... I mean, Belle."

Smooth, Tessa. "No, I don't think so. Have fun, though."

As Nina had promised, the men didn't pressure me at all once I'd given my answer and the three of them plus Tessa all headed off together.

"Did your friend really just abandon you on your first night here?"

An American voice posed the question, and I turned to find a very handsome man in a suit smiling down at me. He was also blond and blue-eyed, just like Dimitri had been, but his smile made him look quite different. His dark suit conveyed confidence but there was a playful twinkle in his eyes.

"May I join you?"

When I nodded, he slid into Tessa's abandoned seat, keeping a respectful distance from me.

"How did you know it's my first night here?" I asked.

"I saw you and your friend with Nina earlier. She always shows the new English-speaking women around."

"It sounds like you know your way around."

He laughed but didn't deny it. "I've been here every night for the last two weeks. I'm only in Vienna for a short time and I want to make the most of it."

We seemed to have that much in common, at least. "What did you do on your first night here?"

"Honestly? We just watched for a while, but that's our thing. We're voyeurs."

I had seen that word during my online research and I knew it meant people who liked to watch others. I definitely liked that too. "We?" I repeated, taking a quick look around. As far as I could see, he was alone.

"My friend left early tonight but maybe you can meet him another night if you're coming back."

He was obviously fishing to find out if I'd be there again, which flattered me. "I'll be back tomorrow," I told him. I didn't want to give away anything more than that.

It seemed to satisfy him anyway. "Perfect. In that case, if you'd like some company until your friend is finished, I'd be happy to take the role."

That was exactly the offer I needed. After chatting a little more, we went together back to the stage that Nina had shown me earlier. A new threesome had taken the place of the women on stage, two men and a woman that time, and the man I walked in with took us right to the front row, where we could see everything clearly and where the people on stage could see us too, watching us watching them.

One of the men lay on the bed on his back while the woman rode him, and the other man fucked her ass from behind. I'd never seen double penetration in person before and I couldn't help imagining what it might feel like, if that were me up there with everyone watching. The man who was in her ass caught sight of me, and he gave me a heated smile as he continued to thrust into her.

Even though I had next to nothing on, my body felt like it was on fire. My nipples tightened, peaking against the fabric of my bra and I shifted in my seat, pressing my legs together to try to satisfy the need for pressure that was building between them.

"You can touch yourself if you want to," the man next to me whispered. "He'll like it."

Swallowing my nerves, I did as he suggested, letting my hand wander to one breast, palming it over top of the black lace to feel my hardened nipple beneath it. The man on stage kept his eyes on me, his tongue darting out to wet his lips as his hips pushed against the woman beneath him.

My heart beating even faster, I brought my other hand to my panties, spreading my legs in my seat so I could rub against the fabric between them. I could hardly believe how turned on I was. My clit was crying for attention, as was the aching entrance just beneath it.

Giving in to my body's demands, my hand slipped beneath the fabric, and a shiver of pleasure and need ran through me as my fingers made contact with the sensitive skin there. The man on stage groaned aloud, his attention now entirely focused on me even though his body was attached to someone else.

As my fingers pushed inside my warm and wet hole, three people reacted to it: me, the man on stage and the man beside me too.

Nothing in my life had ever been hotter, and the only one touching me was me.

The man on stage pumped faster, his own orgasm building as mine did too.

"You're driving him crazy," the man next to me whispered in my ear, his breath hot and heavy. "He's imagining it's you he's fucking right now, not her."

I got that impression too. Suddenly, he pulled out of the woman's ass, stroking his cock as he released all over her, and the sight broke the dam inside me too, my whole body shuddering with fulfilment in my seat.

"Fuck, that was hot," the man next to me groaned. He hadn't made any move to touch me, I realized. He just liked watching it happen, exactly as I wanted.

After giving me some time to recover, my new friend, whose name I didn't even know, took me to one of the nearby restrooms where I could clean up, and then we returned to the Plaza where Tessa was already waiting. She didn't look nearly as satisfied as I felt.

"What happened?" I asked, worried that something had gone wrong.

Luckily, she shrugged, looking only disappointed rather than unhappy. "They were too bossy. I told them to fuck off."

I couldn't help laughing. "They're doms, Tessa. I think they have to be bossy, it's in the job description."

The man with me laughed too. "Sorry it didn't work out. I'm Tate, by the way."

He held his hand out to Tessa, who shook it, eyeing him with obvious interest. "Tiffany."

Grinning at us both, Tate turned to me. "I never got your name, did I?"

"Belle. Thank you for your company, Tate."

"My pleasure, quite literally. I need to head out now but I hope I'll see you back here tomorrow."

"With your friend?" I asked, remembering what he'd said earlier. If he did indeed have a friend, it might work out well for me and Tessa.

"We'll both be here," he promised. "Have a good night, ladies."

Tessa looked at me with wide eyes once he'd gone. "What did you guys do?"

"I'll tell you about it at the hotel," I promised. "Right now, I think I'm ready for bed."

Chapter Six

RECONCILIATION

~Noah~

Tate's good mood was the first thing I noticed when I met him for breakfast in the staff dining room the next morning.

"You missed out last night," he told me as soon as I sat down with my coffee. "Luckily for you, tonight should be even better."

At that moment, I didn't feel any more excited about that night than I had about the previous one, but I'd decided in the shower that morning that I wouldn't waste any more time feeling sorry for myself or brooding over what I could never have. Seeing Olivia had thrown me off, but in the end, it really didn't matter if she was there in Vienna or at home. It didn't change the relationship between us, or lack thereof, so I was just going to have to keep living my life as I usually did. As best as I could, I would try not to think about her at all that day.

"Did you get up on the stage last night?" I asked Tate curiously.

He shook his head. "Of course not, I'm not doing that without you there."

I felt kind of touched by that, as odd as it sounded. We had been each other's wingmen for so long, it wouldn't seem right to me to do something big like that without Tate being there to see it, and it pleased me that he felt the same way.

"So, what happened then?"

"I spent a bit of time with someone new, and I've gotta tell you, she's something special."

That definitely piqued my curiosity. Normally, to Tate, one girl was the same as the next. He charmed them while picking them up, loved them while he was fucking them, and they never crossed his mind again afterwards. I wasn't sure I'd ever heard him talk about a woman again the next day.

"Special?" I repeated, keeping my voice low so the others in the room wouldn't hear us over the clatter of silverware and chatter of their own conversations. "What does that mean? Did she have some kind of gold-lined pussy?"

Tate laughed, momentarily distracted by the image. "Would that even be comfortable?"

"Gold is pretty pliable when it heats up," I pointed out. "It'd be better than most metals."

"Maybe if it melted enough it would transfer over like gold leaf and you'd end up with a golden dick."

I grinned at the thought. "Now that *would* be special." We were getting off topic, so I brought us back to what he'd said. "What's the deal with this woman? The sex was really that different?"

"Actually, nothing happened between us. We talked a bit and then I got to watch her get herself off. She didn't even take her clothes off and it was incredible. I think she's pretty new to the scene but she was obviously made for it. I've never seen anyone react so naturally, and I think we could show her a really good time. Maybe she's the one we're meant to go on stage with."

If I hadn't been intrigued before, I definitely was after that description. "You got all that from one night where you didn't even touch her?"

He shrugged. "Like I said: she was special. And the best part is she's got a friend too. I'm not sure what her kinks are, but I'd like to find out."

It sounded like he had our night all planned out, and thanks to his enthusiasm, I'd started to look forward to it too. At the very least, I wanted to meet this woman for myself.

First, though, we still had to get through the day of work. "Where are you shadowing today?" I asked him, glancing up at the clock on the wall. Our shift was about to start in just a few minutes.

"Housekeeping." As Tate grimaced, I had to laugh. He had been dreading that part of the internship. He had never been so happy as when he moved in with me and found out I paid a housekeeper to come clean the house every other day. "What about you?"

"I'm doing one of the excursions." The hotel arranged trips to local attractions as part of its guest services. Normally, the trips were full of older couples or groups who liked the convenience of the arranged trips, but to me, it sounded like a version of hell. I would much rather explore a city on my own.

Tate was obviously of the same opinion as he grinned over at me. "Have fun."

I narrowed my eyes back at him sarcastically. "Yeah, you too." Neither of us was in for a fun day, so hopefully, that night would make up for it.

Half an hour later, I stood by the bus in front of the hotel under the watchful eye of the tour director, greeting the guests as they got on board. That day, we were taking them to Schönbrunn Palace, the former imperial summer palace. I had been there as a child with my family but I didn't remember much of it. Hopefully, I would find it more memorable that time around.

Charming my grandparents' generation came pretty naturally to me and the tour director soon left me alone to greet any latecomers while she went to check on things inside. As our departure time approached, the bus seemed pretty full, so I was just starting to climb on board myself when a lone figure came running out the front doors. "Excuse me, sir? Is this the Schönbrunn tour?"

I would know that voice anywhere, and I turned back to find Olivia standing there, slightly out of breath, looking as beautiful as ever in her white winter coat and hat, her newly-brown hair spilling over her shoulders and her cheeks tinged pink.

So much for getting through the day without thinking about her.

"It is," I confirmed, giving her a smile as though finding ourselves thrown together once again was perfectly normal. "Though I don't think the 'sir' is necessary."

Her eyes widened in surprise for just a second before she caught herself. "Good morning, Noah. I didn't realize it was you."

Obviously. "Good morning," I replied, glancing behind her to look for her friend, but there was no one else there. "Are you on your own?"

She nodded, her lips pursed. "I've been trying to drag Tessa out of bed but she is very aware of the fact that it's only 3 am in New York, and she's not budging. She told me to go without her, so here I am."

There she was indeed, like some kind of punishment for me and a reward at the same time. "Well, you can sit with me if you'd like. I'm on my own too, though I'm technically working."

Though she seemed surprised by the offer, she agreed anyway and followed me onto the bus. After letting her take the window seat just behind the driver, I sat down next to her.

"I didn't have you pegged as the organized tour type," I observed as the bus pulled away from the hotel. "I thought you'd be doing all your own research and have lists and schedules and the whole nine yards."

Our family snowball fights were just one example of how Olivia had always liked to be prepared.

She smiled a little sheepishly. "I do have a guide book full of tabs and highlighted sections back in my room."

That was the Olivia I knew. "So then, why are you here?"

"We just arrived yesterday," she reminded me. "And I didn't know how late we'd be out last night, so I thought I'd book something easy and stress-free for our first day here. I wasn't counting on the stress of having to get Tessa out of bed though!"

We both laughed and I couldn't really believe how natural it felt to be sitting there and chatting with her like that. It appeared she was going to pretend the previous Christmas had never happened, and I was happy to follow along.

Something she'd said had caught my attention though. "Did you go out somewhere last night?"

The smile on her face faltered a little bit, but only for a second. "Yeah, we just went to this club I'd heard about during my research."

The idea of her at a club, on a crowded dance floor, other men touching her as she moved, immediately turned me on, and I shifted a little in my seat as my dick began to stir. I was going to have to change the subject.

The first words that came into my head immediately spilled out of my mouth. "I heard you broke up with your boyfriend recently."

Fuck, that wasn't any better. She looked surprised and a little confused that I knew about it, or perhaps just that I would bring it up. "Yeah, I did. I guess my dad still likes to talk, huh?"

I couldn't deny it, since that was where I'd heard about it. "Jackson sounded disappointed. How are you feeling?"

She shrugged casually. "It's fine. He was a nice guy but we just weren't right for each other in the long term. Being together was fun while it lasted and then we moved on. Not everything needs to be forever, right?"

My mind instantly flashed back to Christmas Eve, to her in her underwear in my bed, telling me she didn't need a lifetime commitment. At the time, I thought she was being naïve because of her inexperience, but maybe she truly believed it?

The idea that she actually might not have a problem with casual sex was a real surprise to me. Even though there was still a wide gap between that and the kind of thing I was into, for the first time all year, I felt a little bit of hope.

Maybe she wasn't quite the good girl I'd imagined her to be?

~Olivia~

Noah and I continued to chat for the rest of the bus ride to the palace, talking casually about school and our mutual acquaintances as if we hadn't spent the past year avoiding each other. He didn't bring up anything about the previous Christmas so I didn't either. It surprised me when he asked about my boyfriend, but I figured he probably didn't know many other things about my life at that moment to ask about. My parents hadn't told me much about him in the last year either, since I stopped asking, though I thought they would have at least mentioned that he worked in the same city I planned to vacation in.

Noah seemed impressed when I told him my team had reached the finals of the NCAA volleyball tournament that year and he laughed and teased me about how mad I still was that we'd lost. He asked curious questions about the classes I was taking, and when we pulled into the drive to the front of the palace, it felt like it had only been a couple of minutes we'd been talking rather than half an hour.

Everyone piled off the bus and Noah had to leave me to go and help the tour director, but as soon as we were inside the palace and following the local tour guide, he returned to my side, walking through the rooms beside me as we listened and made comments to each other on the things we were seeing.

"The palace was modelled after the palace of Versailles in France," the tour guide told us. "Which is interesting because one of the most famous people to have been born here, Marie Antoinette, ended up calling that palace her home, at least for a while, when she was sent to marry the French dauphin."

"Aren't you glad arranged marriages aren't common anymore?" I asked Noah as we moved into the imperial bedroom.

He shrugged. "Sometimes they worked out and sometimes they didn't. Sounds like just about any marriage to me."

I couldn't tell if he meant that seriously or not. "How can you say that? Your parents have an amazing marriage."

Just like my own parents, Gemma and Cole hadn't lost any of their passion for each other over the years. I often saw Cole whispering in Gemma's ear, and though I couldn't imagine what he said, her eyes always sparkled afterwards, like they had some kind of secret only the two of them knew.

Noah's green eyes looked down on me, not exactly sparkling but gazing at me with interest, at least, just as engaged in the conversation as I was. "They got very lucky. Finding someone who's your match on every level is pretty rare, from what I've seen."

"What levels are you concerned about?" I was very curious to know what he looked for in a woman, even though I no longer flattered myself that I might figure on his list.

"Well, first, there's the professional side," he explained, pointing up at the portraits of the Emperor and Empress on the wall above the bed. "That's why these arranged marriages were made in the first place. You need someone who's going to fit into your world and have business interests that align with yours."

Noah and I would definitely have aligning interests if I ended up working at Stamer Hotels, though lately I hadn't thought about that nearly as much as I used to. "Okay, that's one. What else?"

We followed the tour into the dining room next and Noah gestured to the table as he made his next point.

"The social and personality side of things. Ideally, they'd be someone you'd like to spend time with, someone who's interesting and makes you think and makes you laugh too. You're going to have a lot of meals together, a lot of time spent in each other's company, so it should be enjoyable. That's harder to find."

I had never had any trouble making Noah laugh, or vice versa, but I didn't bring that up. Why was I even thinking about it? I had left my dreams of me and Noah behind a long time ago.

At least, I thought I had.

Before I could ask about his next criteria, the tour guide started talking about Empress Maria Theresa and the sixteen children she gave birth to over nineteen years, and I couldn't help wincing at the idea. Noah noticed it and laughed.

"You'd have to have the same ideas about kids too," he teased me. "That's important in a marriage."

I had no idea how Noah felt about kids and asking him didn't seem like a good idea. "Anything else?" I asked instead.

"Well, there's the way the kids are made, of course. You'd want someone who's compatible with you in the bedroom."

Besides the night I had 'accidentally' shown up in his bed, that comment marked the first time Noah and I ever talked directly about sex. And not just sex, but the kind of sex that people liked.

My heart beat a little faster as my mind raced, trying to figure out what to say to him that might help to clear the air between us. I wanted him to know that I didn't judge him for what I'd seen the year before, but I didn't know if he would appreciate me bringing it up. Would it be easier to just keep pretending the whole thing had never happened, or should I address the elephant in the room and bring it out into the open?

Before I could decide how to reply, the guide announced the end of the tour and told us that we had some free time to explore the gardens and the Christmas market outside. Noah excused himself to check in with the hotel's tour director but he came back a few minutes later.

"She says I'm free for the next hour until we meet back here for lunch, so do you want to go walk in the gardens for a while?"

I quickly agreed and we walked together out of the palace into the bright December sunshine. A thin layer of snow covered the impressive formal gardens that stretched from the rear of the palace up a large hill where an imposing yellow monument stood guard.

"It's supposed to be a really good view from up there," I said, pointing to the Gloriette on top of the hill.

"Let's go take a look," Noah suggested, taking my hint.

We walked side-by-side, our hands in our pockets to keep warm as I tried to find the words I wanted to say. "We didn't quite finish our conversation inside about marriage."

Noah glanced over at me curiously. "Didn't we? We covered business, leisure and pleasure. I thought that was pretty much it."

His pithy summary made me smile. "Those are all important, but I just wanted to say that sometimes you can't judge all that about a person right away. You need to spend some time together and give things a try before you see how truly compatible you are. That's what makes choosing your own partner better than an arranged marriage, because you have a chance to see if you can grow together before you're stuck together forever."

"You shouldn't have to change who you are for anyone," he replied, sounding a little guarded as he tried to work out where my words were leading. Maybe he thought I was going to suggest that he give up his kinks to be with someone, but that wasn't what I meant at all.

"No, you shouldn't," I agreed. "But sometimes, people don't know they're interested in something because they haven't been exposed to it. Someone who's only ever worked in a fast food restaurant, for example, might not know she'd be great at running a hotel empire, simply because she's never had a chance to try. Does that mean you shouldn't give her a chance?"

"So, I should be trolling my local McDonalds for dates?" he teased, taking my argument to its most extreme conclusion.

"Maybe," I shot back, wrinkling my nose at him. "Though you'd have to eat there too so it didn't look too suspicious, and I'm not sure that's on your diet."

I poked him in the stomach to make my point, and even through the layers of his suit and his winter coat, my finger hit solid muscle. The vision of him shirtless in his bed came rushing back to me, sending a wave of desire through me that almost made me groan in frustration. I thought I was past that. Those kinds of thoughts about Noah were supposed to have been shelved for good.

He pressed his hand to his stomach, pretending I'd hurt him. "And do you think that applies to all levels of the relationship? That things can develop even if they aren't there in the beginning?"

That was just the opening I'd been waiting for, so I summoned all my courage and looked him straight in the eye. "I think with sex especially, a lot of people don't know what they like until they try different things. I don't imagine your first time was with a room full of people."

Noah's feet nearly tripped him up again, just as they had that night back at Isabel's farm when he nearly fell down the stairs. Being with him made that whole night seem so close, like I could almost reach out and touch it. Like I could blink and find myself back there again.

His eyes were wide with surprise as he regained his footing and looked over at me. He obviously hadn't expected me to bring it up and I forced myself to stay silent to see what he would say.

"My first time wasn't like that," he confirmed, the words coming out of his mouth slowly. "I'm sorry if seeing that made you uncomfortable, Liv. I didn't know you were coming that night."

Of course he hadn't, and I quickly hurried to explain myself. "I know, and you don't owe me any apology. I'm sorry for showing up unannounced. What I walked in on did shock me, as I'm sure you guessed, and I've been avoiding you because I was embarrassed, but I'm not upset with you. I hope you haven't been worried about that."

He blinked quickly a couple of times as he thought over my words. I had obviously taken him completely by surprise by bringing it up so bluntly.

"I was worried that you thought less of me," he finally admitted. "And I was embarrassed too, not because of what I was doing but because I wasn't just honest about it with you in the first place."

"I understand," I assured him truthfully. After everything I'd been through in the last year, I understood him better than ever. "And I don't think less of you at all, Noah. That's what you're into, and that's okay. It's not for me to judge."

"Thanks, Liv." He looked away from me, like he didn't want me to know how much that affected him, but I knew him better than that. I didn't need to see his face to know he appreciated my support. When he looked back at me, his smile was softer and more natural. "I've missed you."

"I've missed you, too. Now, let's see who can get to the top of this hill first."

Without any further warning, I took off up the path while Noah shouted out behind me that I was cheating. By the time we reached the top of the hill, me just ahead of him, we were both out of breath and laughing as I claimed victory.

Looking out over the view of the palace and the city beyond with Noah beside me, I felt better than I had in a long time. Maybe friends were all Noah and I would ever be, but at least I had my friend back. That almost made the whole trip to Vienna worthwhile all on its own.

Chapter Seven

GLORY HOLE

~Noah~

By the time we got back to the hotel, I felt a hundred times better than I had that morning. Olivia and I finished our walk in the garden and had lunch together, along with a group of women in their sixties from Kansas who were on a big European Christmas market tour. Everyone was in a good mood, laughing and joking together.

When Olivia asked the ladies what they thought about the empress who had sixteen children, one of them looked over at me with a knowing smile. "If my husband had looked like your boyfriend here, I would have done the same."

That set the women off laughing again while I waited for Olivia to correct the woman and tell her that we weren't together. However, she didn't say anything, simply carrying on with the conversation as if it were true. I supposed she must have figured it wouldn't be worthwhile trying to explain, but to my surprise, I found that I really didn't mind them making the assumption either.

After lunch, we had time to look around the Christmas market stalls in front of the palace. Olivia picked out some things for her family and friends while I bought my mom a pretty ornament with a hand painted picture of the palace on it and a painted glass nutcracker for Eve. She always used to threaten my balls when she got mad at me, so I figured the metaphor was appropriate.

My dad was always the hardest to buy for, but after coming up empty at the market, I wondered if The Playground had some tongue-in-cheek Christmas stuff for sale. It was certainly possible. They did sell merchandise, so I decided to check with Nina that night, thinking he would probably get a kick out of something like that.

"I've got to get back to work," I told Olivia as we got off the bus back at the hotel. "But if you're free tonight, maybe we could grab dinner? I know the best schnitzel in town."

As I expected, that made her laugh. "I don't think you've had time to try all the schnitzel in Vienna yet, unless that's all you've been doing here."

I definitely hadn't been spending my free time that way, and for just a moment, I was tempted to tell her about The Playground to see how she'd react. When she told me that my kink didn't bother her, it honestly meant the world to me, but I knew there was still a big difference between being okay with it and wanting to do anything like it herself. In the end, the temptation passed and I kept my mouth shut.

Olivia turned me down anyway, though she sounded apologetic about it. "Tessa and I actually have plans tonight. Maybe tomorrow?"

I swallowed down my disappointment, reminding myself that we both had other obligations; she had her friend to think about and I actually had plans that night too, and just about every other night for the rest of the month. Tate owed me a favour or two, though, so I ought to be able to convince him to spend one night doing something else. "Tomorrow would be great. I've actually got a friend here with me too so maybe the four of us could hang out. We could go visit the big market down at the Rathaus, unless that's what you're doing tonight?"

For some reason, her cheeks turned slightly pink. "Uh, no, we're doing something else tonight, but that sounds great for tomorrow."

With that agreed, we set a time to meet in the lobby the next evening and I let her go, watching her retreating back as she headed for the elevator. The day had definitely taken an unexpected turn but I couldn't be happier about it.

When my shift ended, I went to my room, showered, and changed into a fresh suit. As usual for The Playground, I didn't bother with a tie, leaving the top two buttons of my shirt undone. Everything would be coming off at some point anyway.

After a quick meal in the hotel restaurant, Tate and I grabbed a cab to the club, where he groaned when I told him I'd made other plans for us the next evening. "Trust me, after you see the girls we're hanging out with tonight, you're going to wish you hadn't done that."

He actually pictured us spending more than one night with these women? My curiosity got even stronger about exactly what had impressed him so much.

"Where are we meeting them?" I asked as we went through the club's security and left all our stuff in the lockers. The wristbands the club gave us acted as our payment method; all drinks were charged to it so we didn't have to carry cash or cards with us. Everyone had as little on them as possible.

"We didn't set up anything specific, so we'll just wait for them in the Plaza, unless they're here already."

A quick survey of the room told us they weren't, so Tate and I sat down at one of the booths where we'd be left alone and ordered some drinks from the bar.

"Look, they're doing glory holes in the viewing rooms tonight," Tate pointed out as he scrolled through the electronic menu where the club also advertised their special events. "Do you want to sign up?"

"How does it work?" He raised his eyebrows at me and I rolled my eyes. "I know what a glory hole is. I just mean: how does the club set it up?"

He scanned through the information on the tablet. "You sign up and say if you want a man or a woman. There's fabric hung across the middle of the room with a hole just big enough for your dick, so you can't see who's on the other side but the people in the viewing area can see both sides. In other words, the crowd can see who's sucking who off, but you and the woman would have no idea."

That sounded like fun. The people watching me turned me on more than the person touching me, to be honest, so it didn't really matter to me who sucked me off. I could imagine the mouth belonged to anyone. Hell, I could even imagine Olivia there if I really wanted to.

My dick immediately began to harden at the idea, making it clear that I had definitely recovered from my lack of sex drive the night before. That evening, I felt completely ready for it.

"What about these women we're supposed to meet?" I reminded him.

He shrugged. "Maybe they'll want to take part too, or at least watch. Even if they don't, we can't wait all night for them."

That sounded more like the Tate I knew. "Sign me up, then."

Glancing around the room as he booked us a time, I saw Nina chatting with some of the regular customers by the bar and I remembered I wanted to ask her about a present for my dad.

"I'm going to go talk to Nina for a few minutes. I'll be back soon."

"Okay, but I got us in for twenty minutes from now," he warned me. "Don't be late."

Though I shouldn't take that long, I didn't want him to stress about it. "Go without me if I'm not back. I'll find you afterwards."

After he nodded in agreement, I headed over to the bar.

"Hey there, Noah," Nina greeted me with a friendly smile as I approached. "What can I do for you tonight?"

Most people at the club used fake names but Tate and I hadn't bothered. If someone saw a picture of me, they'd recognize me no matter which name I used, so it didn't seem worth the trouble. The nice thing about a place like The Playground was the high level of discretion. Even if people did recognize me, they wouldn't spread it around. The chance of anyone I knew ever finding out I'd been there was infinitesimally small.

Nina's hand rested on my arm as she asked her question, with clear interest in her eyes. Although she worked there, she'd made it plain to me that she'd be willing to take a break to play with me if I wanted to, but honestly, I didn't. As soon as I got to know a woman, my desire to have sex with her lessened considerably. I much preferred when I didn't know a thing about my partners.

Olivia was the obvious exception to that general rule, though I still didn't fully understand why.

I explained I was looking for a gift for my dad and she promised me the club had exactly the kind of thing I wanted. Leading me to one of the offices, she sat me down at a desk where we looked at the merchandise together until I picked out some gold-plated cufflinks that at first glance looked like an abstract pattern but on closer inspection were actually a couple in a tantric position. My dad would love them.

"That's perfect, thanks for your help, Nina."

"I'm more than happy to help. With anything."

Her eyes moved across my body in invitation, but *my* eyes went to the clock on the wall and I swore beneath my breath. "Fuck, I didn't realize the time. I'm booked into one of the viewing rooms in two minutes."

Nina smiled through her disappointment. "Maybe I'll come and watch."

"That sounds great. See you later."

Tate would have already gone by then since I told him not to wait, so I went straight to the rooms in question. They had the 'backstage' area divided by curtains too so we really couldn't see who was in the other half of the room.

"Sie sind spät," the staff member admonished me in German, letting me know I was late. I apologized as she directed me through a temporary curtained hall leading to a door. Opening it up, I stepped inside to find the room just as Tate described it. The wall in front of me was half-window, with a small crowd of people gathered on the other side. A chair in the room was the only furniture other than the silk curtain which hung to my right, dividing the room in two. A circular hole had been cut into the centre of the curtain, but I could only see empty space on the other side.

Standing in front of the window, facing the onlookers straight on, I removed my shoes first, then my belt, and unzipped my pants. The eyes watching me, and the eager anticipation and enjoyment on their faces, got me hard as I pulled my pants and underwear down, letting my dick spring free. My pants, I removed entirely, leaving my legs bare, but I kept my shirt and suit jacket on. My dick was really all that I needed out, and every eye on the other side of the glass was fixed on it.

My body hot with anticipation, I stepped over to the hole and stuck my dick straight through it.

~Olivia~

When I got back to the hotel room after saying goodbye to Noah, I found Tessa still lounging around in her robe. "Did you just get up?" I asked in disbelief. "Half the day is over."

She shrugged, looking completely unapologetic. "I was having the hottest dream about that guy from the club last night until the housekeeping staff woke me up. The guy apologized when he saw me in bed and left right away, but I could have sworn he even *looked* like the guy from the club, the dream was that strong."

I tried my best to follow all of that. "Which guy from the club? Andrei?"

She wrinkled her nose. "No, the one you were hanging out with: Tate."

I hadn't realized he'd made such an impression on her. "Well, it's lucky for you we're seeing him again tonight, then. But first, we're seeing some of Vienna, so hurry up and get dressed!"

With a groan, she went off to shower and get ready and eventually, we did manage to make it for a tour of the opera house and for dinner, cake and coffee at the historic Sacher hotel before the time came to get ready for our night at The Playground.

I had been tempted to accept Noah's offer of dinner when he made it, but in the end, I was glad I hadn't. I didn't need to drop everything for him, and Tessa was really looking forward to that night. To be honest, it excited me too. The night before, we'd really only dipped our toes in the kink pool, but that night, I was ready to get a little wetter.

That evening, I wore a pink babydoll set from my new lingerie collection. Lace covered my bust, held in place with thin straps over my shoulders, and sheer fabric floated down beneath my breasts to the top of my hips, with a pink thong beneath it. Tessa chose a red and black corset with black panties and as we stood in front of the hotel mirror to check ourselves out, I had to admit we looked pretty damn good. If Tate and his friend didn't show up for any reason, we wouldn't have any trouble finding other willing partners.

The Playground seemed a little busier than it had been the night before, I noticed, as we walked out into the Plaza in our high heels. Maybe the day of the week made a difference; that night was Wednesday, and I already knew that weekends were the busiest. Maybe by Friday or Saturday, I'd be ready to do one of the viewing rooms or even the main stage with a big audience. Just the idea sent a thrill of excitement through me.

"There he is!" Tessa spotted Tate first, sitting at one of the booths along the wall and he stood up to greet us with a smile.

"You both look amazing," he told us as he kissed our cheeks, one after the other, his eyes roaming freely and shamelessly across both our bodies. Wearing a suit as he had the night before, he still looked just as good as I remembered, but for a moment, I wished Noah's eyes were looking at me that way instead.

No. I was *not* going to spend my time thinking about him, I admonished myself. I'd promised Noah the next evening, but that evening was all about me.

"Where's your friend?" I asked Tate as we took a seat next to him. He'd already ordered us some drinks, which was kind of him. In a place like The Playground, we didn't need to worry about anyone spiking our drinks. Security was tight, not to mention the fact that we were all there to have sex anyway. "Or did you just make him up?"

Tate laughed. "I promise you, he's real, he just stepped away for a minute. I'm glad I caught you, though: we've signed up for a special event tonight and there's still room if you'd like to take part."

"What kind of event?" Tessa asked curiously.

Tate explained about the glory hole viewing rooms, and the more he described it, the more turned on I got. I didn't have a huge amount of experience with blowjobs, but I had done my research on them once I became sexually active, the same as I did research on everything, and my boyfriend had always been satisfied. The idea of people watching me do it while also not knowing anything about the person I gave it to seemed doubly taboo and therefore even more exciting.

"What do you think?" Tate asked when he had finished his explanation, his face alight with anticipation.

"I'd love to," I told him honestly. "But not with you, if that's okay. I'd rather not know who it is."

That didn't offend him at all. In fact, he completely understood. "Of course, that's part of the fun. Tiffany?"

It took Tessa a moment to realize he was talking to her, and I had to bite my lip to keep from laughing. She would be terrible undercover.

"I don't know," she replied when she finally figured out the question was meant for her. "I've never had anyone watch me before."

"It's absolutely fine if you don't want to," he assured her. "Not everyone's into the same thing, which is why places like this exist. You could watch if you want to instead."

"I wouldn't mind watching you," she told him, making his eyes light up even more, the idea obviously appealing to him too. "Watching Liv would just be weird for me."

"Liv?" Tate repeated, looking curiously between the two of us.

I groaned internally. "It's a nickname," I explained, semi-truthfully. "It's a long story, but she means me."

"Sorry, Belle." Tessa shot me a sheepish smile.

Tate pressed a few things on the tablet on the table before using it to scan my wristband. "There you go, Belle, you're all signed up. One random dick, coming your way."

That made me laugh even as my body began to pulse with excitement. This was really happening. I was going to give a complete stranger a blowjob in front of a crowd of people. What would Noah think if he could see me?

Oh my God. I *really* needed to stop thinking about him. As Tate told us we should get going, I slammed back the remaining contents of my glass.

"What about your friend?" I asked, getting to my feet.

"He'll find us," Tate promised. "Don't worry about him. Just enjoy yourself."

I certainly intended to.

With Tate leading the way, we made our way back to the exhibition area we'd visited the night before, and Tate found Tessa a prime viewing spot in front of one of the rooms before he and I headed 'backstage', as he called it. A woman with a tablet scanned our wristbands before directing Tate to one room and me to another.

"Should I take my clothes off?" I asked her, my stomach filled with both nerves and excitement as I looked at the closed door in front of me.

"It's up to you," the woman told me. "Personally, I think you look great just as you are."

The heat in her eyes told me the compliment wasn't random. She found me attractive, and that thought turned me on even more.

Taking a deep breath, I stepped into the empty room. While the night before, the viewing rooms had been full of furniture that the occupants could use as they pleased, that night, the room was completely empty other than the silk curtain hanging down the middle of the room with a hole cut into it, and a plush mat on the floor just beneath it.

The mat was there to protect my knees, I realized, and another shot of desire ran through me. *Fuck.* I was really doing this.

A crowd had already gathered on the other side of the window and though I didn't know if I should acknowledge them or not, I finally decided to give them a little wave. Several of them waved back, confirming they could definitely see me just as well as I could see them.

The seconds ticked away, dragging into minutes, and the dual feelings of nerves and excitement both grew stronger. Why was it taking so long? Was this normal? Should I be doing something else?

I licked my lips to try to moisten them, and that brought some catcalls from the other side of the glass, the noise muffled by the wall between us but not completely blocked. Emboldened by that reaction, I ran my hands down my body, over top of the fabric, which was met with more sounds of approval.

The enjoyment I could see and hear from the gathered onlookers only made me hotter.

At last, I heard the door open and close on the other side of the room, and my heart beat faster as I tried to imagine the person behind the curtain. However, no matter what images I tried to keep in my head, the one I kept returning to over and over was Noah. I could almost see him in his suit, greeting the crowd with a smirk before getting his cock out.

And suddenly, it appeared: a rather long, thick cock jutting through the hole in front of me, and my mouth began to water.

Dropping to my knees, aware of every face watching me, I took hold of the base of the cock in front of me. A very impressive specimen, I had to admit; certainly bigger than my boyfriend's. For a moment, I wondered if I could even get my lips around it, but there was only one way to find out for sure.

Using my thumb to push it upwards, I licked along the underside of the shaft first, starting at the base and working my way to the tip. Again,

I could hear the cheers and encouragement from the other side of the glass, giving me confidence as I reached the head, letting my tongue flick along the ridge as the cock jumped eagerly in response. Whoever it belonged to was obviously enjoying himself too.

Looking over at the gathered crowd, making eye contact with them one by one, I opened my mouth wide and took him in deep.

~Noah~

Everything about the glory hole was incredible. The woman on the other side of the curtain must have had some kind of magic tongue because I had never been so hard so soon into a blowjob. Or maybe it had to do with the people watching us, and watching her, especially. Though they did look at me to see my reaction, most of their attention was focused on the other side of the curtain since all the action was taking place there.

As her warm, wet mouth wrapped around my head, the cheers of encouragement from the crowd, egging her on, only got me harder. Several of the men at the window were touching themselves, and some of the women too. From their expressions, I could see the jealousy of some of the men, wishing *their* dick was the one in this woman's mouth, but that pleasure belonged to me.

Her tongue vibrated against my shaft as she took me in deeper, until I could feel the back of her throat, the tightness there making me even harder. I tried to hold in my sounds of pleasure, not wanting to break the spell of anonymity between us, but I couldn't stop a low groan from escaping as she went faster, her hand pumping me too.

Fuck, this was going to be over very soon if she didn't slow down. I couldn't remember the last time I had been so turned on.

And suddenly, in my mind's eye, Olivia was on the other side of the curtain, down on her knees sucking me off as the whole crowd watched, and that only made me harder still.

"Scheisse," I muttered, about the only German word I'd picked up from the women I'd fucked in the club so far.

The woman must have heard me, or maybe she just felt how hard I was getting, because she slowed right down, obviously not wanting the blowjob to be over so quickly any more than I did. Her mouth left me but her hand took over, slowly and firmly, maintaining my desire but not heightening it just yet. Fuck, she really knew what she was doing.

I couldn't imagine Tate being nearly as lucky with his match.

Turning my head, I made eye contact with one of the men on the other side of the glass. "Is she hot?" I mouthed to him, gesturing to the curtain in front of me.

He laughed, clearly having understood me. "Gorgeous," was his mouthed reply. "Lucky bastard."

At that moment, I almost felt he was the lucky one. At least he knew what she looked like so he could try to track her down later on. I had no idea who she might be and I already knew the club staff wouldn't tell me. The whole point of the room was to keep the encounter completely anonymous, but as my pleasure built, I was tempted to tear the curtain down so I could see for myself just who that unbelievable mouth belonged to.

~Olivia~

The muttered curse from the other side of the curtain brought me back to my senses. I'd been so caught up in what I was doing, so turned on by the people watching me, that I almost missed how close he was to orgasm.

I definitely wasn't ready for the experience to be over yet, so I turned it way down, pumping him slowly with my hand until it felt like he had regained some control. My tongue played along his shaft, licking and kissing him before sucking just his head in as he moaned again.

His voice was deep, and in my turned-on haze, he almost sounded like Noah. However, the only word he'd spoken had been in German, so my mind had to be playing tricks on me. Even so, I couldn't help imagining Noah's face looking down on me, the desire in his eyes as I began to deep throat my mystery man's cock again.

That time, I had no intention of stopping, working him harder and faster until I felt his balls tightening. At the last moment, I pulled back, finishing him off with my hand so everyone could see it. The crowd wanted the money shot. They wanted to see him coming, they wanted to see him come *on* me, and I was happy to oblige.

The warm strands shot onto my chest, giving me a pearl necklace that pleased the crowd immensely. Everyone watching broke into applause, sending my own need even higher. *Fuck, I was turned on.* That had been one of the sexiest things I had ever done and no one had even touched me.

Getting to my feet, I gave the crowd a small bow and a wink before heading back out the door to go get washed up. The quicker I finished, the quicker I could find my own satisfaction.

I needed to get fucked, and I needed it soon.

~Noah~

Despite the amazing orgasm I just had, the whole experience left me feeling a little unsatisfied. Not knowing the identity of the woman on the other side of the curtain was driving me crazy. Though I would have loved to come in her mouth, the way she finished me with her hand and the applause from the crowd afterwards told me that she'd made a show of it. Being in public wasn't just about making me come. Enjoying the performance was equally important, and she must get the same rush from being in front of the crowd that I did.

A dozen other ways we could entertain people together popped into my mind. I didn't consider myself a selfish lover and I'd be more than happy to return the favour she'd just done me. What a shame there was no equivalent of the glory hole for the woman. Maybe it could be done with a curtain across her stomach? I should suggest it to Nina as another event for the club.

Those and a host of other random thoughts ran through my head as I acknowledged the crowd outside the window with a wave and pulled my pants back on, rushing out the door as fast as I could to see if I could catch sight of the woman who must have left just before me. Frustratingly, I couldn't see any sign of her backstage. Undeterred, I went around to the front of the viewing room to see if I could talk to someone who'd been watching us, but they'd all dispersed as well, quickly moving on once the show ended.

I did, however, see Tate through the window of one of the other rooms. His blowjob was still going on, which must have meant, as I'd suspected, that he wasn't getting quite the amazing treatment I had. From what I could tell, the woman was working hard at it, but maybe a little too hard. I tried to catch Tate's eye, but his gaze was locked on someone at the front of the crowd. From where I stood, I could only see the back of her head and her reddish hair. Was that the girl he'd been telling me about before, the one who was special?

Before I could find out, another man approached me, a complete stranger, and spoke to me with an Australian accent. "We need some eyes in one of the private rooms. Are you interested?"

That was a typical request in that area of the club. Tate and I had been pulled into plenty of rooms during our time there. If people were at the club on their own or with just one other person, as Tate and I were, but wanted a slightly bigger crowd for their scene, they would simply ask whoever was close by. Most people were happy to oblige, just as I was. Glancing over at Tate again, I could tell he would still be a while. We'd catch up with each other later.

"Sure. Lead the way."

As we walked down the hallway to the private rooms, he waxed poetic about the woman we were about to see. "Wish I'd got in there first, but watching will be almost as good. She's fucking gorgeous."

Most of the women there were. They needed to have a certain level of self-confidence to do what we did, and more often than not, that confidence came from knowing just how good-looking they were. Or maybe, the confidence just made them even sexier.

As we entered the room, a few other people had already gathered: two couples and a couple of other men on their own. The scene had already begun, and as my eyes landed on the woman on the bed, I had to admit that the guy who brought me there had been right. She was incredible, or at least her body was. At that moment, I couldn't see her face.

She knelt on the bed, on her hands and knees, so that we were looking at her from the side, and she was still fully clothed, or at least as clothed as most of the women were. Her pink babydoll top highlighted her firm breasts perfectly as the material beneath them floated down onto the bed below her. The sheerness of the top made the shape of her completely visible beneath it, and that shape couldn't be any better.

The matching pink thong didn't hide much either, and as we entered the room, the man in the scene with her pulled the thin fabric aside and licked a long line from top to tail, his thick tongue sliding across her exposed skin slowly and firmly.

The woman's head, which had been hanging down between her arms, her long, brown hair obscuring her face, raised up as he tasted her, and a sweet moan of contentment came from her lips. At last, she turned to face the crowd and as our eyes connected, the whole world shifted around me.

Chapter Eight

DISCOVERY

~Olivia~

Almost as soon as I reentered the public side of the viewing room area, a man appeared in front of me, wearing a slate-blue dress shirt with the sleeves rolled up. "That was amazing," he said appreciatively, his eyes lingering on my chest where the mystery man's cum had been until I washed it off. "You deserve a reward after a show like that, and I'd love to be the one to give it to you."

Well, fuck, that was direct. And since he'd offered exactly what I was looking for, I had no reason to refuse. He was good-looking, tall and tanned, with a slightly exotic accent, maybe from South Africa or New Zealand. I couldn't pinpoint it exactly but it really didn't matter. I didn't need his life story, I just needed to come. My body already throbbed with anticipation and as his eyes travelled across it once more, the sensation only got stronger.

"What are you suggesting?"

He grinned as I asked for more details, understanding that he had my attention. "I've got a private room already booked for tonight. My friend, Ken, would like to watch."

He pointed to a blond man nearby who gave me a nod and a smile. He actually looked a bit like a Ken doll with his perfectly styled hair, tanned skin and muscled physique. Was that where they came up with the name for him to use? I suspected Ken wasn't his real name, no more than Belle was mine.

"I'd like more people to watch," I blurted out before I'd even realized I meant to say it. Having the crowd in the viewing room had been very powerful for me, and I'd found that I liked to vary the experience by looking at different people. Having just one person there almost felt more intimate, like some kind of connection existed between us, and I didn't want that.

I wanted the anonymity of the crowd. I wanted to get lost in it.

"Of course," the man in front of me quickly agreed, gesturing his friend over to us. "Can you pick up a few extra eyes? Room 17."

Ken nodded and went on his way while the first man put an arm around my shoulder and led me towards the hall where the private rooms were located.

"What do I call you?" he asked. "Other than beautiful?"

The compliment made me smile as I stuck to my false name. "Belle."

"French for beautiful? That's even better. You can call me Derek and trust me, you're going to remember it after you scream it for me in front of everyone."

He grabbed hold of my hips, pressing me against his stiff cock straining against his pants, and my knees almost buckled as the dampness between my legs got worse. I had only had one drink but I felt almost drunk anyway, high off the adulation of the crowd and the lust of this man I'd never met before.

The room he took me into had a single bed in the middle of it with crisp, clean sheets. "Do you have any ground rules?" he asked as he let go of me and began to undo the buttons of his shirt. "Any limits?"

The chest that revealed itself beneath was hard and defined, with a tattoo covering most of the left side. The pattern was intricate and I couldn't quite make out what it signified.

Despite the aching, insistent thrumming of my body, I forced myself to focus on his question. I had given the subject a lot of thought beforehand

and I did have two rules, which I laid out for him plainly: "Condom for penetration, and no anal with your cock. Fingers are okay."

The condom was simply a matter of intimacy. Everyone at the club had been STD-tested, and I had birth control covered so pregnancy didn't really worry me. I just didn't particularly like the idea of some guy I didn't know coming inside me. Considering everything else I was willing to do, perhaps it didn't make much sense, but it was still a limit for me.

And the anal rule was simply because I hadn't done it before. I wouldn't mind trying it, but I figured my first time wasn't going to be particularly sexy and I definitely didn't want a man just going in there without preparing me properly first. It would have to be someone I really trusted.

I had asked my boyfriend once if he wanted to try but he had no interest. And since, up until that night, he was the only man I'd ever had sex with, I was still an anal virgin, and I intended to stay one for the next two weeks unless something truly unexpected happened.

The part about never having sex with any other guy was definitely about to change, though, and within the next few minutes by the looks of it.

Derek agreed to my rules without complaint and he helped me up onto the bed, positioning me on my hands and knees so he'd have full access to me and the other people in the room would have a good view too. His hands ran across my ass, almost completely bare to him besides my tiny thong.

"Fuck, Belle, I'm looking forward to this," he muttered, driving my need even higher.

A few people began to drift into the room as Derek continued to explore my body. I watched the couple who stood closest to me as Derek's big, warm hands cupped my breasts, and two more men entered the room as Derek's fingers slid between my legs, rubbing the fabric of my thong against my clit, making me moan as my head dropped between my arms. Closing my eyes for just a moment, I tried to savour every sensation, not only from his touch, but the way every inch of my skin felt alive and sensitive knowing there were others watching every movement.

The gentle click of the door closing let me know that the rest of our audience had arrived, and with my head still hanging, I felt Derek pull my thong to the side, followed by the sensation of what could only be his tongue, tasting me intimately and deeply in front of all those other people.

The experience was everything I'd hoped for and exactly what I wanted and needed. As I let out another small moan, I raised my head to look at the people gathered, wanting to share it with them. The pleasure wasn't only mine; it belonged to them too, and that was what made it so good.

A second later, I locked onto the green eyes at the back of the room, staring at me in total shock.

~Noah~

For just a moment, I thought I had to be seeing things. After all, Olivia had been on my mind all day. Hell, I'd literally just been thinking about her while I had my dick in some unknown woman's mouth. That had to be the reason that I saw her face on the woman in front of me. Nothing else made sense.

But when her blue eyes widened in surprise and her moan of appreciation died in her throat as she got a look at me, I knew she was no hallucination. That *was* Olivia up there. The girl I'd known my whole life, the one who used to blackmail me into playing dolls with her, the one I'd spent Christmases and birthdays and holidays on the beach with, the one who got crazily competitive about everything, the one who made me laugh like no one else, and the one I never, ever thought would even know that a place like this existed, *she* was the girl on her hands and knees in front of a roomful of strangers, looking like a goddess in her sexy pink lingerie, with another man's tongue inside her.

And she was *loving* it.

At least she had been, until she saw me. As the reality of the situation hit her, just as it hit me, fear, confusion, and maybe even a bit of shame flashed across her face, and that was the last thing in the world I wanted her to feel. Though it seemed to me almost impossible that she would actually be there, I couldn't deny my own eyes, and if she wanted the crowd, if she craved it like I did, I was the very last person in the world to make her feel bad about it.

The irony of the situation wasn't lost on me. A year earlier, she walked in on me, and twelve months later, on the other side of the world, there I was, surprising her. The circumstances weren't the same but they were close enough, and I had no intention of making her feel that she'd done anything wrong.

Especially when I felt the complete opposite.

In fact, once the initial shock began to fade and some feeling began to return to my body, I found the whole situation sexy as hell.

My fantasy had literally come to life. In fact, the scene in front of me was better than anything my mind had ever dreamt up. In my daydreams, it had just been me watching her and another man in the privacy of her room. Even in my wildest dreams, I couldn't have imagined that she would get off on having strangers watch her, that she would want to be completely public in that way.

It would have seemed way too far-fetched.

So, when she hung her head again, not in pleasure but in uncertainty, I knew I had to do something. Audience participation wasn't usually encouraged in a private room but I would have to make an exception. Nothing seemed more critical than making sure she didn't think I was upset or disappointed with her or that I judged her in any way. She'd made it clear to me earlier that day that she didn't judge me, and now, I understood exactly why.

She was kinky too.

She was just like me.

Since I didn't know what name she'd used in the club and I didn't want to use her real name in a room full of strangers, I didn't bother with a name at all. I just spoke directly to her, pretending for a moment that no one else was there.

"Look at me."

My words had the desired effect. Every head in the room turned my way, including Olivia's, and I ignored everyone else to focus on the woman before me. She was all I could see.

"You look incredible. I wish you could see just how gorgeous you are with his tongue in your pussy. I bet you taste divine too."

The man with his lips on her groaned in appreciation and agreement. "So fucking sweet, Belle."

Belle. My mind flashed back to rainy Sundays in my parents' apartment, watching Disney movies while raindrops dripped down the windows, me teasing Olivia that she'd end up married to someone ugly like the Beast rather than a prince.

"It doesn't matter what he looks like," her stubborn 10-year-old self retorted. "It's how he makes her feel."

The image faded and the grown-up Olivia's face was back in front of me, watching me watching her. My words and the encouragement of the man behind her seemed to be helping. The embarrassment that had briefly appeared on her face began to fade, replaced with curiosity and perhaps a bit of arousal as well.

She wanted me to keep going. She wanted to hear what else I had to say.

I did my best to give her what she needed. "You're a star up there. Nobody here can take their eyes off you. We all want to see you enjoying this. Everyone in this room is turned on right now because of you."

A jolt of pleasure hit her, her body contracting as her eyes stayed fixed on me. Maybe my words had caused it, or maybe the other man's tongue had found a sweet spot. Either way, seeing her enjoying herself sent a shiver of excitement through me too.

"There's nothing more beautiful than a woman who can share her pleasure with others. We all want to be there with you for it, Belle. We want to see you come, we want to see you let go all over his face. You must be close."

All the telltale signs of an approaching climax were there. Her nipples were hard against the lace of her lingerie, she had instinctively spread her legs a bit wider, and her arms were beginning to tremble. I'd watched those arms on the volleyball court often enough to know that supporting her weight wasn't making them shake. The pleasure building inside her was doing that.

That same pleasure built inside me too. Although I'd enjoyed my own orgasm not very long ago, my dick had grown hard again. How could it not, while I witnessed the sexiest thing I had ever seen in my whole life? Groans of enjoyment were coming from the man with his face between her legs as Olivia's eyes stayed on me, her beautiful pink lips parted and her cheeks flushed.

"Show me, Belle." My voice had gotten quieter, barely louder than a whisper, but I knew she could hear me anyway. "Let me see you give in to it. Let him give it to you."

The man's hands gripped her tighter as he pressed his face in, and whether his touch did it, or what I said, or the combination of both, something took Olivia over the edge. Her elbows buckled as her orgasm took her, and she moaned out a name as her body shook.

Not his name, whatever the hell it might be.

My name, murmured from somewhere deep inside her. "Noah."

With her eyes closed, she couldn't see just how much that affected me. Pride and desire shot through me, pure and strong. That orgasm was for *me*.

Nothing had ever made me fucking happier.

The man continued to lap at her as Olivia firmly pushed herself back up, and she gently moved forward, separating herself from him.

"That was amazing, Derek," she said to him, her smile sweet and sincere. "But I think I'm finished."

He must have been disappointed, but he took it well. Things were only fun as long as both partners were into it; everyone who was serious in the scene knew that. "Sure. It was my pleasure."

Realizing the show was over, the others in the room began to disperse, but I stepped forwards without even meaning to, drawn towards her like I always had been and like I'd never been before. The movement caught Derek's eye and he looked over at me with a bit of a smirk. For the first time, I saw his face unobscured by Olivia's body, and I realized with surprise that he was the man I'd interacted with through the window of the viewing room, the one who told me how gorgeous the woman going down on me was.

Had Olivia been there watching too? Surely I would have noticed her?

"I didn't know you were here with someone," he said to Olivia, looking back and forth between the two of us curiously. "But if you guys want a third sometime, let me know."

Of course he would assume we were together after the way I had just taken over their scene. I didn't bother to correct him and Olivia didn't either. How could we explain the truth? That was far too complicated, and nobody's business but our own.

"Thanks for taking such good care of her." There were a lot of decent guys in the scene but some that weren't. Though I was glad Olivia seemed to know the difference, I had a million questions. How many times had she done this? Did she go to clubs like this at home? Was this the reason she came to Vienna in the first place?

How did I never know that we shared something this big in common?

I wanted answers to those questions and a whole lot more as I turned to her and offered her my hand. "Come with me, Belle. I think it's time for us to talk."

~Olivia~

It felt like I floated back down the hallway with Noah's hand holding mine. We had never held hands before, but it didn't exactly feel romantic. It felt more like he was afraid that I was going to disappear if he let go of me, and honestly, I kind of felt the same. Without him holding me down, I might just leave the ground entirely.

Was this really happening? It seemed so close to some of my dreams that it couldn't be real, but the lights of the club, the other people around us and all the smells and the sounds were too detailed for my mind to come up with on its own.

When I looked up and saw him in the room, when I saw the moment he recognized me, it felt as though someone had dumped ice water over me. All the heat that had been building inside me, the lust and the need created by the glory hole experience and Derek's unabashed interest in me, not to mention the people watching us, it all seemed to freeze as Noah stared at me in complete and utter shock.

What was he doing there? I knew the chance existed that he would be at the club, but right there, in that room? He didn't like to watch, did he? I thought his preferences ran to the group scenes. It honestly never crossed my mind that I would run into him in a private room like that.

And as I watched him process what he was seeing, I realized that must have been what my face looked like when I walked in on him the previous Christmas. In his shock, I could see exactly the message that my reaction would have sent him: that he wasn't who I thought he was.

That I was disappointed in him.

It felt awful.

The blood drained down to my hands and knees, to the lowest parts of me as I hung my head, waiting for the sound of the door closing to let me know that he had left. I didn't even know if I still wanted to go through with the rest of the scene. Derek's tongue continued to explore my exposed slit, but I couldn't concentrate on that. All I felt at that moment was uncomfortable.

But when the sound finally came from the back of the room, it took me completely by surprise. Rather than the sound of the door closing, Noah's voice rang out, calm, in control, and full of authority. When he told me to look at him, I had no choice. And when he told me how beautiful I was, how much he and everyone else were enjoying watching Derek eat me out, and especially when he told me he wanted to see me come, all the fire of my arousal came roaring back, even stronger than before.

The heat in his eyes and the tension in his body told me those weren't just idle words. He really wanted it. Watching me affected him too, in a good way, so when my orgasm finally took me, the words he spoke adding a stick of dynamite to the fire Derek stoked between my legs, Noah was foremost in my mind, his face that I saw behind my closed eyelids, and his name on my lips.

The experience was everything I had imagined it would be, as taboo and hot as my wildest dreams, but where did it leave us? How did we go back to being just 'childhood friends Noah and Olivia'?

Did I even want to? Did he?

"There you are. I thought I'd lost you." Tate appeared in front of us as soon as we stepped back into the main exhibition lounge, and Noah and I both stopped short.

I opened my mouth to reply, but to my surprise, Noah responded instead. "I'm sorry I disappeared. Something came up."

Curiously, I looked back and forth between the two of them. "Do you two know each other?"

The colour seemed to drain from Noah's face as he glanced between us as well. "Tate is my friend. How do you know him, Liv?"

"Wait, he calls you Liv too?" Tate looked just as confused as the two of us, all of us looking at each other with uncertainty.

Tessa stepped in to explain, obviously seeing things clearer than any of us from her outsider position. "Noah and Liv have known each other forever," she told Tate before turning to Noah. "We met Tate here last night. He told us he had a friend but we didn't know that friend was you."

Noah was Tate's mystery friend? That was unbelievable. It seemed we were destined to run into each other, though whether fate was lending a hand or playing some kind of cosmic prank, I still hadn't decided.

Noah seemed to agree as he squeezed his eyes closed for a moment. When he opened them again, his jaw was set firmly. "I think we should go talk back at the hotel, without any of this... distraction."

He gestured around us to all the club's attractions, and at that moment, I couldn't really disagree. It would be a lot easier to concentrate with my clothes back on, for one thing.

"We're leaving?" Dismay flashed across Tessa's face. "But we just got here."

"Noah and I are leaving," I clarified. "You can stay if you want to, if Tate doesn't mind looking out for you."

Now that I knew he was Noah's friend, I trusted him even more than before, though it also seemed a bit strange that he had watched me finger myself the night before. Did friends do that?

"It would be a pleasure," Tate agreed chivalrously, but something else lurked in his eyes as he looked between me and Noah. "I'll bring her home safe and sound, but I can't guarantee she won't be a bit worse for wear."

Tessa giggled, clearly on board with that idea. "Okay, I guess we'll see you later then."

The two of them went off together while Noah and I walked back to the Plaza, his hand still holding mine. He asked which changing room I was in, and only when we were at the door of it did he finally let me go. "I'll meet you in the lobby as soon as you're ready."

As I pulled my clothes back on, alone in the little room, my hands began to shake and my stomach started to churn. Was I really that nervous about talking with Noah, or was I getting sick? I had only had one drink, so it shouldn't be that, but I didn't really know what else to think. I really didn't feel well all of a sudden.

By the time I got out to the lobby, I felt even worse, and Noah immediately came over to me, concern in his eyes. "What's wrong, Liv?"

"I don't know," I told him honestly. "I just don't feel great."

Putting a strong arm around my waist, he helped me out to the waiting taxi. The ride back to the hotel was a short one in the night-time traffic, and once we were there, he practically carried me up to my room. He probably would have picked me up if I'd let him.

As soon as we were inside my suite, he took off my coat and placed his hand on my forehead, checking my temperature. "You're not warm," he murmured, the scent of his cologne strong and enticing as he stood close to me. "How do you feel?"

"Cold, actually," I tried to explain. "Tired. Nauseous. Weak. A little dizzy."

A look of understanding settled across his face. "Liv, was that your first time in front of a crowd like that?"

What did that have to do with anything? I didn't understand why he asked, but I didn't lie to him either. "Yes."

"I think you're just having a comedown," he guessed as he led me over to the couch and sat me down. "Let me help."

Moving quickly, he grabbed a glass from the small kitchen in the suite and filled it up with water, bringing it over to me along with a banana that he found in the fridge. He also grabbed a blanket from the bedroom and laid it over my lap.

"Have something to eat and drink, you'll feel better," he promised me.

"Why is this happening?" I asked, my hands still shaking as I took the water from him. The liquid was cool and refreshing as I swallowed it down and I did feel a bit better almost immediately, although I couldn't say if the improvement came from the water or from Noah's tenderness in taking care of me.

"Performing like that is a real rush for the people who enjoy it," he explained, watching me carefully as he sat down next to me. "Your body produces adrenaline and endorphins, which makes you feel amazing in the moment, but after it's over and the natural chemicals leave your system, you have a big drop, an anti-climax. It's kind of like what rock stars feel on stage, and why so many of them drink or do drugs afterwards. It's such a big let down when the high ends that you feel worse than if you hadn't had the high at all."

"So, this is normal?" I asked, peeling back the top of the banana and bringing it towards my mouth.

Noah's eyes were fixed on my lips as they encircled the banana and he swallowed hard, his Adam's apple bobbing. "It's completely normal for people like us. It gets easier with time as you learn to regulate it better."

"Like us?" I was beginning to feel like a parrot, repeating everything he said, but I didn't want to jump to any conclusions. What did he mean by 'us'?

His eyes raised to meet mine. "People who get off on having other people watch them."

Excitement raced through me once again to hear him state it so plainly, without a hint of judgement, but his words also confused me. "That's what you like? I thought you were into the group scenarios."

He smiled, shaking his head. "That was one night, Liv, one moment you happened to walk in on. I enjoyed it, but it's not typical for me. What I really like is watching one other couple, or having people watch me. And based on tonight, I'm guessing it's what you like too."

The air seemed to be growing thicker around us, as though my confirmation of his assumption mattered to us both.

"This is all still pretty new to me, but yes, I think so. That's why I'm here, Noah. I came to try to figure out if this is who I really am and if this is what I need."

Heat flared in Noah's eyes, along with something that almost looked like pride. "In that case, I think I'm just the person to help you figure it out."

Chapter Nine

COMEDOWN

I didn't miss the way Olivia's pupils dilated when I offered to help guide her during her exploration at The Playground. My dad taught me that lesson, too: how to read people's body language to figure out what they were really thinking. It could be important in business to know when people told you what you wanted to hear instead of actually being ready to commit to a deal. There were all kinds of tells, but the eyes were the biggest one, and in Olivia's case, I didn't have any doubts.

She liked the idea. It turned her on, just like it did for me.

Even so, she didn't agree right away. "I don't need a babysitter, Noah. I'm not a child anymore."

That much was for damn sure. "No one's talking about babysitting. A lot of people, and especially women, have a partner for backup when they start out in the clubs."

Her eyebrows raised in her familiar, challenging way, but I kept talking before she could object.

"It's not a sexist thing, it's just a fact. You need someone who's been around for a while and understands the way things work. There are guys out there who have been doing this a long time, who can make you think you want something or who don't respect your boundaries. It's important to choose the right people to play with."

The idea of anyone taking advantage of her made me feel a little queasy. As much as I was all for her exploring and having fun, I wanted it to be a good experience.

"And you don't think I can make those choices on my own?" Her arms crossed as she leaned back against the couch, making me smile. When we were younger, I always knew that if I wanted her to do something, all I had to do was tell her that she couldn't do it. Nothing would make her move faster to try to prove me wrong.

In a place like The Playground, that kind of spirit could get her in trouble.

"This is exactly what I'm talking about, Liv. You need to approach each partner and each scene critically rather than emotionally. They're the ones getting the real prize. Anyone who gets to fuck you should be grateful for it and follow your lead. And sometimes, they'll say all the right things but do something different anyway, and you might need some backup."

She still didn't look fully convinced, so I tried to bring it back to specifics.

"Why did you choose to go with that Derek guy tonight? What did he offer you?"

Her lips twitched in a subtle sign of guilt, letting me know that she'd been more impulsive than she wanted to admit. "I was turned on and he said he'd give me a reward."

That wasn't much of an answer. What had turned her on in the first place and what was she getting a reward for? Although curious, I didn't want to get distracted from the main point I was trying to make. "Nothing more specific than that?"

Defiance flashed in her eyes. "No, but we talked about limits when we got to the room. There were other people in the room and I had my wristband if I needed help. I did my research, Noah. I chose The Playground because it takes safety seriously."

I was glad to hear she had considered all that, and honestly, I had expected nothing less from her. The mention of her limits made me curious about what they might be, but she was still missing my main point.

"I'm not suggesting he would have tried to rape you, I'm just saying that sometimes, there's a fine line between seduction and coercion. In the heat of the moment, it's easy to let someone push things a little further than you wanted to go, and that leaves you feeling awful afterwards. This comedown you're having sucks, right? Well, imagine that combined with feeling upset or embarrassed by what you did too."

Her finger tapping against the glass of water in her hand was a sign that she was considering my words. "Has that ever happened to you?"

The question took me by surprise, but she had every right to ask it, and the truth was that I *was* speaking from experience. If I wanted her to trust me, I'd have to trust her too. "Yeah, it has. It happened one of my first times at a club like this in New York."

Her eyes went wide and she couldn't help interrupting. "You go to places like this at home? What if someone sees you?"

The genuine concern in her voice made me smile. "This particular club is very private, and everyone wears masks over the top half of their face. The non-disclosure agreement they have you sign is intense and legally binding. I've taken it all into consideration, Liv. I don't want anyone else stumbling across my secret."

The allusion to the previous Christmas made her smile, and she nodded before bringing me back to the story. "What happened?"

The memory wasn't one of my fondest, but I owed it to her to be honest. "I was invited to join another couple in a private room with a small audience. Threesomes aren't my favourite thing, but as I said, I hadn't been to the club many times before, I was horny from watching all night and eager to get started with anything, so I agreed. We talked about ground rules and I told them I wasn't interested in anything between me and the other guy. It's just not my thing. They both agreed to that, but once we were into the scene, he kept touching me. At first I thought his hand slipping was accidental, since there wasn't a lot of room with what we were doing, but as the scene went on, it got more blatant. I should have said something but I didn't want to spoil the moment for us or for the people watching, and just as I was about to come, he kissed me and shoved two fingers up my ass."

Olivia gasped in dismay as she leaned forward. "What did you do?"

"Well, at first, I was just in shock, and before I could do anything, I heard the crowd cheering. They loved it since they thought everything was part of the show. You might think having the crowd there would stop things like that happening, but it actually did the opposite. It made me not want to disappoint them, so I didn't punch him or tell him off like I wanted to. I just pushed him away, not too hard, and finished the scene, but afterwards, I felt really upset about the whole thing; upset with him and with myself."

Her blue eyes were full of sympathy and a lot more understanding than they'd been showing a few moments earlier. "Did you tell anyone?"

I shook my head. "No, mostly because I was embarrassed. I'm supposed to be the one in control. I'm Noah Stamer, for fuck's sake. Not even Tate knows about it. I guess that makes you the first person I've told."

She seemed touched by that, in a way. "How do you prevent something like that from happening again?"

"Well, I'm a lot more picky about doing threesomes," I said, giving her a smile to let her know I was only half-serious. "But more than that, I usually have someone I know in the room with me, someone to have my back if I start to look uncomfortable. Tate has stepped in for me before, and I've done the same for him. There's no shame in it, Liv."

Once again, she nodded and I could tell she was coming around to the idea. "It's not just because you think I'm a helpless little girl?"

That idea made me laugh. "Helpless is not a word I would ever use to describe you, and I haven't thought of you as a little girl in a long time, Liv. Definitely not since you showed up in my bed in your underwear."

Her cheeks turned slightly pink at the memory even as she smiled. "That was a bit forward, wasn't it?"

"Maybe a little," I agreed, still grinning. "But I appreciate someone who knows what they want and goes for it."

A flicker of heat seemed to pass between us as our eyes met, but I quickly moved on. There was still a lot we needed to talk about.

"I don't want to scare you off the scene; that's not what I'm trying to do at all. It's amazing when it's done right. It's the absolute fucking best, actually, and I can't imagine not having it as part of my life. 'Regular' sex behind closed doors just doesn't do it for me."

Her brow furrowed as I spoke. "Is that what you meant about being with one woman every night not being right for you?"

I was surprised she remembered my words after all that time, but she had it right. "Exactly. I just don't get turned on unless there's someone watching."

"Would you let me watch you?"

The idea made my cock immediately jump to life, and I answered her with blunt honesty. "I would love you to watch me, Liv. I loved watching you tonight. I meant every word I said in there: seeing him pleasure you was incredibly hot. I'm hard again just thinking about it."

Her eyes immediately dropped to my lap, looking for proof, and I couldn't resist teasing her just a little.

"You don't believe me? Why don't you touch me and see for yourself?"

~Olivia~

Noah's green eyes sparkled mischievously as he invited me to touch him to see how turned on he was. The words were a dare and I knew it.

There were a lot of reasons the challenge tempted me. To show him I wasn't afraid, for one. To turn the tables on him was another, since I was pretty sure I could make him a whole lot more turned on if I started touching him. And the last reason, and perhaps the most tempting of all, was simply because I wanted to. I'd dreamed of being able to put my hands on him for so long, and he'd just gone and offered me my heart's desire on a silver platter, so to speak.

But that last reason was also exactly the reason I hesitated. It had taken me a long time to put my dream of Noah and I as a couple to rest, and what he had just said confirmed that his position on that hadn't changed. He wasn't looking for any kind of relationship. He thought 'regular' sex was boring, and the idea that we could sleep together and it would mean nothing to him had the potential to break my heart all over again.

All things considered, going down that road at all was probably not the best idea.

I still wanted to watch him at The Playground and I definitely still wanted him to watch me. That evening had been incredible. The things I'd felt in front of that audience were everything I'd been missing with my boyfriend, and the things Noah said about needing a guide, or a partner, or a buddy, whatever he wanted to call it, all made sense too. I *was* new to this and there was still a lot I didn't know. Having someone who'd been there and done it all, by the sounds of it, would be a smart idea.

And maybe, depending on how things went, we might even do some things together in public, where the focus was on the show and the sensations, not on emotion, and I could be satisfied with that.

There in my hotel room, though, just the two of us with no audience, it felt dangerous. It felt like I was on the edge of falling for him all over again, and I didn't want to, not when I knew he wouldn't be there to catch me.

With all that in mind, I leaned back and crossed my arms again. "I'll take your word for it."

Noah laughed, though I could have sworn there was a little bit of disappointment in his eyes. "I think that might be the first time I've ever seen you back down from a challenge."

"I do have some self-control," I told him sarcastically. "But I hear what you're saying about why having a backup at the club is a good idea. So, if you're offering, then I accept. I'd be happy to explore with you."

That seemed to genuinely please him. "Good. We'll make a plan at the club tomorrow to make sure you get to try everything you want to."

"I thought we were going to the Rathaus market tomorrow?"

His eyes widened in surprise before he laughed again. "I almost forgot you were the same girl I made those plans with."

Was that supposed to be a compliment or not? "I'm still the same Liv, Noah. Nothing's changed."

The way he looked me over, head to toe, suggested he might not agree with that. "Well, in that case, you've got a couple of days to decide where you want to begin. You should get some rest now. Are you still tired?"

I was. The water and food had helped, and so had Noah's support, but the mood swings had left me feeling drained. "I could sleep."

Noah knew me well enough to know that was code for 'I'm exhausted', so he leaned forward and kissed my cheek. "Sleep well, Liv. I'll see you tomorrow."

He let himself out of the suite and I sat there for a few more minutes, reviewing everything that had just happened in my head. The whole trip had taken a completely unexpected turn but all things considered, I wasn't upset about it. I still got to explore my new kink, and now I had someone to help me, someone I trusted and someone who turned me on just by watching me.

He had told me the year before that he didn't think I could keep sex and emotions separate, and on that point, at least, I was determined to prove him wrong. When it came to Noah, they were two completely different things.

~Noah~

My sleep that night was restless, filled with images of Liv on stage with other men, her eyes watching me the whole time. Their hands were on her, their dicks inside her, but whenever she came, my name was on her lips.

Every single detail was unbelievably sexy, right up until someone new joined her on stage, someone whose face I couldn't see. She turned her attention to him, ignoring me completely, and as he took her, she moaned out his name instead and my eyes shot open, my heart racing in the darkness of my hotel room.

Tate.

I could still hear the echo of her cry, and my stomach twisted at the sound. Why the hell did I feel that way? I had never minded sharing anyone with Tate before. More times than I could count, we had fucked a girl one after the other, or swapped partners when we were done.

There were no emotions involved. Our encounters were just about the sex, only about the moment.

And I wasn't planning on having sex with Liv myself. I was just going to guide her and watch. So, why did the idea of him and Liv make me feel like I was going to be sick?

Maybe it had to do with what he'd said before he knew who she was, about how there was something special about her. He was right: she *was* very special, but how did he know that, and what exactly did he mean by it?

I was going to have to find out.

When I got down to breakfast, he was already there, digging into his food as usual, so I grabbed my coffee and sat down across from him. "It seems like we've got some catching up to do."

He raised his eyebrows at me. "I'd say. Tessa filled me in a bit on you and Liv, but I imagine there's more to the story."

Even the sound of Liv's name on his lips made me grimace. What the hell was wrong with me?

I would have to give him some kind of explanation, but first, I wanted to find out more about what he might be thinking. "How did you meet them?"

He explained how he saw the men approach them in the Plaza and Liv's friend went with them, leaving Liv alone, which was when he went to talk to her. The story had my chest swelling with pride; obviously, the men had offered something Olivia wasn't interested in, so she said no. It made me glad to know she was being selective, though I shouldn't have doubted it.

Tate went on to describe in more detail exactly what happened when they went to the stage together, how Liv had got off on watching the couple on stage, and my own excitement flared up again. I couldn't wait to see her touching herself while she watched me.

"It's rare that I see a woman who gets off on it the same way we do," Tate explained to me. "You know how it is. They're happy enough to take part, but it's not a need like it is for us. With her, I think she needs it. She craves it just like we do."

It still sounded too good to be true, even though all the evidence pointed that way.

Tate wasn't finished yet. "She's exactly the type of woman I see myself with for the long term: someone who owns their kink and isn't afraid to indulge it, but is fun and intelligent and successful outside of it too.

You'd meet her in the street and never know what she was into. She's the whole package."

My coffee tasted far more bitter than usual as I forced myself to swallow. "Since when are you thinking long-term?"

"Since we're growing up, Noah. I know you're not looking for anything like that, but we're graduating in just a few months and I'm going for it all. I want the life your dad has: rich, powerful, with a beautiful woman who shares his kink."

I almost regretted telling Tate about my parents' dungeon if it had somehow led to his interest in Olivia.

"I've been paying attention to the women we've been with lately, but either they're not right or they don't truly understand the kink, they're just going through the motions. But Liv... like I said, she's got it all."

"How can you possibly know that from spending one evening with her?" I could hear how angry I sounded though I truly didn't understand why. "What about her friend? She's beautiful and she seemed to like you."

Tate shrugged. "Tessa's gorgeous, for sure, but she doesn't like the same things. We went to watch the action on the stage last night and she kept wanting us to go somewhere alone. She's into me but not the scene, and that won't work. I think the real question is: why are you so upset about the idea of me going after Liv?"

Fuck, I hated how well he knew me sometimes. "I'm not upset, I'm just surprised. You've never mentioned anything about wanting to settle down before."

"Well, I've been thinking about it for a long time even if I didn't say anything. I don't think that's the reason it makes you angry, though. I think you don't think I'm good enough for her."

The undertone of hurt was clear in his voice. Tate was used to people in our circle putting him down because of his family background and where he came from, making snide remarks about his lack of wealth or connections, but that had never bothered me. "That's not it."

"Then what is it?" he challenged. "The truth, Noah."

The truth? I had no idea. I just knew that the thought of the two of them together in a relationship made me feel unwell, but that was hardly something I could say to my best friend without it sounding awful.

"She's brand new to the scene," I tried to explain. "I've offered to help her find her feet. This is the time she should be exploring and having fun, just like we did. A relationship isn't on her radar right now."

That sounded plausible to me and luckily, Tate seemed to agree once he gave it some thought too. "You're going to stick close to her while she's here?"

"Yeah, as long as she wants me to."

He nodded slowly, still thinking it over. "That could work. I could get to know her a bit better outside the club while you spend time with her there and keep an eye on her. By the time we're ready to move things to the next level, she'll already have some fun under her belt and we can see what it's like to try things out as a couple."

The word 'couple' made my stomach drop once again. "You're assuming an awful lot. What if you're not her type?"

He shrugged again. "Then no harm done, but I'm interested and I'm going to make it clear to her. Tonight's the perfect time when we go to that market. Turns out you setting that up was a good thing after all." He gave me a grin before glancing at the clock. "Shit, I'm going to be late. I'll catch up with you later. Have a good day, Noah."

"Yeah, you too," I managed to mumble as he took off to go start his shift. I should have been going too, but I still felt off. As soon as I brought my coffee cup to my lips, I had to put it back down again as the smell turned my stomach.

What the fuck was wrong with me?

~Olivia~

When I opened my eyes to the bright winter sun coming through my window, I knew immediately that I had overslept. Worn out by the highs and lows of the previous day, I had fallen asleep almost immediately and slept deeply through the night. If I dreamed, I couldn't remember it, though now that I thought back over it, most of the previous evening felt like a dream.

Did that all really happen? Did I give a complete stranger a blow job, then let a different one make me come in front of a half dozen other people, including Noah Stamer?

I was pretty sure I had, and I quickly searched my emotions, looking for a sign that I felt embarrassed or ashamed of what I'd done, but I couldn't find anything like that. It had been exactly as exciting as I'd hoped it would be, and not only did I not regret it, I wanted more. Just the thought of being back there again, with Noah beside me, had my whole body humming in anticipation.

It didn't surprise me at all that Tessa was still in bed by the time that I showered and dressed, so I let myself into her room and jumped onto the bed next to her to wake her up.

"Morning people are the worst," she grumbled as she tried to roll over and pull the covers over her head. I quickly pulled them back down before she had a chance.

"It's almost eleven, so it's barely even morning anymore. Besides, you owe me all the hot details from last night. What did you do after Noah and I left?"

That got her attention, and she immediately sat upright. "Fuck, I almost forgot! What happened with you and Noah? I can't believe he was there. How crazy is it that Tate is his friend? How did you find him? How did he react when he saw you? Did he make you leave? Did you guys fight? Is he going to tell your parents?"

That was way too many questions for me to keep straight so I stuck to the basics, telling her what happened with Derek, how Noah found me, and the gist of what we'd talked about back here in the suite. Her eyes were wide as saucers by the time I was done.

"He's really into the same stuff you are?"

"Yeah, I guess so. I'll know for sure once we spend some time together at The Playground." Once again, a thrill went through me at the thought. "Enough about me; what did you do last night?"

Her lips pressed together in a pout. "Nothing very exciting. Tate and I talked for quite a while. I dropped the whole Tiffany thing with him, by the way, since he already knows you're not Belle. Hanging out with him was nice, but I wanted more. I'm beginning to think I'm the only woman in the world who can spend two nights in a sex club and not get laid."

Her exaggeration made me laugh. "I haven't exactly been laid yet either, and obviously, you just haven't found the right space for you yet. Back up and tell me exactly what happened."

She explained how she watched Tate get his blowjob through the glory hole. Unable to contain my curiosity, I asked if she had seen the man I was with, but she hadn't. She hadn't looked over into my room at all. Next, I asked if it turned her on to watch Tate through the window, like it would have done for me.

"Yes?" She didn't sound completely certain. "The woman he got wasn't great at it though. I could have done a better job, and I told him so."

Of course she did. Tessa never had a problem saying what was on her mind. "What did he say to that?"

"He told me we could try it out in one of the rooms sometime, but I don't really want to do it in front of other people. I just want to be alone with him."

My heart sank a little bit as I remembered what Noah said about 'regular' sex not being enough. If Tate felt the same way, it sounded like my friend was setting herself up for disappointment. "Maybe your kinks just aren't that compatible," I suggested gently. "I thought you wanted to try some of the BDSM stuff anyway?"

"Yeah, I guess." She could hardly sound less enthusiastic, but a moment later, her eyes brightened. "But we're hanging out with them tonight, right? Maybe I can work my best seductive moves on Tate outside the club."

"Maybe." I still wasn't convinced but I gave her a bright smile anyway. "But first, you'll need to get up."

With a groan, she did as I asked, and we finally made our way out into the Vienna sunshine. We visited St Stephen's Cathedral in the heart of the city and the nearby Mozart house museum where the famous composer had lived for a while.

"I can't believe Mozart was only 35 when he died!" Tessa exclaimed as we made our way back onto the busy streets. "He did so much."

"He didn't waste any time," I agreed. "He started young, but he also worked hard. He knew what he wanted and he went for it."

That was how I wanted to be too. Life was far too short, and none of us were getting any younger. Wasting time on futile efforts made no sense, and Noah had already proven himself to be a dead end for me. Now that we were friends again, maybe I could truly start to move on.

Chapter Ten

DOUBLE DATE

~Noah~

Tate and I met Olivia and Tessa in the lobby just before seven, ready for our evening out together. They were both dressed warmly since we'd be spending a lot of time outside, and I couldn't help noticing how amazing Olivia looked in her fitted red coat and white hat. Somehow, she managed to look just as sexy fully-dressed as she did in her lingerie. From Tate's expression, I felt pretty sure he noticed it too.

"Did you guys have a good day?" I asked as I gave them both a kiss on the cheek. "Nice to see you again, Tessa."

I hadn't really had a chance to talk to Olivia's friend yet and I realized as I greeted her that I didn't know a thing about her.

"We did," Tessa replied, but her eyes were on Tate, not me. "I'm starving though. You said something about dinner?"

"You're definitely getting food," I promised. "Liv didn't believe that I know the best schnitzel place in the city, so I'm going to prove her wrong."

I gave her a teasing wink and she scrunched up her face at me in response, just like when we were kids.

The place I had in mind wasn't far from the Rathaus, or City Hall, the site of the big Christmas market that we would visit later, and boisterous chatter, mostly in German, greeted us as we walked into the small, family-run establishment. We sat at a circular table, Olivia on one side of me and Tessa on the other as we stumbled through our orders in very poor German.

When our beer arrived, I offered a toast: "To discovering new things with old friends."

Olivia's lips twitched as she picked up my challenge. "And trying the oldest things with new ones." She gave me a wink as she clanked her stein against mine before taking a drink.

Conversation over dinner flowed smoothly as we all got to know each other better. Tessa was funny and outspoken and I could see why Olivia liked her. Tate was his usual charming self, having both the girls eating out of the palm of his hand as he told them stories about our time in college together. He mostly kept things clean, flirting with the risqué at times but never getting outright dirty. They both asked Olivia and I about growing up together, so I shared a few of my favourite stories and Olivia did the same.

The entire experience felt relaxed and fun and *normal*. In fact, it truly surprised me how normal it felt to be sitting there and chatting with Olivia like nothing had happened between us, after almost a year of silence and after everything that had happened the night before.

Maybe she was better at keeping her emotions under control than I had thought.

In the dim lighting of the cozy restaurant, she looked as sweet and wholesome as she always had. As Tate said that morning, no one would ever guess by looking at her that the night before, she'd been on display in front of a small crowd as a total stranger brought her to orgasm.

She was almost like two women in one, the same way that I was two different men, I supposed. No one had ever fully known both sides of me except for Tate, but now Olivia did too and it hadn't scared her off.

Why would it, when she was just the same?

As we made our way to the market afterwards, we were quickly swallowed up in the crowd. Hundreds of stalls spread out beneath a massive Christmas tree that sparkled in front of the neo-Gothic city hall. Christmas carols played and the smells of wine, chocolate, sausages and fried dough filled the air. The mood was festive and fun and I immediately thought of my mom and all the amazing Christmases she'd given me as a child.

Naturally, any thought of childhood Christmases led me back to thoughts of Olivia. She'd always been there, and I'd taken it for granted that she always would be.

There were too many people for us to all walk together, so we broke up into two sets of two, and to my frustration, Olivia ended up with Tate. They walked just in front of me and Tessa but I couldn't hear what they were saying. I could, however, see the way they leaned towards each other as they pointed out different things in the stalls, and the way Tate's hand went to her waist as he steered her out of the way of distracted people in her path.

"You've gone quiet," Tessa observed after a few minutes. "Am I that boring?"

"Of course not," I apologized. "Sorry, I've just got a few things on my mind."

She raised her eyebrows at me suspiciously. "A few things like a certain best friend of mine, perhaps?"

Fuck. Was I really that obvious? I tried to deflect and redirect the conversation to cover up for it. "How long have you and Liv known each other?"

"We were roommates our first year," she explained before giving me a sly smile. "Which means I know *all* about you."

That didn't sound like a good thing, but I couldn't contain my curiosity about what Olivia would have told her. "What do you know?"

"I know you've got your head up your ass when it comes to Liv," she told me bluntly. "And I know that, despite how much she's tried to move on, she's still hung up on you too."

That didn't seem likely considering how she'd pushed me away the night before, but I couldn't deny that the idea made me happier than it should have.

"I'm glad you guys have made up or whatever you've done," she continued. "But if you're not ready to be serious about her, don't lead her on."

"I'm not," I promised, rather taken aback with the turn the conversation had taken. It brought to mind Jackson threatening me all over again. "I've always been completely up front with her about what I want."

"Maybe," Tessa said, still eyeing me warily. "But how up front have you been with yourself?"

To emphasize her point, she looked over to where our friends were laughing together as they looked through a stall of humourous street signs, and my chest tightened again at the sight.

Was Tessa right? Was that the reason the idea of Olivia and Tate together bothered me so much?

Was I really just jealous that he saw before I did just how perfect she really was?

~Olivia~

"Did you know there's a village here in Austria called Fucking?"

Tate asked the question so innocently as we looked over the street signs at the market stall that I honestly didn't know if he was pulling my leg or not. He stood very close to me because of the crowd, but I couldn't read the look in his blue eyes. "Really?"

He nodded seriously before offering me a grin and a qualifier. "Well, it's not called that anymore. They changed the name in 2020 because too many people were trying to steal the town sign. Now, it's called Fugging, but for almost a thousand years, the town was Fucking."

"And what do you think goes on there?" I asked with a laugh. "Is it worth a visit?"

He laughed back. "Actually, I think only a hundred people live there, so it's probably really boring. The Playground is way more exciting."

I couldn't argue with that. Although I was really enjoying our evening, there had been a few times over dinner when my mind had drifted to the club instead, usually when I noticed the way that Noah's shirt stretched across his chest or the way he licked his lips after taking a swig of his beer.

Noah wasn't what I wanted to focus on, though, so I changed the subject as Tate and I moved on to the next booth. "Oh, these are beautiful!"

The whole stall was full of white and gold Christmas ornaments, and even though I had already bought my mom and sister some ornaments at Schönbrunn Palace the day before, I couldn't resist getting them more. My suitcase was going to be full of Christmas decorations by the time I went home.

"Is there anyone that you're buying for?" I asked Tate as I paid for my purchases.

"Are you asking me if I have a girlfriend?" he teased. "You don't have to make up an excuse, you can just ask me."

"I actually meant family," I retorted, matching his tone. "But now that you've brought it up, *do* you have a girlfriend? I just assumed you didn't because of how we met, but I don't really know how things work with people who are into the kind of things we are. It's all still pretty new to me."

Luckily, Tate seemed to understand my somewhat convoluted question. "Well, first off, I don't have a girlfriend. But if I did, it would definitely be someone who would be okay with me doing the kinds of things that happen at The Playground. Ideally, she'd be right there with me, doing them too."

That was interesting. I had kind of assumed that things would have to be either/or. I didn't really know there were people who had both a private and public sex life like that.

"You wouldn't have a problem with your girlfriend having sex with other guys in front of you?" I asked, lowering my voice so no one else could hear us.

"Not in public. In fact, I'd find it sexy as hell, but if she went off with someone and had sex in private, that would be different."

That interested me even more, but I completely understood the distinction. I wouldn't go home with a man I just met, and yet, I had gone to the room with Derek the night before with hardly a second thought.

Privacy made it more intimate, more emotional. In public, the focus was on the performance and the energy from the crowd. Everything was more physical, more purely carnal. Maybe that was why Noah didn't enjoy sex in private. He told me he didn't think I could separate sex from emotion, but maybe he couldn't *combine* them. Maybe he didn't know how.

"Does that mean you're not seeing anyone either?" Tate asked me, and I supposed my questions had kind of given that away. "I don't see how a woman like you could possibly be single."

Even though he was obviously buttering me up, the compliment made me smile. "I just got out of a relationship, actually. He wasn't interested in trying things like this and I wanted to explore it, so we went our separate ways."

He looked impressed. "A woman who knows what she wants, huh? No wonder Noah's been hiding you away."

What was that supposed to mean? A tight feeling settled over my chest as I tried to figure it out. "He doesn't talk about me?"

Tate immediately shook his head. "He's never even mentioned you."

That hurt far more than I expected it to. I knew Noah didn't think of me in any kind of romantic way, but I thought we were at least close enough that he might have talked about me to his close friends, the way I had talked about him with Tessa.

Maybe I meant even less to him than I realized.

"How long have you guys known each other?" I asked, trying to distract myself from the bitter taste in my mouth.

"A few years. We've been sharing a house for the last couple."

My eyes went wide before I could stop them. Tate lived with Noah? Based on that and the kinds of things I knew he was into, that meant he was probably there the night I had shown up to see Noah. And even then, Noah still didn't tell him about me?

"Hey, Tate." Speaking of the devil, Noah tapped his friend on the shoulder from behind us. "I'm going to grab a bratwurst, you want one?"

"Hell, yes." Tate's eyes lit up as he saw the stall just ahead of us.

"Seriously?" I gawped at the two of them. "We *just* ate."

Tate grinned. "What can I say? We've got big appetites, in more ways than one."

He gave me a wink as he and Noah walked away, and Tessa came up beside me, linking her arm through mine as she muttered under her breath, "I'd like a taste of *his* bratwurst."

My giggle made Noah and Tate turn around, but I shook my head at them and they continued on their way.

"Did you manage to put in a good word for me?" Tessa asked once they were completely out of earshot.

Oh, shit. I'd totally forgotten she'd asked me to talk her up to Tate if I had the chance. I had let Noah distract me, once again.

That ended immediately. If he didn't waste any time thinking about me when we weren't together, I wasn't going to waste my time either. He was a friend of the family and my new kink mentor, but nothing more.

He wanted to know how good I could be at keeping sex and emotions separate? Well, he was about to find out.

~Noah~

Although I had a dozen things to say to Tate as we stood in line for our sausage, I didn't know how to begin. I didn't want it to sound like I'd suddenly become interested in Olivia simply because he had, even though there was a sliver of truth in that. Jealousy didn't fully explain it, though. The fact of the matter was: I had always been interested in her, I just hadn't been able to see how it could work.

After the revelations of the previous night, what Tate had said to me earlier that day and what Tessa had just helped me realize, I had finally started to see just what an idiot I'd been. She was the girl I'd always wanted, the one I thought would be right for me 'if only'. Since it seemed like 'if only' was a reality, I would have to be a complete idiot not to do something about it.

If I let her get away without even giving it a chance, I would regret it the rest of my life.

However, Tate was interested too, he'd made that perfectly clear to me, and I didn't want to mess up anything between us. There were very few people in the world I felt completely comfortable being myself with, and I didn't want to lose him as a friend.

"We need to talk about Olivia," I finally started, and he looked over at me in surprise.

"Liv? What about her?"

He didn't even know her full name. He didn't know anything about her, not the way I did, and it felt like that should give me some kind of advantage, but I knew it didn't work that way. He'd recognized something special in her the very first time he met her, and my years of history with her meant nothing if he made a move before I did.

"There are a few things I haven't told you about her." That was an understatement, but I had to start somewhere.

"I got that impression," he agreed mildly. "She seemed really surprised when I said you'd never mentioned her."

Fuck. Why would he say that to her? I glanced back at her as if I could see her reaction for myself, but she wasn't paying any attention to me. She and Tessa were at another stall, laughing and talking as they looked at the things for sale.

I'd never mentioned her, but not for the reason it probably sounded like, and I immediately made that clear to him. "Well, that's because she means a lot to me and I wanted to protect her from the kinkier side of my life."

His eyebrows raised in amusement. "Looks like you missed the boat on that one."

"Yeah, thanks," I said sarcastically. I didn't need him to tell me that. "My point is: I like her. I've always liked her, I just never thought we could work together because I didn't think that she'd be into the same kind of shit we are. Now that I know she is..."

"Now what?" he challenged. "You want me to back off because you saw her first?"

Pretty much, yeah, but I realized how petty that made me sound. "I'm asking you to respect the fact that we've got a history and there are still some things we need to figure out. Maybe she's not interested anymore, but I want to find out..."

He cut me off curiously. "Anymore? She was interested before?"

Grimacing, I gave him an abbreviated version of what happened the previous Christmas as we got to the front of the line and placed our order.

"You're a fucking idiot," was his brutal summary.

"I know." I couldn't argue with that when it was true. "But I really had no idea she would be open to this. It's like you said: looking at her, you'd never guess."

He had to concede that point, at least. "Well, what do we do now?" he asked bluntly. "I might not have known her my whole life, but I like her, Noah. I really like her."

"I suppose our mutual good taste was bound to bite us in the ass sooner or later."

That made him smile, but it didn't solve the problem. "So?" he prompted again.

"So, I guess it's up to her," I said, my chest tightening at the thought. "I'm going for it, but I can't stop you from doing the same. Whatever Liv decides, whether it's one of us or neither, we'll have to live with it."

"And we'll still be friends by Christmas?" he asked, only half-joking.

"I don't see why not. As long as it's a fair fight, may the best man win."

~Olivia~

It took me a lot longer to decide what to wear to The Playground on Friday night than it had on Tuesday or Wednesday. First of all, I knew that night would be a lot busier. Friday and Saturdays were the big nights and I wanted to wear something that would make me stand out from all the beautiful women there.

And second, I knew that whatever I wore, Noah and Tate would see me in it. There was a very good chance that at least one of them would see me out of it as well.

After Tate and Noah got their bratwursts the night before, I managed to send Tate and Tessa off together, as Tessa wanted, leaving me and Noah alone. As we walked, Noah shared that he'd told Tate about offering to be my guide, and Tate had offered to join us at The Playground so that the three of us could explore things together. I wasn't really sure why that would be necessary; was Noah simply trying to get out of spending time alone with me?

Whatever the reason, I agreed since I had already been planning on hanging out at The Playground with Tate anyway before I knew he and Noah were friends, and he seemed like a genuinely nice guy.

"What about Tessa?" I asked, gesturing to my friend as she tried on winter hats while Tate offered his opinion. "We can't leave her alone but she's not into the same stuff we are. She needs to have some fun too."

"I've been thinking about that," he replied, which took me by surprise. "Tate told me she's interested in BDSM, but nothing too heavy. Is that right?"

I nodded. "She's not entirely sure what she likes, but she wants to give it a try."

"Well, we've gotten to know a guy at The Playground who's into that kind of stuff, but he likes to do it with an audience. If she'd be okay with the three of us watching, we could set something up for tomorrow. That way, we'll be there if it doesn't work out, but hopefully it does and we can all have some fun."

I promised to ask Tessa about it, which I did as soon as we were back in our hotel suite for the night. "It would be in one of the private rooms in the exhibition area," I explained, passing on what Noah had told me. "Only the people invited would be there, which would be me, Tate and Noah."

"Tate would be watching me?" I could tell that idea tempted her, even if she wasn't sure about the rest.

"It would really turn him on," I assured her.

"But... you'd be watching me too," she added, chewing on her lip. "Won't that be weird?"

I had given it some thought already and, strange as it may sound, I really didn't think it would be. "Honestly, no, not for me. If you're having fun, I'll enjoy it too. Tate and Noah watch each other all the time and they like it, but if it makes you uncomfortable, just say so and I'll go. You won't know until you try, right? We'll consider it an experiment."

She agreed, and with that settled, we called it a night. On Friday, she and I spent the day at the Prater amusement park, going on rides, eating candy and playing games. It was a completely different kind of playground to the one we'd be going to later that night, but doing something mindless and fun for a while made a nice change. We took lots of pictures and posted them to our social media, letting everyone at home know what a good time we were having.

What we were doing that evening would have no photos involved.

Finally, I settled on a red and black corset with the same black stockings and garter I'd worn on our first night. Tessa went for a more innocent look in white lace, and we certainly made a contrasting pair. She looked like an angel, with me as her corrupting devil, and maybe there was some truth in that since the whole trip had been my idea in the first place.

Noah and Tate were waiting for us in the lobby when we got downstairs, both dressed in their suits. "Men have it so easy," I complained as the four of us got a taxi together. "You can wear the same thing night after night and nobody notices."

"You can say that again," Tate agreed with a grin. "This is the exact same suit I've worn the other two nights you've seen me. Noah, on the other hand, has a different one for every night."

Noah rolled his eyes but didn't contradict his friend, leading me to believe it must be true.

"I can't wait to see what you two are wearing tonight," Tate continued, giving Tessa and I both appreciative looks as his eyes scanned us, as if he might be able to see beneath our clothes right there in the taxi.

"You won't have to wait for long," Tessa promised with a smile.

At the club, we all went to a changing room together and the men left their few things in the small lockers while Tessa and I disrobed. Noah's eyes were on me as I finished undressing, and I gave him a little teasing twirl. "Do I live up to Stamer standards?"

His gaze was heated as his eyes met mine. "You live up to anyone's standards, Liv."

The four of us walked out together into the Plaza, where it immediately became clear how different that night was going to be. There were no free tables and dozens of people mingled around the bar already. The air was thick with anticipation and our approach caught the attention of more than a few people. If Tessa and I were there on our own, we would have been inundated with offers, but the presence of Noah and Tate seemed to keep people at bay and they simply watched us from a distance.

"There he is." Tate steered us towards an older man by the bar who wore a suit just as expensive as Noah's. Tall, with dark hair and a closely trimmed beard, I would have guessed he was in his late 30s or maybe even early 40s. Everything about him suggested power and control. "Hey, Lewis."

"Tate. Noah." Lewis had a British accent, not too different from my mom's or Gemma's, the words crisply and cleanly enunciated. With no attempt to pretend otherwise, he openly assessed me and Tessa, his steely gaze taking in every inch of us. "Which of you is Tiffany?"

We were still using our fake names in the club, it seemed. I gave Tessa a little nudge to remind her she was Tiffany, and she raised her hand, like we were in school, as I tried not to smile.

Lewis' expression turned even more critical. "Stand up straighter," he instructed and immediately, Tessa's back stiffened. She seemed to be responding well to him, which was a good sign, but I noticed something else as he took a drink, his eyes still fixed on my friend.

Noah was closest to me so I leaned over to him and whispered in his ear. "He's wearing a wedding ring."

Noah nodded, looking unconcerned as he whispered back. "She's not looking to marry him, is she?"

I supposed not, but I still didn't really like the idea. Where was his wife? Did she know he was there?

Just as quickly as the questions and disapproval entered my head, I tried to push them away. Those were emotional responses, I reminded myself, and none of this was about emotion. The Playground was purely sex, and I needed to keep that in mind, not just for Tessa but for myself too.

It didn't take long for Lewis to establish that he could work with Tessa, and we all ordered some drinks and took them with us to the private room that had been reserved for us.

A few toys and instruments already waited inside on a table next to the bed in the centre of the room. To one side of the room, there was a couch where Tate, Noah and I took a seat, with me in the middle.

My drink was strong and it didn't take too long for the corners of the room to begin to blur as I watched Lewis and Tessa together. He started by laying out his ground rules: she had to call him 'Sir' at all times, she was only to speak when he asked her something, and any violation of the rules would be punished. They agreed on a safeword for her before he offered one last instruction.

"No one in this room exists for you except me, unless I tell you otherwise. You won't look at them or acknowledge them in any way. Do you understand?"

"Yes, Sir." Tessa seemed to relax a little at the idea that she didn't have to engage with us, and I wondered if Lewis had done it on purpose, knowing she wasn't completely comfortable with the exhibition side of things.

With the scene set, Lewis grabbed a riding crop from the table and began to run it up and down Tessa's body, correcting her posture so that her back was arched, her chest stuck out, her legs slightly apart and her hands behind her head. Each word from his mouth was an order, uttered with total confidence and command, and she seemed to enjoy it, doing her best to obey him.

"What do you think?" I got a whiff of whiskey and cologne as Tate leaned over to whisper in my ear. "Would you like someone controlling you that way?"

I shook my head as I whispered back. "I don't think so, but it looks like it's working for her."

"Liv doesn't take orders well at all," Noah added from the other side of me, making it clear he could hear every word. "She likes to come up with the plan."

Since he was right, I didn't argue. I simply settled back and took another sip of my drink as Lewis began to remove Tessa's clothing, bit by bit until she stood naked in front of us. If she planned to ask me to leave, I thought she might do it then, but her attention was completely focused on Lewis, as he'd instructed. She seemed to have forgotten the rest of us were there.

Tate shifted in his seat next to me, letting me know that he was getting turned on by what we were watching, and I could see why. Tessa looked amazing, and as Lewis ran the riding crop up between her legs, pressing it against her and sliding it back and forth against her clit as she tried to keep still, I could almost feel it between my legs too. My body began to respond in almost the same way while Noah adjusted his pants.

The combination of the drink and the scene in front of us was intoxicating, making me forget about everything other than the moment, a moment where I sat between two hot, horny men who were only interested in the same thing I was: feeling as good as we possibly could.

Emotions didn't matter, I reminded myself. In that small, dream-like room, I wasn't Olivia Hanmer, I was merely a woman enjoying herself next to two men who were doing the same.

So, before I could put too much thought into it, I placed my drink on the floor. With Tate on my right side and Noah on my left, I needed both hands free, and as we all continued to watch the scene in front of us, I reached out and placed my hands directly on their hardening cocks.

Chapter Eleven

REALIZATION

~Noah~

Dominance wasn't usually my thing. Maybe it had to do with the fact that I thought of it as my dad's kink and every kid naturally rebels against the things their parents like. As a teenager, I discovered my parents' dungeon in our apartment by chance. I'd always known the locked door was there, and I'd tried to break into it as a kid just out of curiosity, but my parents always insisted it simply contained confidential work information and I'd never really questioned it. I never saw them going in and out of the room, so they must have always used it after Eve and I were asleep.

One day in high school, though, I came home earlier than expected in the afternoon and was on my way to the kitchen as they came out of the room together and I caught enough of a glimpse through the door to see that it definitely did not contain business files.

My mom's face turned bright red but my dad was cool about it, as usual, holding the door open wider. "You might as well take a look."

That all happened after the conversation we'd had about my own kink and my own research on the subject, so I wasn't as shocked as I might have been. Surprised that it had been there right under my nose the whole time, sure, but not shocked.

After the surprise faded, I had to admit there was something pretty cool about how they found something they enjoyed together and were still doing it despite their age.

That kink wasn't for me though, so it surprised me how turned on I got from watching Lewis and Tessa together. As he slid the crop through the wetness between her legs and brought it to her mouth, telling her to lick it off, a sudden rush of blood ran to my dick, so strongly that I had to adjust myself before it got painful.

Was it actually the scene in front of me that had me hard, or was it knowing that Olivia sat next to me, watching it right along with me and clearly enjoying it as well?

Tate and I had decided the night before that neither of us would make an immediate declaration to Olivia about how we felt. We didn't want to scare her off or to make it about us when her trip was supposed to be her chance to discover herself and what she liked. If she knew we were fighting over her, no matter how gentlemanly we tried to be about it, it might put her off or make her not want to be around either of us, and neither of us wanted that. Her enjoyment came first and foremost.

So, we agreed that we would keep it quiet for at least a few days, but that we would both get to spend time with her in and out of the club. That was why we were all together in the private room, but if the opportunity came to ditch Tate, I planned to take it, and I was sure he had the same idea.

"Does it taste good?" Lewis asked Tessa as she obediently licked the riding crop clean. When she nodded in response, his expression hardened, and with a firm thwack, he brought the crop down on her bare ass. "Answer me out loud when I ask you a question."

"Y-yes, Sir," she stuttered, her eyes wide with surprise but also with arousal. She was obviously enjoying herself, and that made it good for us too.

My attention was so fixed on them that I didn't notice the hand reaching for me until it made contact. Olivia's palm pressed against my growing dick, making it almost instantly swell even larger, and I looked over at her in surprise.

The night before, I'd invited her to touch me but she hadn't. Now that we were in the semi-public setting of the private room, her qualms about it seemed to have disappeared. She wasn't looking at me, her eyes still facing forward as she watched Tessa and Lewis, but a hint of a smile graced her beautiful face.

She knew just what she was doing to me.

And to Tate, apparently. A moment later, I noticed that her other hand was on him, rubbing him through his pants just as she was doing to me, and that only made me harder. Fuck, she was sexy. Her confidence and her willingness to dive in, not to mention the absolutely unbelievable way she looked in her corset and stockings that evening, combined to form a vision of my perfect kink dream.

I spread my legs a little more, giving her complete access to me as my hand went to her thigh. In front of us, Lewis placed some lube on a butt plug, and as he bent Tessa over to place it inside her, Olivia's hand pressed harder against me, making me groan.

Tate's hand had gone to her chest, his fingers playing across the top of her breasts, so I slid my hand between her legs, pressing against her just as she did to me. As her hands stroked both me and Tate through our clothes, my hand mimicked the action, rubbing against her through the damp fabric of her panties. She let out a sweet little sigh as I took hold of her knee and lifted it over mine, spreading her legs wider.

All three of us looked straight ahead as our hands explored each other, still watching the scene playing out in front of us, drawing our own pleasure from what we could see and hear and smell as well as the sensations of our own bodies. The experience was all-encompassing and intense, and it felt like time had stopped, like nothing in the world mattered but that moment and the satisfaction it would ultimately bring.

"You're going to fuck me now with that plug still in." Lewis' firm voice filled the air as he gave Tessa her instruction. "Do you want to use your safeword?"

Her body seemed to tremble in anticipation. "No, Sir."

Satisfied with that answer, he undid his pants, pulling them down just far enough to get his dick out before he laid down on the bed. Tessa climbed on top of him and lowered herself onto his waiting dick, the plug still filling her ass, and she cried out as she took him in. "Oh, fuck!"

Lewis turned to the three of us watching. "She needs something to fill her mouth. Which of you will it be?"

We hadn't anticipated that request, and there was a moment's hesitation on our end as I tried to decide if I wanted Olivia watching me or if I wanted to stay there touching her while we watched Tate. Since he remained silent too, he must have been having the same dilemma, but finally, Olivia decided for us.

"Tate, you should go."

Faced with her direct request, he didn't refuse, getting to his feet and pulling his own pants off as he stepped up onto the bed, standing over Lewis' head so his dick was in front of Tessa's face. She took him in immediately and eagerly as Lewis took hold of her hips and began to thrust up into her.

Left alone with Olivia on the couch, I slid my hand beneath her panties, the heat and wetness at her centre making me even harder. My own pants were getting very uncomfortable, so I quickly pulled my hand back and unzipped them, letting my dick breathe a little freer, though my underwear still restrained me. Olivia's stroking grew faster as my hand returned to her, flicking lightly across her clit as we both watched Tessa being fucked by both men on the bed in front of us.

"You're taking us so well," Lewis praised her, his face lined with concentration as he watched her body react. "Such a good girl."

Tessa seemed to like the praise, her body jolting in response to it, and Olivia did too. She really *was* a natural. Tate had been exactly right: her pleasure came almost entirely from what she was watching, feeling it along with the other person. There was no pretense; this was truly her kink, just as it was for me.

Tessa came as Olivia and I continued to watch, but neither man stopped, and a moment later, Olivia pulled my underwear over my dick, freeing it entirely. As her warm hand connected with my skin, my head fell back in pleasure and I couldn't help moaning out the one word I'd used most often since we started coming to the club. "Scheisse."

For some reason, Olivia's hand froze, and a moment later, she pulled back from me entirely, shuffling away from me on the couch so that my hand slipped out of her panties too. When I opened my eyes, I found her staring at me in disbelief, ignoring the scene in front of us that would soon reach its climax.

"Liv? What's wrong?" The sudden change in her made no sense. We had just been getting to the good part.

"It was you," she whispered, looking down at my exposed dick before raising her eyes back to my face.

"What was me?" I'd definitely missed something.

"The other night. In the glory hole."

The glory hole? I hadn't thought about it again since that night, not with everything else that had happened in the meantime, but as it crossed my mind, my dick got even harder as I recalled just how good it had been.

And finally, belatedly, the meaning of her words sunk in. "Wait. Are you saying...?"

She nodded, her eyes full of uncertainty. "I think so. This is... I don't know, Noah. This is a lot. I need a minute."

She got up and left the room just as Lewis pulled out of Tessa, finishing himself off as he came on her, his groans of satisfaction echoing around the room as the door clicked shut.

Well, fuck. That was intense, in more ways than one, and the night had only just begun.

~Olivia~

I felt like such an idiot as I rushed down the hallway from the private rooms back to the busy lobby of the exhibition area. I really thought I could do it. I thought I could forget who I was and forget who Noah was, and just be in the moment, surrendering to the avalanche of sensations coming in at me from all angles.

And for a while, it worked. Being there with him was thrilling and titillating and everything I wanted it to be. I even got to touch him as I'd always dreamed of doing. I had just got his cock out, just started to touch it, when Noah muttered that word next to my ear, that word I'd heard a couple of nights earlier in a different situation but said in exactly the same tone. As soon as I realized that it had been him on the other side of the curtain, it suddenly hit me with full force: things between us were never going to be that simple.

Noah and I were connected. We always had been, from the moment I was born. There was a picture of him holding me when I was a day old, for crying out loud! And somehow, fate had conspired to bring us there together and to put us on opposite sides of that curtain. For years, I had dreamt about being naked with him, being the one who got to make him happy, and the first time I saw his cock, I didn't even know it belonged to him.

It felt like a trick, even though I knew he hadn't done it on purpose. He'd been as clueless as I was, that was clear to me from the look on his face when he put it together, but somehow, that made it even worse.

Nothing about it had been special to him. Now, I was just another girl who had sucked him off, just like that girl I walked in on him with the previous Christmas. I would bet he didn't even remember her name, and though she might be nameless, I had been literally faceless. I was a mouth to him and nothing more.

And that bothered me, emotional distance or not. Fuck, it hurt like hell.

Which meant that no matter how much I had tried to convince myself that I wanted nothing more from him than being friends or kink buddies, or whatever the hell we were at that moment, there was more to it than that. Somewhere deep inside, I still wanted to be important to him in the way that he always had been for me.

That was never going to happen. It felt like my heart had broken all over again, and along with the pain I felt, I was also frustrated and embarrassed.

Why couldn't I just get over him?

Why did it *always* have to be him?

"Woah, slow down, Belle. You okay?"

The accent, exotic but familiar, caught me by surprise and I looked up to find Derek standing there along with his friend from the other night and a few other people, both men and women. They all had drinks in their hands and Derek and the other men were all dressed as Santa, with the hat, red pants and jacket, though their jackets were hanging open with nothing underneath. His hard, planed chest and abs, right at my eye level, made a very enticing distraction, making me momentarily forget my own turmoil.

Reluctantly, I lifted my eyes to his, which were full of concern as they scanned me. "Is someone bothering you? Where's your boyfriend?"

My boyfriend? He must have meant Noah. *What a joke.*

"I'm fine," I lied. "I just needed a change of scene. What are you guys up to?"

Without asking, I reached over and took his drink from his hand, taking a swig of it. Straight and strong, it burned on the way down, which was just what I wanted. A little physical pain would help me forget everything else I felt.

I handed the glass back to him and he took it with a smile, not minding that I'd helped myself. "We're just waiting for our time on stage, it's starting any minute. We've got a little show planned."

As soon as he said the words, I realized that the women with them were dressed in red and white lingerie to go with the Santa suits the men were wearing. Obviously, they'd put some effort into whatever they were doing that night, and I found myself rather intrigued by the whole thing.

"If you're not busy, you could come and watch," he offered. "I'll find you a good spot."

"That sounds perfect."

"Belle." Noah's voice was suddenly right behind me. With my back to him, I hadn't seen him approach. Randomly, I thought him using my fake name was kind of sweet, but it didn't change the way I felt overall, especially the need to get away from him. "Can we talk for a minute?"

Before I could reply, a member of staff came up to the group. "We're ready for you now. Have fun."

That gave me the perfect out. "We'll talk later," I said to Noah, not looking back at him. "The show's about to start."

Giving Noah a friendly nod, Derek put an arm around me, his other arm encircling a different woman, and we walked together into the theatre. It didn't come as much of a surprise that most of the seats were already filled on a Friday night. Even so, Derek found me a spot at the front, like he'd promised, and with a wink, he bounded up on stage with the others to cheers from the crowd.

I hadn't seen any of the other performances on stage from the beginning, and I was surprised to see they set it up like a play, with dialogue and a storyline, and though none of them were brilliant actors by any stretch, the crowd was really into it. The basic premise was that the men, five of them in total, had all turned up to audition to be the next Santa. What none of them knew was that Santa didn't just make toys; he also had to keep all the female elves satisfied year-round since male elves had tiny cocks, apparently.

It all felt light-hearted and really cute, and I found myself smiling as the women bantered back and forth about what they were looking for in the perfect Santa.

The three women set themselves up behind a table like they were a judging panel, asking the men questions, until finally they got to the crux of the matter and all the men were asked to pull their cocks out so the female elves could compare.

The mood quickly shifted from cute to steamy as the men began to show the women exactly what they had to offer. They were all impressive examples, I had to admit, taking the time to examine each of them one by one.

"Liv." My name whispered over my shoulder nearly made me jump. Somehow, Noah had ended up right behind me again, in the row behind mine. "I need to talk to you."

"Not now," I hissed back. "I'm enjoying this."

It would be hard not to be. As I watched, two of the Santas lifted one of the women up onto the table, on her hands and knees as they spit-roasted her, one man taking her from behind while the other pushed his cock into her mouth.

Two small beds had been set up on the stage, and both were quickly put into use. One Santa was going down on one of the elves while another Santa let the third elf ride him.

And the fifth, Derek... well, he was looking over in my direction.

With a crook of his finger, he beckoned for me to come and join him onstage.

Hundreds of eyes suddenly turned to look at me, to see who Derek was looking at, and it almost felt like I was in a trance as I got to my feet and climbed the steps up to him. His smile of anticipation and the gaze of the crowd as I approached had my body on edge already, not to mention all the carnal acts going on all around us.

"I've been fantasizing about you using your mouth on me ever since I saw you in the viewing room the other night," he whispered, quiet enough that only I could hear him. "If you do it now, it would make my fucking night."

The thought of giving him a blowjob in front of all those people, a much bigger crowd than had watched me the other night, made my heart beat faster and the throbbing between my legs stronger too.

And then there was the fact that Noah would be watching. Maybe I could send him a message, as clear as the one he'd given me earlier. He hadn't known I was the one who got him off the other night, but I hadn't known it was him either, and I would do it for another guy just as readily.

He wasn't anything special to me either.

Without a word, I dropped to my knees on the hard stage and a few cheers and some applause filtered in from the crowd. I looked out over them all with a teasing smile, drawing out the suspense just a little, until my eyes locked onto the man in the second row, the one with the bright green eyes watching me intently.

Keeping my eyes on Noah, I licked my lips, slowly and dramatically, before wrapping them around the head of Derek's cock.

~Noah~

Olivia was obviously upset with me, but I really didn't understand why. Being in the glory hole room together wasn't my fault. I hadn't planned it, but now that I knew she had been there, I was even more impressed with her than ever. From the reaction of the crowd that night, I knew she had performed well, and from my own side, it felt fucking amazing.

She was incredible. My image of the sweet, innocent girl braiding tinsel in her hair was quickly being combined and melded with that of a confident, sexy, kinky woman who was even more appealing to me. The fact that she was both of those women at the same time made it even better.

But I still didn't know why she was so bothered that it had been me on the other side of that curtain. She didn't seem to have any problem touching me earlier, so it didn't make sense to me that she would be upset about having been with me in an intimate way. I wanted to talk to her and understand it, but she kept putting me off, and suddenly, she went up on stage with the guy from the other night in front of hundreds of people.

Getting up on that stage was no small thing. Even for seasoned veterans of the scene like me and Tate, the stage was on a different level, so for her to do it on one of her first nights there took real guts.

Her bravery had never really been in question though, so if she really wanted to do it, I wouldn't interfere. Hell, I'd fantasized about it enough times that my dick had already begun to swell as she climbed the steps to the stage, my body reacting to the idea that my daydreams might be about to come true.

But when she made eye contact with me just before beginning, my stomach sank.

She wasn't doing it for the thrill of performing or the pleasure she'd get out of it. She had gone up there for some kind of revenge for whatever wrong she thought had been done to her, and that was never satisfying in the end. I'd seen enough people do something like that after breaking up with someone or having a fight with their partner, and the comedown was terrible. They always regretted it.

That wasn't the experience I wanted Olivia to have. I'd promised to be her guide and watch out for her, so if she was going to let herself be swayed in the moment by an emotional response, I would have to step in. That was my job.

Still, I didn't want to embarrass her in front of the whole crowd by just storming in, so I would have to proceed very carefully.

"Oh, fuck, Belle." The guy whose dick was in Olivia's mouth was obviously enjoying himself, as he should be. I knew from experience just how good it felt. "You've been such a good girl this year."

As those words sank in, I realized they were my ticket into the scene.

Getting up from my seat, I climbed over the front row and headed up the steps, aware of everyone watching me. The guy in the Santa suit looked over at me as I walked up, but Olivia hadn't seen me yet, still on her knees with her back to me.

"I'm sorry to interrupt, Santa. I'm from your accounting department, and I'm afraid there's been a mistake in the list this year. Belle here has actually been very naughty, and as you know, only good girls get to suck Santa's dick."

Olivia stopped what she was doing as soon as I started speaking, turning to look at me in surprise. Her expression grew harder as she processed my words and realized I wanted to remove her from the scene. I recognized her stubborn look immediately, the look she always gave anyone who told her she couldn't do something.

"I have been nothing but good," she argued with me.

I made eye contact with the guy above her who nodded at me. He obviously recognized me from the night before and he understood I had Olivia's best interests at heart. He wouldn't stop me.

"Don't make it worse by lying," I warned Olivia, keeping in character. "You can come with me and check the file if you want."

She got to her feet, crossing her arms defiantly across her chest. "Make me."

I had to smile at the perfect opening she'd just given me. "I was hoping you'd say that."

Before she could react, I had her up and over my shoulder as I walked back off the stage to hoots and cheers from the crowd who all thought our departure was part of the show. People offered encouragement as I carried her back out of the room with her squirming the whole time and yelling at me to put her down, while the guy on stage simply joined in with one of the other couples, resuming his fun as if nothing had happened.

Outside the door, I called over a member of the club staff and asked if there were any private rooms free. Only when we were inside one of them with the door closed did I put Olivia down.

Her face flushed red with anger when she finally got free of me. "What the hell, Noah? You had no right to do that. I was just having fun! It had nothing to do with you."

Though she shouted at me, I kept my voice calm and level. "If you were having fun, that would have been fine, but you weren't."

"You don't know what I'm feeling! You never have. You always treated me like a little kid, and now you've just done it in front of all those people too. They're all going to think I can't do anything for myself."

Did she really believe that? Nothing could be further from the truth. "Nobody thinks that, and trust me, no one who saw you up there is thinking of you as a little kid. They all thought me hauling you out of there was part of the show, that this is how you and I get off. They all imagine we're somewhere fucking each other right now, so forget about them. I want to talk about you."

She flopped down onto the bed in the room, her arms still crossed defensively. "What about me?"

Keeping a bit of distance between us, I took a seat on the bed next to her. I didn't want it to feel like I was talking down to her, but I needed to clear the air between us. "You weren't ready for that. You did it because you're upset, but I don't know why. Was it because of what we were doing in the other room? Because of the glory hole? Talk to me, Liv. What's wrong?"

For a moment I thought she might stick to her denial and try to tell me there was nothing wrong, but slowly, her arms uncrossed and her expression changed from anger to disappointment. "I've messed everything up, haven't I?"

Her comedown was kicking in, the adrenaline leaving her body, so I did my best to buoy her up.

"You haven't messed anything up," I assured her. "There's no harm done. Like I said, no one out there knows there was anything wrong. It's just you and me here now, with no judgement. I want to understand what the problem is so I can help you through it. I want you to enjoy yourself here, Liv. That's the whole point, right? So what's going on? Is it me?"

Although I asked the question, I really didn't expect her to agree with me, so her response took me by surprise. "Yes. It's you."

It almost felt like something cracked inside me with those words. Was she rejecting me before I'd even had a chance to tell her how I felt? If she'd left it there, I wasn't sure what I would say, but luckily, she kept talking.

"And it's me too. It's the two of us together. I thought I could do this, but I can't."

That didn't make things a whole lot clearer. "What can't you do? Being here at the club with me? You don't want me to watch you?"

"No, it's not that."

That was something, at least. "So you're okay with me watching, but you don't want to be sexual with me? Is that why you're upset that I was the one in the glory hole?"

"No, it's not that either."

Fuck, she really wasn't giving me a lot to work with here. "You're going to have to help me out, Liv. I'm running out of ideas."

Her face scrunched up like she was trying to hold something in, but a moment later, she blurted it out anyway. "I don't want to be just another fuck to you, Noah. That's why I'm upset. In the glory hole, I was just some random girl, and that girl hasn't crossed your mind again since. If anything ever happened between us, I wanted it to be special, and it wasn't. It was nothing."

Her gaze dropped to her hands as she finished, so I reached over and cupped her face, lifting her chin up so she had to look at me. "That blowjob wasn't nothing. You were amazing. You were amazing when I didn't know who you were, and it's even more amazing now that I know it was you."

She tried to look away, but I held her firmly in place so all she could do was purse her lips at me. "You're just saying that because I'm upset."

"I'm not. You know me better than that, Liv. I don't do bullshit. I've never lied to you and I'm not doing it now. When we were finished in the glory hole, I tried to find you. I went looking for the girl who had been on the other side of the curtain because I wanted to know who she was. I wanted more of her."

Uncertainty clouded her face as she tried to judge if I meant it or not. "You did?"

I nodded. "The only reason I didn't try harder to track her down was because I ran into you right afterwards, and it kind of rocked my world. I haven't been able to think of anything other than you since then. The only thing that made me forget about you was... you."

Somehow, we had moved closer to each other. I wasn't even entirely sure how. "This isn't real," she whispered, her sweet blue eyes looking straight into mine. "You never say things like this to me."

"That's because I'm an idiot," I told her, relaying Tate's assessment of me. "But if I ever made you feel like I didn't think you were special, I didn't do it on purpose. If anything, I thought you were too special for me."

That made her smile, at last. "That's stupid."

I moved a little bit closer. "Yeah, it kind of is."

She was so close to me, I could feel her breath on my face. "This still feels like a dream."

It did to me too, but I wasn't about to let that stop me. "How about now?"

Leaning forward the last couple of inches, I kissed her, right there in the private room with no one else there to see it.

Chapter Twelve

MIXED MESSAGES

~Olivia~

My head swam with everything that had just happened, the emotions running through me, and the lingering effects of the alcohol. Between the stimulation of watching Tessa and Lewis while touching Noah and Tate, finding out I had given Noah a blowjob without realizing it, the excitement of Derek and his friends' performance, the adrenaline of getting up on stage with him, the anger and frustration I'd felt when Noah interrupted and literally carried me away, the argument we'd just had, and the sweet and completely out-of-character things he'd just said to me, I honestly didn't know which way was up or down anymore.

And to make matters even more confusing, Noah kissed me.

He'd never kissed me before. I kissed *him* that night back in his room at Isabel's farm the previous Christmas, the night I waited for him in his bed, and he kissed me back, but he had never been the one to start it.

If I had handed him the lines ahead of time, he couldn't have said anything closer to what I had always dreamed of hearing from him, and though it made me happy, doubt still lingered in my mind. What had changed his mind? Was this all part of the performance?

I honestly didn't know, but neither could I bring myself to care too much, not when it felt so good to have his lips on mine and his hand still holding my face while the other went around my waist, pulling me closer to him. I could taste the alcohol on his tongue as he slipped it into my mouth, firm and commanding, and his assuredness sent a thrill of excitement through me.

He wanted me as much as I wanted him, at least in that moment, and I clung onto that knowledge like an anchor in the sea of uncertainty I seemed to be floating in.

Wrapping my arms around his neck, I lowered myself back onto the bed we were both sitting on, pulling him down with me. There was no resistance as he settled down next to me, his mouth still attached to mine. One elbow propped him up while the other hand made an exploration of my body, over my corset, all along the edges of it, and finally finding its way back between my legs, where it had been in the other room before I freaked out and ran away.

His fingers insistently pushed my legs apart, and I willingly obeyed, spreading them wider as the aching there grew stronger. All the adren-aline that had left my body during our argument returned with a rush as I practically trembled in anticipation. At last, he was going to touch me. After all the years of waiting and dreaming about it, it was finally going to happen.

Noah broke our kiss for just a second, his mouth sliding across my cheek to whisper in my ear. "You made me feel so good when you made me come the other night, and I'd love to return the favour. Can I?"

I appreciated that he asked permission. Despite the fact that I wore next to nothing, lying on a bed in a literal sex club, he didn't assume he could do what he wanted with me. He wanted to make sure I wanted it too, and fuck, I really did. I wanted him to have his way with me and do everything I had always dreamt of him doing. If we couldn't have forever, at least we'd have that one night.

"Yes, please, Noah. I want you to make me come. I know you can."

A low sound, almost like a growl, came from his throat as he kissed me again, his fingers pushing my panties to the side as they made contact with me, slipping through the wetness waiting for him there.

"Fuck, Liv." The sound of him groaning my name was the sexiest thing I'd ever heard, making my whole body shudder with desire.

He teased me for a moment, his touch feather-light as he ran his fingers up and down, avoiding my clit just enough to make me even more aware of it than I had been before. Just before I begged him to touch me properly, he finally did, giving me the pressure I so desperately wanted as he rubbed down on the sensitive spot.

"Oh, God." The words were murmured into his mouth, swallowed by his possessing kiss as he finally pressed a finger into me.

Noah Stamer was finally right where I'd wanted him for years: inside me. It might have only been his finger, but it was a start, and he showed no signs of stopping.

Deeper he pushed, his finger swirling and exploring until it couldn't go any further, his thumb still caressing my clit at the same time. "You feel amazing," he whispered before kissing me again as another finger joined the first one, filling me further, though it still wasn't enough. I still needed more. I wanted *all* of him.

His fingers fucked me slowly at first, like he was memorizing every inch of me through touch, but as I spread my legs even wider, pulling him closer to me as my need grew stronger, he took pity on me and began to pick up the pace. His thrusts were strong and sure, his thumb working my clit to perfection as his tongue continued to tangle with mine. There wasn't a single part of me that wasn't completely tuned in to what he was doing, and my legs began to tremble as his fingers pressed against my g-spot.

"Yes, Noah!" I cried out his name as my back arched in the heights of my pleasure, holding me in its grip for a few perfect seconds before it broke and wave after wave of the most blissful relief washed over me. My body contracted around his fingers that were still deep inside me, making him groan in appreciation.

"Fuck, you're beautiful when you come."

I opened my eyes to find him staring at me, a look of satisfaction and desire on his face that was everything I had always dreamed it would be.

"I still haven't seen what you look like," I reminded him, the words coming out shakily as I tried to catch my breath. "All I saw was the curtain."

That made him smile even as his gaze turned more heated. "That definitely needs to be remedied."

He removed his fingers from me, leaving me feeling colder and empty, but only so he could roll over onto me, letting me feel just how hard and eager he was. He had obviously enjoyed himself too; maybe not quite as much as I had, but there could be no question he had gotten something out of it.

Just as he bent down to kiss me once more, a knock on the door made him pause.

"Does someone else have the room booked?" I whispered, as if the person on the other side might hear me.

"They shouldn't," he said with a frown. He waited a moment longer, not moving, and when no further sound came, he leaned down again.

That time, our lips did manage to connect, but just for an instant before the knock came again, accompanied by a voice. "Noah? Liv? Are you in there?"

Noah groaned in frustration as he rolled off me.

"Is that Tate?" I asked, sitting up and straightening out my panties. Noah hadn't actually taken anything off me, so I was still as clothed as I had ever been.

"It is," Noah confirmed, his jaw clenched as he looked away from me. "And he's probably going to be pissed at me."

He'd lost me. "What? Why?"

"Because I wasn't supposed to go this far with you, not right away."

That didn't make things any clearer. "Wasn't *supposed* to? According to who?"

"According to our agreement."

An uneasy feeling settled in my stomach, dislodging the butterflies that had previously been in residence there. "What agreement?"

Noah turned to me with an expression somewhere between regret and embarrassment. "He likes you, Liv. He wants a shot with you, he told me yesterday."

My stomach dropped even further as I started to put the pieces together. Tate told me Noah had never even mentioned me, and suddenly, Noah was telling me he couldn't stop thinking about me... the day after Tate told me that he was interested in me. "Is that what brought on this sudden interest in me? Because he likes me?"

"No, of course not," he assured me quickly. "It just helped me to see a couple of things..."

The knock sounded again, louder this time. "If you're in there and want us to go away, just say so. I just want to make sure you're okay."

'Us'? Tessa must be with him too. *Fuck.* I had completely abandoned her during her own scene. Tate would have looked out for her, but that wasn't the point. I had to stop being so selfish, so I got to my feet and headed to the door to open it.

"Liv, wait," Noah's voice pleaded behind me. "Let me explain."

I didn't want to hear his explanations. I'd already heard his side of the story, and I needed to hear the rest of it before I could figure out for myself exactly what the truth was.

~Noah~

All the ups and downs of that night were starting to give me whiplash. Just when everything had calmed down and we were finally connecting, and I got the amazing privilege of making Olivia come, Tate showed up and we got thrown off course again.

At least that time, I understood why; I heard the way the words sounded as they came out of my mouth and I knew what it must have sounded like to her. Tate had pretty much accused me of the same thing the night before: of being the spoiled rich kid who only wants his toys when someone else shows an interest in them. But that wasn't where my feelings came from and I needed to explain that to Olivia properly, if she would just sit down and listen to me for a minute.

Instead, she went to the door, unlocked it, and let Tate and Tessa in. Tate had his arm around Olivia's friend in a supportive gesture and he looked around curiously as he entered. "You guys are on your own in here?"

Of course that would come as a surprise to him, but I didn't want to get into it so I asked a question of my own. "How did you know where we were?"

"I asked Nina if she'd seen you," he explained. "I was worried after you both ran out earlier. Is everything okay?"

"We're fine," Olivia answered, a little too quickly, before turning to her friend. "How are you? I'm sorry I left before you were finished but it looked like you were having fun."

Tessa nodded, still leaning on Tate. "It was... intense."

That word could apply to a lot of things that evening. "I think we could all use some time to decompress," I suggested. "If you're ready to go, I have an idea where we could relax."

Everyone agreed, and as we collected our things from the changing room, I noticed we'd already been there for over two hours. Time could be a slippery thing in The Playground, it often disappeared with little warning.

In the taxi on the way back to the hotel, Olivia, Tate and Tessa chatted while I placed a quick call to the hotel's on-duty manager. "I know the spa is closed for the night, but I'd like to use one of the jacuzzis. You can bill the cost to my dad."

I rarely played the boss' son card. For the most part, I wanted people to treat me as much like any other employee as they could, but I also wasn't above using my influence when necessary.

As I expected, she didn't refuse me. "We'll have it ready for you in a few minutes, Mr Stamer."

"I'll need some bathing suits as well, for two men and two women."

With that arranged, I turned my attention back to the others while Olivia described the on-stage show we'd watched to our friends, though she left out her own starring role in it and my cameo appearance.

Tate grinned over at me. "That sounds awesome. Were you taking notes for our own performance?"

Her eyes filled with curiosity, Olivia looked between us. "Are you guys planning something like that?"

I answered for the both of us. "We haven't entirely decided what we're doing, but we do want to do *something* on stage before we leave. We were thinking about doing it next weekend."

From the spark of interest on her face, I could tell she was intrigued. I would love for her to take part in it, but the next weekend seemed an awfully long way away. A lot could still happen before then.

When we arrived at the hotel, a member of staff was waiting to take us to the spa where the jacuzzi already bubbled away in the soft mood lighting of the small room. Olivia and Tessa went into one of the changing rooms to get their bathing suits on while Tate and I changed where we were. We'd definitely seen each other naked before, so we had nothing to hide.

"How did things go with Tessa and Lewis?" I asked him once we were on our own.

He shrugged as we settled down into the warm, soothing water. I'd barely realized how tense I felt until the heat soaked into my skin.

"Things were going well until you guys ran off and left us without an audience."

Though some people might not understand what he meant by that, I immediately did. "You didn't get off?"

He shook his head in confirmation. "No, and I think it might have upset her. Lewis gave her some aftercare but she was pretty quiet with me."

That did sound like she might have been upset. From my few interactions with her, quiet was not a word I would have used to describe Tessa.

"Why *did* you leave?" Tate asked, leaning forward curiously. "What happened?"

That wasn't a short story and I didn't know how much time we had before the girls joined us, so I tried to sum it up quickly. "Liv was the girl in the glory hole with me the other night. We didn't know, and when she figured it out, it freaked her out a bit. We talked things over and we're okay now."

"She blew you without realizing it?" When I nodded, Tate whistled. "What are the odds? And didn't you say she was really good?"

I had definitely said that. "Yeah. She was amazing and the crowd loved her. Like you said, she's a natural."

Appreciation flashed in his eyes, and I groaned internally. I wasn't trying to make him more interested in her; that was the opposite of what I wanted.

"But listen, about what we said about not making any move right away..."

Before I could finish my sentence, the door to the changing room opened and Olivia and Tessa came out, both dressed in the simple one-piece suits the hotel had left for them. Tate immediately understood that whatever I had been about to say wasn't meant for their ears, so he quickly changed the subject. "They really need to get some hot tubs like this at The Playground, hey, Noah? This is perfect."

"I'm surprised they don't have any," Olivia said as she and Tessa slowly lowered themselves into the water to join us. "They have pretty much everything else."

"It's probably a hygiene issue," I suggested. "How many times would you want to have to drain cum out of a pool?"

That made the girls smile, and Tessa looked more relaxed as she sank down fully, letting her head lean back against the jacuzzi's rim. However, when she looked over at Tate, who gave her a smile in return, her own smile vanished and she raised her head again.

"You really don't like me at all, do you?"

That was the blunt Tessa I recognized from the night before, and I didn't envy Tate as his brow furrowed in confusion. "What? Why would you think that?"

"Tessa..." Olivia tried to interject, but her friend didn't pay any attention to her.

"I have never failed at a blowjob before, but I couldn't make you come tonight, and Liv just told me that you like her instead? Was that the only reason you were with me tonight, so she could watch you?"

Tate's eyes moved to Olivia in surprise before coming to rest on me. *Fuck.* That wasn't how I wanted to let him know about my conversation with Olivia. I had been trying to be honest with her, but telling her how he felt before he could was still kind of a dick move.

"She's still a little drunk," Olivia told us by way of apology before turning to Tessa and whispering to her. "This isn't exactly what I meant by telling him how you feel."

Obviously, they'd been talking about us in the changing room while we were talking about them.

Tate quickly recovered from his surprise, speaking to Olivia first. "It's okay. I'm all for being honest." Next, he turned to Tessa. "Of course I like you. You're beautiful and funny and fierce. What's not to like?"

His answer seemed to both please and confuse her. "Then why didn't you come?"

That was harder to explain to someone who didn't share the same kink, but he gave it his best shot. "There was nothing wrong with what you were doing, and you looked amazing doing it. I just need the audience or it doesn't work for me, ever. It's nothing to do with you in particular. Noah's the same way, right?"

He looked over at me for confirmation, and though I met his gaze, I was fully aware of Olivia's eyes on me too, awaiting my response.

It *had* always been true for me too, but that night, in the private room with just me and Olivia, with my fingers inside her, watching her come, I had been pretty fucking turned-on even though there was no one else there. Would I have come if we'd had sex? I couldn't say for certain, but it definitely felt possible.

My mouth was open to respond, but Tessa jumped back in before I could. "So, if I gave you a blowjob right now with these two watching, that would work for you?"

Tate's eyebrows raised, along with the corners of his mouth. "There's a pretty good chance it would, yeah."

Tessa nodded with determination. "Okay. Take your suit off then."

"Tessa!" Olivia tried not to laugh, but didn't completely succeed, and I grinned over at her as she bit her lip. The night was certainly full of surprises.

"Hey, I don't mind," Tate assured us all, grinning too as he pulled himself up onto the side of the jacuzzi and did as she requested, pulling his suit off to reveal his semi-erect dick. Tessa floated over to him, her eyes fixed on it as she positioned herself between his legs, her head level with his groin.

"She's not usually like this," Olivia whispered to me as we watched Tessa take Tate into her mouth. "I think I'm a bad influence."

"That is never how I would have described you before this week," I whispered back, watching her cheeks flush at both my words and the sight of our friends who were both clearly enjoying themselves. "But maybe it's true. You're a kink goddess-in-training, Olivia Hanmer. I think it's time to accept it."

We fell silent as we watched the private show in front of us, where Tessa seemed to be having no trouble getting my friend hard. Tate's eyes were full of both amusement and enjoyment as he looked over at me, but when he looked at Olivia, I could see something else there too. He kept his eyes on her as his orgasm built and she held his gaze, touching herself beneath the water, just enough to let him know she enjoyed the view.

When he did finally come into Tessa's mouth, his lips formed Liv's name.

As for me, I found the whole thing simultaneously arousing and confusing. Everything was getting far too complicated. We needed to find a way to talk things out and settle everything between us before something that was supposed to be all about pleasure became much more painful instead.

~Olivia~

As Tate mouthed my name, his eyes fixed on me, my gaze quickly dropped to Tessa. She still had her lips wrapped around him, moving slower since he'd just come, and her eyes were down, focused on what she was doing, so she hadn't seen what I saw. She didn't know that he had been watching me rather than her.

I understood it completely, since I've done exactly the same thing the other night at The Playground. When Derek made me come, Noah's name was on my lips. Watching him watching me, I'd felt far more connected to him than I did to the person giving me the physical pleasure, and Tate must have felt the same way.

However, I was equally sure that Tessa didn't understand that, at least not fully. She didn't share the same kink so it just wasn't the same for her, which was why I had tried to tell her earlier that she might want to give up on the idea of Tate entirely.

"It was humiliating," she told me as soon as we were alone to change into our swimsuits, swaying dangerously as she bent down. "I thought Tate was enjoying it and then all of a sudden, he just stepped away, telling me it wasn't going to happen."

From the trouble she was having keeping her balance, she'd obviously had more to drink at the club than I had. Or maybe all the surprises of my night had just sobered me up more.

"It's nothing to be embarrassed about," I assured her. "I didn't see him complaining while I was there. Guys don't have to come every single time to enjoy themselves."

She raised her eyebrows at me in disbelief, and I had to laugh. Maybe that wasn't entirely true, but since we were talking about Tate, there was something else I had to tell her.

"There's more to it than just you. It's the whole kink side of things and..." I trailed off, not quite sure how to proceed without hurting her feelings, but I had to get it out. "Noah told me that Tate might have feelings for me, actually. I haven't talked to him about it, I have no idea if it's true, but that's what Noah said."

That only seemed to confuse her more. "But you like Noah."

"I do. I did. I do." I honestly didn't know which tense to use, my feelings were so mixed up. Did he actually care about me romantically, or was it all some kind of game to him? Did Tate really like me? He barely even knew me. But then, I'd heard my dad talk often enough about how he knew the first time he met my mom that she was the woman for him, though it took him a little while to convince her of that.

I had always compared me and Noah to that story: I was the one like my dad, sure we belonged together, and Noah was like my mom, who just needed a bit of persuasion to come to the right conclusion.

But maybe it shouldn't be so much work. Maybe it could be as simple as someone sitting down for a drink with me at a club and deciding he liked me.

Except there was also Tessa too, who was still interested in Tate despite everything that had happened. She had expressed that interest to me the first time they met, so she deserved a chance to see if there was something there, especially considering I really didn't know how I felt about Tate at all.

"You should talk to him," I suggested to her as we both pulled our swimsuits on. "When you get an opportunity, tell him how you feel. Maybe he'll say no, but at least then you'll know. There are all kinds of other hot guys at The Playground if he's not interested."

She nodded and I thought that we were on the same page, until she confronted him almost immediately after we got in the hot tub. I had meant to wait and do it somewhere privately, but apparently, she didn't want to wait. Tate took it pretty well, I thought, as he tried to explain to her what happened at the club. It sounded to me like he was trying to let her down easy, but that clearly wasn't what Tessa took away from it when she offered to give him a blowjob right then and there.

Tate might be a good guy, but there weren't many guys in the world who were going to say no to that, so I wasn't shocked when he agreed. I glanced over at Noah to try to see what he made of the whole exchange, but he was simply watching them both curiously. Noah and I sat next to each other as Tessa worked Tate's cock, not touching or looking at each other, but I was still very aware of him next to me and the way that his hand rested on his own cock as he watched.

The memory of that cock in my mouth combined with the performance we were being treated to was enough to get my body humming once again. My hands moved almost on their own to the parts of me that were calling out for attention the most, one rubbing over my nipple under the swimsuit while the other slipped between my legs, not too frantic, just applying a bit of pressure.

Everything was fine until Tate mouthed my name. Thankfully, Tessa didn't see him, but Noah stiffened beside me, and I realized how out of hand things were getting. There was nothing wrong with all of us having some fun together if there were no feelings involved, but obviously, that wasn't the case. Feelings were springing up on multiple sides, including mine, and it felt like we were all sinking deeper into quicksand all the time. If someone didn't grab onto a rope soon, we might not all make it out unscathed.

"That was great," Tate told Tessa appreciatively, giving her a warm smile as she let go of his cock. "Thank you."

Her brow furrowed as her reply came out as more of a question than a statement. "You're welcome?"

Clearly, that wasn't the response she'd been hoping for from him, but there wasn't anything else coming. I had to try to find a way to help her see that, as gently as possible.

Leaving Noah behind, I moved over to Tessa, putting my arm around her shoulder and pulling her back to the bench on the other side of the jacuzzi as Tate pulled his suit back up and lowered himself back into the water.

"You see, Tessa? What happened earlier had nothing to do with you." I spoke softly, but loud enough that Noah and Tate could hear me too. "Tate needed the audience. That's what it means to be an exhibitionist, that's what turns him on. But it doesn't turn you on, does it? I don't think you really liked having us watch."

She looked between me and Noah, as if finally registering that we had seen everything she had just done, and her cheeks began to turn red.

"And earlier with Lewis, he told you to ignore us and that made you feel better, didn't it?"

Wincing, she gave me a nod. "I just blocked you guys out and focused on him."

I figured as much. "And that's totally fine, there's nothing wrong with that. I loved watching you, but I wouldn't want anyone giving me orders the way he did with you. We've all got our own kinks, that's the whole point of coming here and trying things out. But I think if you're looking for more than just a bit of fun, you need someone who shares the same kinks with you and truly enjoys the same things as you. It'll be way more fun for both of you in the long run."

Her eyes moved over to Tate, letting me know that she was following what I was trying to say without stating it outright. She, however, seemed to have no problem with putting it more bluntly. "So, you don't want to date me because I don't get turned on by people watching me fuck?"

Although I winced, Tate didn't seem to be offended or put off by the question. Instead, he answered her with total honesty. "I didn't know you were interested in me like that, Tessa. If I'd realized, I would have told you before, but Liv is right: I don't usually do relationships because I don't usually meet anyone who would truly fit in with my life."

His eyes rested on me for just a second before he continued talking to my friend.

"I think you're gorgeous and fun and I really like you. I'd love for us to be friends, and if you wanted to have some fun too, I'm totally up for it. Obviously."

He gestured down to his waist beneath the water, to his cock that she had just drained.

"But if you want something serious, I don't think it would work. I'm sorry if I gave you the wrong impression."

Though he didn't know it, he had come very close to repeating Noah's words to me from the previous Christmas. Was Noah thinking about that too? I stole a quick glance at him and his green eyes were on me, the look in them completely inscrutable.

I quickly looked away.

Tate held out his hand to Tessa in a peace offering. "Friends?"

Obviously, she'd hoped for a different outcome, but after all the craziness of the evening, she seemed to accept it. "Friends," she agreed, shaking his hand before returning to her seat and looking around at all of us. "I just feel like the odd one out, I guess, since you guys all like the same thing."

I could understand that. We would need to find some other people for her to hang out with at the club, preferably ones who enjoyed the same things she did and who *weren't* married.

Tessa wasn't quite finished yet. "And speaking of liking the same thing..."

The mischievous look that crossed her face made me nervous, and for good reason once the next words came out of her mouth.

"How exactly are you guys planning on working out this little love triangle you've got going on?"

Chapter Thirteen

LOVE TRIANGLE

~Noah~

I kept my mouth shut as Olivia helped Tate and Tessa work through whatever was going on between them, but it didn't mean I wasn't paying attention. I noticed the way Tate's eyes moved to Olivia when he said he didn't usually meet anyone who would fit in with his lifestyle, and I didn't miss how closely the words he said to Tessa matched what I'd said to Olivia a year earlier when I stupidly pushed her away, thinking she'd never understand a guy like me.

If I had only known then what lay beneath her innocent surface, this could have all been so much easier.

Because at that moment, things weren't easy. In fact, they were complicated as hell. When Tessa asked how we were getting out of the mess we'd gotten ourselves into, I desperately wanted to know the answer to that too.

Tate and I both instinctively looked over at Olivia, since she seemed to be the one with the answer, though putting her on the spot like that was hardly fair.

She quickly pointed out the same thing. "Tonight has brought up a few things I didn't know before. I think we all need some time to figure it all out."

Part of me was disappointed, since I would have loved for her to just choose me right then and there, but I also recognized it would probably be better if she wasn't impulsive about it. I'd already seen that night what her knee-jerk reaction could look like. Olivia was usually the kind of woman who planned things out, studied them in detail, and made lists of pros and cons, so it really didn't surprise me that she'd want to take some time to think things over.

I could only hope I'd done enough to get myself a few items in the 'pro' column.

"What are you guys doing tomorrow?" I asked, trying to help her out by changing the subject and also because I was genuinely curious. "Tate and I have the day off if you'd like some company."

It would be good for us to spend some time together again outside of the club and the world of fantasy it created. Tate said he wanted to be with Olivia in the real world, and I had started to believe that was possible for me too, but The Playground was hardly the best place to figure that out.

"We're going to the House of Music," Olivia replied. "Have you already been?"

I shook my head. Besides work and The Playground, Tate and I hadn't done much in the city at all. "That sounds great. We can grab a late breakfast in the restaurant and then go."

Everyone agreed and the girls left to go back to their room while Tate and I stayed a few minutes longer. Once they were gone, he turned to me with his eyebrows raised. "Do you want to tell me exactly what happened tonight?"

Though some of what happened was private between me and Olivia, I did owe him some explanation, and I tried my best to give him one. "Well, I already told you that Liv and I figured out we were in the glory hole together. She was upset because she thought it didn't mean anything to me, so I tried to show her that's not true and that she's special to me. That's when you found us and I realized I'd unintentionally gone against what you and I had already agreed by declaring my feelings for her, so I told her you like her too. I wasn't trying to go behind your back, Tate. I just couldn't take that look on her face when she thought I didn't care."

Thankfully, he seemed to understand that and didn't appear to be too upset about it. "Well, she didn't shoot me down, at least."

No, she hadn't, to my disappointment. Fuck, I would love to know how she felt about everything. She had never been more of a mystery to me than she was that night.

The next morning, we met for breakfast as planned. Everyone had dressed casually for our day out and we kept the conversation light and casual too. Heavier conversations were still needed, but we all seemed to have mutually agreed, without talking about it, to just enjoy the day without any additional drama.

The House of Music was located in the city centre, just a short walk from the hotel. On the bright, crisp Saturday afternoon, the streets were full of tourists and Christmas shoppers, with Christmas just over a week away.

"What is this place?" Tate asked curiously as we walked up to the former palace which housed the museum.

I expected Olivia to have done her research, and she didn't disappoint. "It's all about sound and music. First, there's a floor with interactive exhibits about how sound is made and how we process it in the ear and the brain. That's what I'm most interested in, but there's also all kinds of stuff about all the famous composers who lived and worked in Vienna."

I had grown up going to classical music concerts with my parents at Carnegie Hall, but I knew Tate didn't have that kind of background at all. I wasn't sure he even knew who any of the composers were, but even so, he didn't seem intimidated. "Sounds like fun," he said simply, making Olivia smile.

Inside, the museum buzzed with the chatter of happy families. "We'll have to fight the kids to use some of the machines," Olivia mused as she looked around, which made me laugh. She really would, I had no doubt.

We went straight to the Sonotopia on the second floor and, as Olivia had promised, the exhibit was full of hands-on stations to play with different sounds and explore how sound was made. She and I made our way to a wall with headphones, each of which played a different sound. "Don't look at what it is," she challenged me. "Try to guess when you hear it."

Always up for a game with her, I put the headphones on and was immediately enveloped in a new soundscape. The sounds of the museum and all the other visitors were completely gone; all I could hear was a muted, whooshing kind of sound.

Olivia had put her headphones on too, meaning she couldn't hear me any more than I could hear her, so when I turned to her, I didn't bother to speak out loud. I just mouthed the words to her. "Is it wind?"

"What?" She laughed as she mouthed the word back at me.

"Wind," I repeated, exaggerating my lip movements. She still looked confused so I tried again, that time adding in some arm motions which made her laugh but also helped her to understand.

She shook her head. "Try again."

I listened harder. Something about it felt very soothing, almost like being in the ocean on a tropical island. "Water?" I tried next.

"Closer." She grinned at me, clearly enjoying the game.

Closer to water than wind; that gave me something to work from, at least. Closing my eyes, I tried to lose myself in the sound entirely. Something felt rhythmic in it, not entirely random. The rhythm almost reminded me of a heartbeat, making me more aware of my own heart beating and the blood pumping through my body.

My eyes snapped open as I thought I figured it out. "Inside the body?"

"What?" Olivia's blue eyes twinkled in amusement, making me smile too. She didn't understand me, and I could definitely have some fun with helping her figure it out.

"The body," I repeated, forming an outline of a woman's body with my hands, curvy and soft just like the woman in front of me. "Inside."

As I mimed putting my hand up inside the body I'd just drawn, Olivia giggled, covering her mouth with her hand. "Lots of kids here," she reminded me, gesturing to the families all around us.

"Where do you think they came from?" I teased her back, knowing she probably wouldn't understand me anyway, and at last, it fully clicked in my head. "Wait, it's the womb, isn't it?"

She nodded as she pointed to the information panel, letting me take a look, and I was exactly right: the sound had been what a fetus could hear inside the womb.

"Impressive," she said as we both removed our headphones. The space suddenly felt a lot bigger when the sound disappeared. "Although, perhaps I shouldn't be surprised. The female body is kind of in your wheelhouse."

I couldn't argue with that, but there was something in the way she said it that gave me pause. She had said the night before that she wanted things between us to be special if they ever got sexual, and now she was talking about my experience with women.

Although I had meant to keep things light that day, I couldn't let an opportunity pass to make my feelings clearer to her.

"How many men have you slept with?" I asked her bluntly, keeping my voice low as we walked into the next room. Tate and Tessa were still playing with one of the other displays, keeping each other entertained.

"How many women have you slept with?" she shot back.

"A lot," I answered truthfully. "Which I think bothers you a bit. That's why I'm asking."

"It doesn't bother me," she countered, but when I raised my eyebrows at her, she sighed. "Well, maybe it does a little. But only because none of them were ever special to you, so what makes you think I would be?"

"Because you're *already* special to me. I don't usually have sex with women I know, for just that reason. It's only about sex. No emotions, remember?"

She knew exactly what I was referring to, that night back at my aunt's farm. "Then how do you know what it would be like with me?"

"I don't," I admitted. "Not exactly, but I do know it would be different. That's why I want to give it a try."

A large group of kids ran up to the displays next to us, forcing us to stop talking for a couple of minutes as we looked over the various instruments in the room. My heart beat faster as I tried to work out from her body language what she thought about what I just said.

When at last we had a second to ourselves, she turned back to me with a little half-smile. "One."

"What?" I felt like I had missed part of the conversation.

"You asked how many men I've slept with," she reminded me. "If you mean full sex, not the kind of stuff I've been doing at The Playground, then the answer is one."

Really? I had to assume that had been her boyfriend, the guy she'd been dating most of the year. I was surprised, and yet not surprised at the same time. It made sense, and it also made me think. She had clearly come to Vienna with the intention of having sex with other men; she wouldn't be at The Playground otherwise. But just like she didn't want to be just one more woman in my bed, I didn't want to be just the guy she used to experiment with either.

She still had some new experiences to discover, some hands-on things to try. If and when we finally slept together, I wanted it to be when she knew for sure what she really wanted, when it would be as special to her as it would be to me.

The more I thought about it, the more it made sense to me: she should have sex at The Playground that night, but not with me. I would be there to watch and guide her through it, but I didn't want us to take that step together just yet.

I just needed to figure out who the lucky guy should be.

~Olivia~

I wasn't sure what I expected Noah's reaction to be when I told him I'd only had sex with one person before, but his response took me by surprise anyway.

"We should change that as soon as possible. You need a much wider base of comparison before you know when it's really good."

He gave me a smouldering wink to let me know that he thought he would definitely fall on the good side, and though the gesture was arrogant as hell, it still turned me on. I was pretty sure he *would* be good. He'd had enough practice.

But that only made his words more confusing to me. It didn't sound like he was talking about the two of us having sex. How wide a range was he talking about?

"Liv, you've got to come try these drums with me!" Tate was trying to hold back a smile as he and Tessa walked up to us.

"I do?" I asked, trying to figure out what was so funny.

Tate nodded. "Of course. I love to watch other people banging."

"Hey, that was my joke!" Tessa objected, smacking his arm. "You can't steal it."

"I wouldn't want credit for that if I were you," I said with a laugh. They certainly seemed to be getting along completely fine after the talk in the jacuzzi, which was good news. Giving Noah an apologetic shrug, I headed over with Tate to the collection of large, hanging drum skins.

"Give this one a smack," he dared me, standing in front of a huge drum hanging from the ceiling, easily twice my height. "As hard as you can."

"You don't want me to do that," I warned him. "I'm a volleyball player with a killer spike, and if I bring that thing down, I don't think I can afford to pay to fix it."

That made him laugh. "Me neither. Okay, just a little tap then. Let's see you find your rhythm."

Tate kept his eyes fixed on me as I started to play a simple beat that somehow morphed into a version of Rudolph the Red-Nosed Reindeer. He joined in as we both sang along, badly, laughing with each other.

"I'm guessing you never had music lessons either," I teased him as we moved on to the next floor where there were displays about the most famous composers from Vienna's history. "You're just as bad as me."

"I never really had any kind of lessons," he said with a shrug. "That wasn't my life growing up."

This was the first personal thing he'd told me about himself, and it made me curious to know more. "What was your life like?"

"You knew Noah growing up, right?" he asked, and I nodded in confirmation. "Well, just imagine the opposite of that. No money, no happy family, definitely no trips to Vienna at Christmas."

Although the picture he drew for me was pretty bleak, his cheerful tone remained.

"You've come a long way then," I pointed out.

"I have, and I've got a long way still to go. I'm going to have it all. We only get one shot at this life, so we've got to make it count, right?"

"Right." I'd come to Vienna for just that reason. "What does 'having it all' look like for you?"

He didn't mince any words. "The corner office, a fancy title with a six-figure salary, a Park Avenue apartment, and an amazing woman to share it with, one who's equally at home in a classical music museum as she is in The Playground."

If his words weren't clear enough, the look he gave me made it obvious he was talking about someone like me. I glanced over at Noah, who was talking with Tessa as they looked at the collection of Beethoven artifacts. "Is this fancy job of yours with Stamer Hotels?"

"It could be. I know the position won't just be handed to me like Noah's will, but I'm willing to work for it. Success in business is 80% confidence, and I've got that."

He certainly did. "Noah's dad keeps telling me he's going to hire me too."

That thought clearly appealed to him. "So we'd be colleagues? Tell me... what's your position on sex in the workplace?"

I couldn't resist that kind of setup. "Any position that works, I suppose."

He laughed loud enough that Noah and Tessa both looked over at us before returning to their own conversation. "This is just what I like about you, Liv. You've got this sweet and innocent vibe, but you're not afraid to get a bit filthy too."

Having him tell me straight out that he liked me was flattering, but I didn't really understand it. "You don't know me very well," I reminded him.

"I haven't known you for very *long*," he amended. "But I'm pretty good at reading people. I knew the first time I met Noah that he was a good guy and someone I could trust, and I had a feeling about you from the moment I first saw you. So far, you haven't proven me wrong."

We were dancing around the issue. He'd pretty much come out and admitted what Noah had already told me: he was interested in me, but he hadn't asked me yet how I felt about him. What would my answer be if he did?

Almost as if he could read my mind, he brought it up. "I know that you don't know me very well yet either, and I'd really like to change that. We're all going to The Playground tonight, but would you let me take you out on a date tomorrow? Just you and me, so we can get to know each other better."

A date? I couldn't help wondering what Noah would think, until I reminded myself he hadn't made me any offer of his own. He didn't have any claim on my time, and why shouldn't I accept? Tate seemed like a lot of fun, and I still had a lot of the city to explore. "That sounds great."

"Perfect."

With that agreed, we joined Noah and Tessa again and the four of us finished looking through the exhibits before heading to the next floor where there was a virtual reality game where we could try to conduct the Vienna Philharmonic. Tessa went first and the musicians quickly refused to play. Tate went next and did a little better but still didn't make it through the whole song.

Noah looked over at me as Tate held out the baton. "You or me?"

"You go first." I wanted to be able to fully size up my competition before I took my turn.

He gamely gave it a try and did the best of everyone so far, but I watched carefully to see what he did wrong, so when my turn came, the orchestra made it to the end of the piece *and* gave me a standing ovation.

"You always have to win," Noah teased me as we headed out of the museum and back out into the city streets.

"I don't *have* to. I just do."

Tessa came to walk next to me while Noah and Tate went on just ahead. Looking at the two handsome men in front of me, so similar and yet so different, I felt like I had found myself in a whole new kind of game. I still wanted to win, but how could I know which of them was actually the prize?

~**Noah**~

As soon as Tate and I had a moment to ourselves, I laid out what I was thinking about that night. "Despite how natural she is, Liv is still new to all of this. She deserves a chance to explore it without any emotional expectations, so I don't think either of us should be in the scene with her tonight."

To my relief, he understood me and completely agreed. "Makes sense to me. I still want to get to know her more outside the club first anyway. That's why I asked her out tomorrow."

He did? *Fuck.* I had been planning on doing the same thing, but I was going to wait until after the club that night to see how she felt about everything. I seemed to constantly be a step behind, and it was getting old very fast.

We went for coffee at one of Vienna's famous coffee houses, Café Central, where the stunning vaulted interior had been decorated for Christmas with real trees and twinkling lights, giving it an even more special feel. Olivia and Tessa debated over the cake selection for a long time before finally deciding, and when we all had our cakes and coffee, I dove in.

"I've been thinking about tonight," I told Olivia. "I offered to be your guide at The Playground, and though a few things have changed since then, I'm assuming you still want to keep exploring there?"

She nodded, looking between me and Tate curiously. "What did you have in mind?"

"Well, I kind of interrupted your scene the other night," I reminded her. "So if you'd like to, we could set up something like that again. In a private room, with Tate and I there and a few other people too."

She jumped straight to the big question: "Who would be in the scene with me?"

"Well, that's up to you. The guy you were with the other night seems nice, if you liked him, or you could choose someone else when we get there tonight. Once you decide, we can make sure they've got a good reputation before you approach them."

"You make it sound like I can just pick anyone in the room," she said almost shyly, sharing a smile with Tessa.

"You pretty much can," Tate promised. "No one's going to say no to you, Liv."

I watched her carefully as she thought it over, looking for any signs that she might be uncomfortable with the idea or feeling pressured into anything, but I didn't see anything like that. Excitement sparked in her eyes as she shifted in her seat, letting me know that just the idea of it was turning her on.

It didn't stop her from taking her friend into consideration, though. "What about Tessa? She doesn't want to watch that."

Tessa made a face at her, her nose scrunching up. "Damn right I don't, but don't worry about me. Last night was enough to last me for a little while, I think I'll just hang out at the hotel bar and have a quiet night."

Olivia's face fell. "I don't want to leave you out."

"I'm a grown-ass woman who's perfectly capable of entertaining myself for a night on my own," Tessa replied. "I'll tell you when I'm feeling abandoned, and it's not now. Go have your weird, kinky fun without me."

Tate and I exchanged smiles. Tessa's bluntness was definitely growing on me.

With that settled, we chatted about other things as we finished our coffee and cake and spent the rest of the afternoon wandering around the historic centre of the city, ducking into shops and churches and anything else that caught our fancy. To anyone passing by, we must have looked like two couples on a double date, but the truth was a lot more complicated than that.

It felt like the evening would never come, but at last, Tate, Olivia and I were in the changing room at The Playground. That night, Olivia wore a striped red and white lingerie set: bra, panties and stockings. Her dark hair hung loose over her shoulders, and she looked amazing, as usual.

"Very festive," I told her, admiring every incredible curve of her body. "You're beautiful, Liv."

"Irresistible," Tate added.

I'd booked a private room for the whole night so we weren't on any particular timeline, and we went to the Plaza first and had a couple of drinks while we chatted with each other. Liv's eyes frequently wandered to the other men in the room as they came and went, sizing them up openly, which made me smile. I loved that she was being picky. I wanted it to be amazing for her.

At last, her eyes landed on someone who brought a smile to her face, and I turned to follow her gaze, immediately recognizing the man she had played with before. If that was who she wanted, I had no problem with that.

"I'll go talk to him if you want," I offered.

Liv nodded. "Sure. His name's Derek."

Probably not, I thought, but that was a good reminder to me to use Olivia's fake name. Derek was grabbing a drink at the bar with another guy by the time I got over to them.

"Hey," I greeted them casually. "We haven't been introduced yet. I'm Noah."

"Derek," he replied, shaking my hand. "And this is Ken."

We made small talk for a couple of minutes about where we were from and how long we were in the city before I got to the point. "The woman I'm here with, Belle, would like to do a scene with you tonight if you're interested. I've got a room booked."

His eyes lit up with anticipation. "Of course I am. I was worried I crossed a line last night with the stage. I didn't mean to make her uncomfortable."

"You didn't," I assured him. "She specifically asked for you tonight."

Any man on earth would be flattered to hear that, so he and his friend quickly finished their drinks while I gestured for Tate and Olivia to join us. We picked up a few more people in the waiting room before heading to the private room which had been set up with a bed in the centre and some sofas along the side of the room.

My heart pounding and my body already primed with excitement, I took a seat and waited for the show to begin.

Chapter Fourteen

WATCHING AND BEING WATCHED

~Olivia~

This was really happening. I had come close a few times, but that night, I would finally have sex in front of an audience. Not just any audience, either, but one that included Noah, as I'd fantasized so often over the previous year, and one that included Tate as well.

I had been a little surprised and maybe just a little bit offended when they told me at the café that afternoon that neither of them wanted to have sex with me that night, but the more I thought about it, the more it made sense to me. They wanted the connection that only the watching and being watched could bring. Though the person I actually had sex with would be important too, they weren't the most important thing.

There were certainly a lot of men to choose from as we sat in the Plaza, and I had started to feel overwhelmed with the decision until Derek walked in. He seemed like a safe choice, though I still really knew nothing about him. All I knew was that he would stop when I said so and had no problem with Noah being there, and for that night, I didn't need anything more than that.

While our audience all took a seat, Derek led me to the centre of the room. "Same rules as the other night?" he asked, and I nodded in surprise.

"You remember what they were?"

"It's hard to forget someone as beautiful as you." With that, he kissed me, wrapping his arms around me to pull me tight against him. He was already getting hard, and the evidence of his arousal turned me on too. There couldn't be any doubt that I wanted this. I'd been thinking about it all day, ever since Noah suggested it, and I could hardly believe it was finally happening. My hands ran over his shoulders and arms as his hands grabbed my ass, his hips grinding into mine.

Though I had sucked him off for a little while on stage the night before, I had been thinking about so many other things at the time that I hardly remembered anything about the act itself. So, when I dropped to my knees and undid his pants, pulling his cock out, I might as well have been seeing it for the first time. His cock wasn't quite as big as Noah's but there was nothing to complain about, and when I took him into my mouth that time, unlike the night before, I only felt pleasure.

Derek exhaled above me happily, but I didn't look at him. My eyes were on the two men sitting next to each other on the couch, both watching me intently. When our eyes met, Noah gave me the slightest of nods. Somehow, he had known when I went on stage that I wasn't doing it for the right reasons, and at that moment, he seemed just as confident that I was truly enjoying myself.

And I was. My body hummed as I sucked and licked and stroked Derek until he pulled me gently to my feet. "Any more of that and the fun's going to be over way too fast," he teased me. "Now, let's see that beautiful body of yours."

I hadn't been naked in public yet, but in his hands, it felt safe and natural to let him undress me. He removed my bra first, his hands running over my bare breasts before he pulled my panties down too.

"The stockings can stay on," he declared. "They're fucking hot."

Lying me down on the bed, he quickly removed his own clothes, leaving us both naked except for my stockings. Climbing onto the bed with me, he knelt between my knees as he took another taste of me, just as he had the first night we met.

"Yes," I moaned as a shudder of pleasure ran through me. He really was very good with his tongue, and my head fell to the side as I looked around the room at each of the people in turn. Derek's friend stood by the door, his arms crossed and his eyes dark with desire. A couple that I didn't know sat on one of the sofas. They had joined us from the lobby and the man had his hand down his partner's pants, mimicking what was being done to me. When the woman and I made eye contact, she smiled at me like we shared a secret, and perhaps we did. We both had the pleasure of knowing exactly what a thrill this was.

There were two other men and another woman, and in the middle of it all, the two men I was most aware of. Tate had started touching himself, his hand slowly moving over his pants while he watched Derek's tongue at work, while Noah had his arms stretched out over the back of the sofa and his eyes fixed on my face.

Derek didn't make me come with his mouth. Instead, after a couple of minutes, he got back up and grabbed a condom from the pocket of his discarded pants, rolling it on before climbing back onto the bed with me. Still on his knees, he lifted one of my legs over his shoulder, lining his stiff cock up with my wet entrance. "Are you ready for me, Belle?"

That was my last chance to back out, but it honestly never even crossed my mind. With my eyes on the two contrasting men watching me, one blond and blue-eyed, the other dark-haired with those deep green eyes, I nodded. "Fuck me, please."

He pushed into me slowly as I inhaled, drowning in the onslaught of sensations. The feel of him filling me was good, but the eyes on me were what really had my heart racing. Every inch of my body felt alive under the audience's watchful gaze.

"So beautiful," Noah mouthed at me, reminding me of our time at the museum earlier, trying to communicate while wearing the headphones. That time, however, I could make out every word. "The sexiest thing I've ever seen."

I couldn't agree more. Him sitting there watching me, getting turned on as he watched another man fuck me, was everything I had always imagined it would be. I had never been so full of need and yet so fulfilled at the same time, and my body found its first orgasm easily, ripples of pleasure running through me as everyone watched. Derek groaned as I came, my pussy squeezing him tightly, but he was in no hurry. He kept his thrusts slow and steady, his fingers playing with my clit until I came again.

As the second orgasm faded, he propped me up on hands and knees where I could still see the audience, and with me in position, he slammed into me harder, making me come once more before pulling out of me, rolling the condom off and finishing himself off with his hand, coming all over my ass and back. The warm strands of his cum seemed to brand themselves on me as every eye in the room fixed on them.

The gathered crowd all applauded and gave murmurs of appreciation as I lay myself down on the bed.

Derek bent down to give me a kiss on the forehead. "That was amazing, Belle. Thank you."

I wasn't sure what I was supposed to say, so I simply returned the sentiment. "Thank you too."

With no need for further words, he got redressed and left along with the rest of the audience until only Noah, Tate and I were left in the room.

In the sudden silence, the room felt a lot smaller. Now that we had all crossed that line with each other, where exactly did we go from there?

~Noah~

Olivia looked incredible as she lay across the bed, worn out and sated by what had just happened. I absolutely meant what I said to her: watching her being pleasured by someone else was the sexiest thing I had ever seen.

A lot of people didn't understand it. My dad would probably cut off his own dick before he'd let another man anywhere near my mom. He was the possessive type, and that was fine for him, and yet, he would happily strike her with the various things I'd seen in their dungeon, whereas I would never want to cause Olivia any kind of pain, even if she agreed to it.

There was a degree of empathy involved in what we did: her pain was mine, and her pleasure was mine too. We shared it no matter who was giving it to her. When her eyes were on me as she came, that orgasm belonged to me even though I hadn't laid a hand on her.

In short, the scene we belonged to wasn't for everyone, but that was what made it a kink. The fact that we both had the same one while also feeling a connection to each other on a deeper level was something wonderful and rare. Watching her in that moment, I felt luckier than ever before and also even more determined that before her stay in Vienna was over, I was going to make her mine, in a way that worked for us both.

Though I could have simply admired her for hours, once everyone else had gone, I got to my feet. When I booked the room, I'd arranged for a few things to be there to help her recover, so I poured out a glass of fresh water and brought over a soft blanket, wrapping it around her shoulders as she sat up and took the glass of water from me.

"How was that for you?" I asked as I sat down next to her. It certainly looked like she'd enjoyed herself, but I didn't want to put words in her mouth. I wanted to know exactly how she felt about it.

"Wonderful," she confirmed, smiling over at Tate, who still sat on the sofa, before turning back to me. "How was it for you?"

Did she really need to ask? "Let's just say that walking over here right now was a little difficult."

Her gaze dropped to my lap before she could stop it, and she quickly looked back up with satisfaction in her eyes. As I expected, she liked knowing how much I had enjoyed it.

"Coming over was very noble of you, then," she teased, glancing over at Tate once more. "Are you in the same situation?"

"I can't even stand up," he groaned, making her laugh.

"What do you boys intend to do about that?" She raised her eyebrows at me in challenge, which gave me the best indication yet that she was completely okay with what had just happened. There was no regret-filled comedown like there had been after her brief time on stage the night before. This was exactly the Olivia I knew.

And I did have an idea about what to do next, which involved finding out how she felt about the voyeurism side of things. I already knew she was an exhibitionist, that had been made abundantly clear, and she seemed to enjoy watching Tessa the previous evening, both at the club and in the jacuzzi too. But what about when it came to me? Would watching me give her the same pleasure that watching her gave me? We would need to find out, and there was no time like the present.

"Why don't you go out into the lobby and see if you can find some women who could help us out?"

When she hesitated for just a moment, looking uncertain as to how she would do that, I threw on the words I knew she couldn't resist.

"Unless you're afraid to."

Her eyes narrowed, letting me know she recognized my reverse psychology, and yet, she couldn't help herself anyway. "I'll be right back."

Handing me the glass of water and blanket, she put her bra and panties back on and strutted out of the room. Tate and I both watched her go, unable to take our eyes off her.

"Fucking hell, Noah," Tate complained as he adjusted himself in his pants. "I know you're my best friend, but I think I'd cut your balls off right now if it meant I had a better chance with her."

My hand moved instinctively to my groin. Why did people keep threatening me with castration? The obsession with my balls was truly bizarre. "It's entirely up to her," I reminded him. "But if you think I'm stepping aside, you are very badly mistaken."

~Olivia~

The night appeared to have another brand-new experience in store for me. How exactly was I supposed to find a couple of women to join us in the room? Did I just walk up to someone and say, 'Excuse me, my two insanely hot male friends are looking for someone to fuck while I watch. Are you interested'?

Actually, that might work. It would probably work for me.

Frustratingly, most of the women in the lobby were with at least one man. Maybe that was why Tessa and I were approached so quickly on our first night. Eventually, as I circled the room, I found a group of three women standing outside one of the viewing rooms without a man in sight, and taking a deep breath, I walked over to them.

"Excuse me? Hi. How are you?"

That couldn't have sounded much more awkward, but the women all gave me friendly smiles before answering me in a language I didn't recognize.

Damn it. "Do you speak English?"

They seemed to recognize that word, at least, but they shook their heads as one of them said something else in the same language as before.

Most people probably would have given up there, but once I got my teeth into something, I couldn't let go. I tried again, using hand gestures to accompany my words, much like Noah had done at the museum that afternoon.

I pointed down the hall first. "In one of the private rooms, there are two men." Here I held up two fingers before miming a man by stroking a fake beard and then a cock. The women all laughed, but I had no idea if they knew what I was getting at. Next, I did what I hoped was a universal symbol for sex, a finger inserting into an 'o' formed by my other hand, and then I pointed at them. "They would like to have sex with you."

The women exchanged glances, talking amongst themselves for a moment before shrugging and turning back to me with a smile.

Was that a yes? I still had no idea but when I started walking down the hall back to the room, they followed after me, so it seemed I was on the right track. Once we stepped back into the room and they got a look at Noah and Tate, there didn't seem to be any objections. They all had big smiles on their faces as they spoke to each other once again.

"I don't know their names," I apologized to the men. "They don't speak English."

Noah raised his eyebrows at me while Tate laughed. "Damn, Liv. You sure can pick them."

I blushed beneath the compliment and headed towards the couch, but Noah stopped me before I got too far. "Do you want to get more of an audience too?"

Thinking about it for a moment, I shook my head. The idea of it being a private performance, just for me, really appealed to me. "If it's okay with you, I'd like to just watch on my own."

"That's more than okay with me." His eyes were full of desire and appreciation as he watched me sit down. A moment later, two of the women came up to him and started to unbutton his shirt.

The previous Christmas, when I walked in on him in the middle of that group scene, neither of us were expecting it, but over the course of the year, my mind had returned to it far more times than I cared to admit. At last, I was going to see something very similar play out right in front of me, on purpose. That time, he knew I was there, and that time, the performance was all for me. That made all the difference in the world.

Tate and the other woman were already practically naked, working fast as their hands pulled at each other's clothing. He was already hard, or still hard, I supposed, since he said he had been turned on by my performance earlier. The tall, blonde woman with him quickly dropped to her knees, sucking him off while they both looked over at me.

Meanwhile, Noah had lost his clothes too as the two women with him, one with brown hair and one jet black, ran their hands all over his body. His eyes never left me either.

I hardly knew where to look as Tate began to fuck the woman he was with. He held up a condom to her first, still in its package, to ask if she wanted him to use it, but she shook her head so he went in bare, both of them still standing as she bent over onto the edge of the bed.

Noah had taken a seat on the edge of the bed next to her while the other two women both went down on him, taking turns sucking and licking him.

My heart racing and my body heating with the visual stimulation, my own need and desire grew stronger again, perhaps even stronger than it had been when I was the one being pleasured. Noah put a condom on, not bothering to ask if they wanted it or not, before laying down on the bed, positioning himself so he could still see me. One woman rode him in reverse while the other moved to join the other pair, sitting on the face of the woman Tate was thrusting into.

The scene was a true orgy, a feast for the eyes and all my senses. The moans and cries of pleasures and the muttered words in different languages created a sensual soundtrack while the smell of perfume, cologne and sweat drifted over to me. I could almost feel the pleasure they were all feeling, my own body pulsing with excitement and longing. When my hand slipped beneath my panties, adding the sensation of my own touch to everything else, Noah's eyes followed it, his heated gaze turning me on even more.

They changed positions and partners a few times until they couldn't hold back any longer. Almost at the same time, both men withdrew from whichever hole they were currently in, Noah discarding his condom as they both stroked themselves to their final release, both of them looking at me while they did it.

I had never felt so powerful, so sexy, or so completely fulfilled.

And I had never been so sure that this was definitely the life I wanted.

~Noah~

The look in Olivia's eyes as she sat alone on the couch, taking in everything going on in front of her, gave me exactly the answer I'd been looking for: she loved to watch me too.

She understood on a primal level that although the woman with me, or women in this case, were the ones touching me, they meant nothing to me emotionally, just as I meant nothing to them. Those women didn't care who I was as a person; hell, we didn't even speak the same language. All they wanted was the physical pleasure of it, and that was all I wanted from them too.

But there would have been no pleasure at all without the audience, without Olivia's eyes on me.

To some people, it seemed complicated, but to me, the solution was utterly simple: I needed both parts, the physical and the visual. I always had.

But it had never been quite as good as when Olivia was the one watching.

Because she *did* know me. She knew who I was probably better than anyone in the world apart from Tate and my family. And the fact that she knew me so deeply and also found me sexy and enjoyed all of this in the same way I did was more than I had ever really dared to hope for.

I also couldn't help noticing that although she did watch Tate as well, her gaze kept finding its way back to me. If that was a part of our competition for her affection, I felt pretty sure I'd won that round.

And with that triumph swelling my chest, my body still flush with the pleasure of my orgasm, it seemed the time had come for me to play a little dirty.

So, once Tate and I got dressed again and took care of the women who had taken part in our scene, offering them some water and something to eat before saying goodbye, I turned to Tate.

"Do you mind going to grab us some drinks from the bar in the Plaza? We've got the room booked for the whole night and I'd rather just stay here and relax for a while rather than trying to get a table out there. It's too busy."

The suspicious look he gave me was fair enough. I *was* trying to get rid of him, but when Olivia piped up with her drink order, he could hardly refuse. "I'll be right back," he warned as he headed out the door, and I quickly locked it behind him.

We had at least ten minutes alone, I would guess, maybe fifteen if I was lucky. I would have to move fast.

Sitting down on the bed once more, I beckoned Olivia over to join me. "Come here."

A little warily, she did as I requested, taking a seat next to me, still dressed in only her bra, panties and stockings. I loved that she felt comfortable around me that way, even when we were alone.

"I could tell you enjoyed that," I started, and she nodded in confirmation. "But although you were close, you didn't come."

She looked away from me for a second, her lips twitching in amusement. "How do you know that?"

She had a point; women weren't always obvious about it, but in her case, the image of her face as I brought her over the edge with my fingers was burned into my brain. "Because I've seen you come a few times now. I know what it looks like and I didn't see it this time."

A beautiful blush spread across her cheeks. "You were paying that much attention?"

"Always. And I hate to see anyone go unsatisfied. It's so... unsatisfying. May I?"

I gestured down at her hips, to the enticing junction between her legs, and goosebumps spread down her arms as she looked down at my lap.

"You just finished," she pointed out, looking back up at me curiously. "You're not super-human, are you?"

Fuck, she could always make me laugh. "I wish I was, but no. I'll have to use a different part of me."

I could almost see her brain working, trying to figure out what I had in mind, but I wanted to keep her guessing just a few seconds longer.

"Lie down," I requested, and when she did, I removed her panties, spreading her legs wide to get my first real look at her. She'd waxed recently, that was clear, her skin soft and smooth, right up to her beautiful pink centre that had never looked as appealing to me on any woman as it did on her. I wasn't sure I could have stopped myself even if I tried, and thankfully, she didn't want me to either. When my tongue connected with her sensitive skin, a shiver ran through her, and through me too. "God, you taste incredible."

My words made her shudder again as I buried my face deeper, inhaling the sweet scent of her arousal. She was turned on from watching me and I got to enjoy the fruits of it. Greedily, I lapped at her, wanting to claim it all, feeling like I could never get enough of her. I had never felt that kind of hunger before, especially not when there was no one else watching.

Except, that wasn't exactly true. Olivia was watching. She propped herself up on her elbows, looking down at my head between her legs, and when I raised my eyes to hers, my tongue swirling around her clit, a moment of pure electricity passed between us, invigorating and exciting.

Damn it, now I really *was* starting to get hard again, but we definitely didn't have time for that before Tate came back. I would have to hurry things along.

My tongue plunged deeper into her as one hand went up to cup her breast and the other played with her clit. Turning her on was like mastering a musical instrument, learning which buttons to press to make the best music, made up of the sweet sighs and moans that were coming from her as she watched and felt everything I was doing to her.

"Fuck, Noah!" At last, her eyes closed as her head fell back, the sensations overwhelming her as she drew closer and closer to her release, and when I switched places, sucking on her clit while my fingers went inside her, that struck the perfect chord. Her body clenched around me as her legs trembled, and all the breath went out of her.

Absolutely perfect, and not a second too soon. I was still licking my fingers clean when there was a thud at the door. "Can you open up, Noah? My hands are full."

"Not as full as mine were," I told Olivia with a wink as she pulled her panties back on. She tried not to smile at me but she couldn't help it, and I couldn't stop my own grin either.

Hopefully, that would give her something to think about while she and Tate were out on their date the next day. I would certainly be thinking about it.

After I let Tate back in, we all sat and drank together for a while, chatting easily and laughing together, and when we were feeling up to it, we went to the theatre to see what was going on there. The performance was surprisingly lacklustre for a Saturday, and when Olivia stifled a yawn, I figured we should call it a night.

We both walked her back to her hotel room, and once she'd gone inside, Tate turned to me, his eyes narrowed shrewdly as we went back to our own floor. "What did you do while I was out of the room?"

He was no pushover. I knew and admired that about him, so I was completely up front with him too. "I returned the favour she gave me in the glory hole the other night."

He looked both surprised and unsurprised at the same time. He wasn't shocked something had happened, but he *was* surprised it had happened in private. "And that worked for you?"

"The scenario wasn't about me," I pointed out. "It worked for her, though."

He rolled his eyes at my not-so-humble brag. "Well, if that's how you want to play it, Noah, game on."

Although I smirked back at him, inside, I *was* a little worried. The thought of the two of them doing what Olivia and I had done, in private like we had, didn't appeal to me in the least. Yet, I had to accept that she was her own woman, capable of making her own decisions. We hadn't made any kind of commitment to each other yet, so if she chose to explore with him, I had no right to complain, just as Tate didn't complain then.

It still didn't mean I wanted it to happen, though, and I was going to be on edge until I found out exactly how their date went. No matter which way I looked at it, the next day was going to be one of the longest days of my life.

Chapter Fifteen

GETTING TO KNOW YOU

~Olivia~

Noah and Tate had to work the next day so Tessa and I had a lazy start to our morning, ordering room service breakfast to be delivered to our suite.

"Did you have a good night?" I asked as we sat down together on the couch in the living room, both still in our pajamas. I really hoped she had since I still felt guilty about going to the club without her, even though she'd insisted.

To my relief, she nodded, giving me a wink before taking a long sip of her coffee, leaving me in suspense.

"Oh, come on already!" I complained after what felt like two minutes, at least. "Give me some details."

Tessa laughed as she lowered the cup. "I met a really nice guy in the bar. He's American too, from the midwest somewhere, and he's here on business. He asked me out again tonight."

"That's fantastic." The development genuinely pleased me, and not just because it would give her something to do that night while Tate and I were on our date. I wanted her to be having just as much fun on our trip as I was. In fact, I had almost suggested that she and Noah could hang out together, but fear held me back; not fear that anything would happen between them, but fear about what she might say to him without me there to act as a filter. "Do you like this guy?"

"For now, at least," she replied with another giggle. "He's a bit older and just looking for some fun, I think, but that's okay. So am I."

Thinking back over the men she'd interacted with at the club – Lewis, the Dom, and the Russian guys she'd gone with on the first night - I realized they all had one thing in common. "Do you have a thing for older guys?"

She thought that over while she sipped her coffee again. "I think I might. I guess they're just usually a bit more sure of themselves, a bit more dominant, but without being full-on BDSM bossy. I think it's sexy."

I could see that. "So, you're figuring out what you like, which is the whole point of being here. That's great, Tessa."

Older men weren't my thing, but then, I had my own kinks to worry about, which my friend quickly brought up. "Are you going to tell me what happened at The Playground?"

As honestly as I could, I told her about me and Derek having sex in front of the crowd, and watching Noah and Tate with the other women. What happened afterwards, with me and Noah alone in the room, I left out. Although the orgasm he'd given me was incredible, I still wasn't sure exactly how I felt about it or what it meant.

She listened intently, but when I finished my recap, she still looked confused. "I just don't get it," she admitted. "Why do you like watching them?"

"Well, it's not really that much different from watching porn or reading an erotic book," I pointed out. "It's not me who's participating, but I can still feel what they're feeling."

"I guess I can understand that, but even when it's someone you like? Wouldn't you rather be the one with them?"

Explaining that part to someone who didn't naturally understand was a little more difficult. "Yes and no. Obviously, when I'm in a relationship again, I'll want to have sex with my boyfriend. But I'd also want to watch him with other people too, and for him to watch me."

With a deep breath, I tried to decide whether to confess the particular thoughts that had come into my head the night before while Derek was fucking me. I wasn't sure Tessa would understand, but maybe it would help to explain just how deep this kink of mine ran.

"I think the ultimate thing for me would be to have my boyfriend right there next to me while someone else was having sex with me. To have him holding my hand or stroking my hair while it happened. That would be incredible."

Of course I didn't mention that when those thoughts crossed my mind, Noah's face had been the one I imagined.

Tessa just shook her head before answering me with her usual bluntness. "I think that sounds like a nightmare, but if it makes you happy, Liv, then go for it. May you be blessed with a man just as weird as you are."

She held up her coffee cup in a toast, and I accepted it as gracefully as I could. "Thanks, I think."

After a lazy morning, we spent a couple of hours at the Albertina Museum looking at priceless works of art, and a couple of more hours exploring the designer fashion stores that were almost equally out of our price range. By late afternoon, we headed back to the hotel to get ready for our respective dates. Tate hadn't told me what he planned on doing, but he was going to come by and pick me up almost right after his shift ended at seven, so I assumed there would be food involved. He'd need to eat too.

Tessa was also having dinner out with her businessman so I wished her a good night and sat down to wait for Tate to arrive. To kill some time, I pulled out my phone and checked in with my parents. My dad had sent me a picture of him and my mom and Noelle visiting the Dyker Heights Christmas lights. We went every year as a family tradition, but this was the second year in a row I had missed it. In reply, I sent him back a picture that Noah had taken of me and Tessa at the House of Music, having fun playing with the different instruments.

Looks like you're having a great time, Livy, he replied with a beaming smiley face emoji. *I'm so glad you're having this experience. Can't wait to see you next week.*

Although a touch of guilt ran through me when I thought about the kind of experiences I was *actually* having, I refused to feel too bad about it. As a grown woman, I was allowed to have whatever kind of fun I wanted, even if I couldn't tell my dad about it.

With Tate's knock on the door, I jumped up and shoved my phone back in my pocket, and he looked around curiously when I opened the door to the suite. He'd dressed casually, as I had, in jeans and a sweater, holding onto his coat for when we went outside. A woodsy cologne, subtle but enticing, reached my nose as he leaned forward to look over my shoulder. "This is pretty swank. I think I was in here cleaning a few days ago."

"Really?" That idea made me laugh. From the look on his face, he obviously hadn't enjoyed it very much. "Did you have to wear a French maid outfit?"

Amusement danced in his blue eyes. "Would that turn you on?"

Almost against my will, my eyes travelled over his body, calling to mind the sight of him completely naked the night before. "Maybe," I answered truthfully.

"We'll see what we can do about that later, but for now, let's go find something to eat. I'm starving."

We took the subway to Karlsplatz, a large square in front of the beautiful Karlskirche where another Christmas market had been set up. Lights illuminated the front of the church and the stalls in the dark winter's evening, shining on the faces of all the other people out enjoying themselves too.

Unlike the market we'd gone to at the Rathaus, this one featured almost entirely handmade arts and crafts with the artists there selling their own goods. There was also food, which Tate was desperate for, so we went that way first. Between the two of us, we shared some raclette, or melted cheese on bread, and Kiachl, which was like a flat doughnut.

Both were dangerously good, and so was the wine we washed it all down with.

As we walked and ate, we talked about the market and about Christmas in general. "What was Christmas like for you growing up, Liv?"

I told him about my dad's enthusiasm which always made it extra special for us, and I recounted the Christmases we spent with the Stamers. When I turned the question back on him, he gave me a slightly sad smile.

"I can't really say I have any good memories of Christmas growing up, but that's what makes this year so special. This is one I'll never forget."

Although he gestured at the setting around us, the market stalls in front of the beautiful Baroque church and the light snow that had begun to fall, his eyes never left me.

"You kind of remind me of my dad," I told him as we moved over to the carousel that was full of excited children, their faces shining in the brightly coloured lights.

Tate raised his eyebrows at me warily. "Is that a good thing?"

"It's a great thing. My dad is awesome. But in particular, I was thinking about how he didn't have the best childhood either. Becoming friends with Noah's dad helped him make a better life for himself."

"That's not why I'm friends with Noah." His voice sounded uncharacteristically tight as he replied and I looked over at him in surprise.

"I didn't mean it in a negative way."

His eyes closed for a second, hiding the pain I'd glimpsed there. "Sorry. I know you didn't. It's just that some people *do* think that I'm using him, or riding his coattails, or whatever. I'm not that kind of guy. I wouldn't pretend to like someone I didn't just to get ahead."

"I know that," I assured him. "I really didn't mean to imply anything like that. It's not like my dad was using Cole either. They were good friends first and they work well together. That's all."

We moved onto safer topics after that and I explained how I was going to London for Christmas with my family. "Have you been there before?" he asked.

"Many, many times. My mom grew up in London and her family is still there so we go about once a year. Noah's mom is British too, so sometimes the Stamers go with us."

I told him about how Noah challenged me to a race inside the maze at Hampton Court palace when I was five or six years old, and how I'd managed to get completely lost. By the time he found me, I was in tears thinking I'd never get out, but he calmed me down, made me laugh, and then when we found the exit, he let me go first so I could tell everyone I won.

"So even back then, he was looking out for you," Tate mused.

I hadn't really thought about it that way, but there was some truth to it. "Yeah, I guess he was. He always knew what would make me happy."

We went inside the church to see the beautiful interior before heading back outside. A band had started to play on a stage set up on one side of the market so we listened to them while we drank some more wine, making light conversation and making each other laugh.

Spending time with him felt very pleasant and comfortable, but I couldn't help noticing my stomach never fluttered when he looked my way. The tingle of anticipation when I thought about what might happen next was missing too. Handsome, sexy, funny and kind, not to mention sharing the same kink as me, Tate should have been everything I wanted but he simply didn't make my heart race.

What the hell was wrong with me?

I didn't have the answer to that, but when we got back to the hotel at around ten o'clock and he invited me to his room for another drink, I thought it best to decline. "I had a really good time, Tate, but I think I'm going to call it a night."

He nodded, his eyes registering a bit of disappointment but mostly resignation. "It's because of Noah, isn't it?"

That felt completely out of the blue. "I didn't say anything about Noah."

"Not right now, but I don't know if we went ten minutes tonight without talking about him."

As I thought back over the evening, I realized he was right, but it didn't mean what he thought it did. "He's the only person we know in common," I pointed out.

"Right, that's it." The light sarcasm in his tone told me he didn't believe that for a second, nor did he hold it against me. "Look, I get it. He's got a twenty-year head start on getting your attention, and I can't really compete with that. It was worth a try though. You're an amazing woman, and he'd be damned lucky to have you as his partner. He's got a lot of things I don't, but I don't know if I've ever been quite as jealous of him as I am right now."

I blinked quickly as I tried to take that all in. "Noah isn't interested in me like that. He never has been."

Tate just laughed. "If that's what you really think, then he's a bigger idiot than I thought."

I had no idea what to say to that, so I simply stood in stunned silence while Tate gave me a kiss on the cheek.

"Goodnight, Liv. Thanks for a great date. I'll see you tomorrow."

As the elevator door closed on him, I still hadn't come up with a response. Did Tate know something I didn't? The last thing I wanted to do was get my hopes up once again, but as Noah came to mind and that familiar flutter rippled through my stomach, I realized it might be too late for that.

My hopes were already up. I just had to hope he wasn't going to shoot them down the same way he did before.

~Noah~

As I expected, the evening seemed to drag on interminably. As soon as I finished work for the day, I headed back to my room, planning to watch TV or read a book to distract myself, but my mind kept wandering, imagining what Tate and Olivia might be doing. The later it got, the wilder those thoughts became, and when I eventually couldn't take it anymore, I picked up my phone and called the one person I thought could help me the most.

"Noah?" My mom sounded surprised as she answered. "Is everything okay?"

That was a good indication of how often I'd called while I'd been away, and guilt immediately joined in with the anxiety I was feeling. "Everything's fine, I just wanted to talk. Is this an okay time?"

Thanks to the time difference, people were still at work in New York, but my mom's architecture firm pretty much ran itself. Unless she was in a meeting, she was usually able to take a break.

"It's always an okay time for you. How's Vienna? Have you seen all the Christmas lights?"

My mom had given me a list of Christmas things to do in the city before I left home, and thanks to Olivia, I could tell her that I had done some of them. "I've seen lots of lights. I went to the market at Schönbrunn Palace and the one at the Rathaus too, and I bought you a few things."

I figured that would make her happy and it did. I could practically hear her smile through the phone. "I can't wait to see what you picked out. So, what's up?"

Obviously, I hadn't called just to chat about Christmas markets and she knew it. "I'm actually looking for some dating advice."

A pause on the other end let me know I'd taken her by surprise, but she recovered quickly. "You usually talk to your dad about this stuff."

"I do, but in this case, I'm looking for a female perspective."

"Well, now, I'm intrigued." Her rich, warm laugh made me feel a little better all on its own. No matter what, my parents always had my back. "Who's the girl?"

As much as I wanted her help, I wasn't ready to name Olivia yet. If things didn't work out, we didn't need our families to know about what went on between us. That would make things very awkward, not to mention I still hadn't forgotten Jackson's threat against me if I messed with his daughter.

Since the full truth was out of the question, I told a half-truth instead. "A girl I ran into here. For the first time, I'm thinking about getting into a proper relationship, and now that I am, I've realized I don't have a clue what I'm doing. I was wondering: how did you and Dad go from just hooking up to being in a real relationship? What did he say to you to let you know he wanted more, and what made you believe him?"

I hadn't meant to ask so many questions all at once, but my mom seemed to take it all in stride. "Well, to be honest, I was about to tell him the same thing but he got there first. We were already on the same page, even though we didn't know it, which helped. As for the exact words, I don't remember precisely what he said, but the gist of it was that he hadn't been looking for a relationship but he wanted to be with me anyway."

It didn't sound all that great to me. "And that didn't send you running in the opposite direction?"

She laughed again, the laugh of someone secure in knowing they'd made the right choice. "Not at all. I appreciated it because his words were honest and straightforward, and true to what I knew of him. If he'd suddenly gone all flowery and told me he could see our whole future together and he had no doubts, I would have been suspicious. Since he was real and earnest instead, it made me trust that he would always tell me the truth, even when it might not be exactly what he thought I wanted to hear."

That did make some sense, I supposed, and I had always tried to be honest with Olivia too. As far as I could see, she wouldn't have any reason to suspect me of lying if I told her what I wanted.

"If this woman is interested in you, then she's interested in *you*," my mom continued. "So just be yourself. Don't try to do what anyone else would do, not even your dad. Do what feels right to you, and if she's the right girl, she'll know what you mean even if the words aren't perfect."

I supposed that meant there were no shortcuts, but it took some of the pressure off too. I could be myself. That was how I tried to live my whole life, embracing who I was; I just hoped that when it came to Olivia, I hadn't left it too long. "Thanks, Mom. I appreciate it."

"Anytime." She hesitated for a second, as though debating with herself whether to say anything else, but in the end, she couldn't help it. "Are we going to get to meet this girl soon? I've been waiting a long time for you to bring someone home, Noah. I hope we'll all get along."

"I'm pretty sure you'll like her," I replied, trying not to smile. My mom had always loved Olivia. "But I'll have to see what she says first. Say hi to Eve and Dad for me."

She promised to and, as we hung up, the time flashed across my phone. Still only 9:30. *Fuck.*

With restless thoughts swimming around my head, I went for a walk, roaming the streets of the city with the elegant Christmas lights overhead and thinking over the different things I might say to Olivia. A lot depended on how her date with Tate went. If they'd really connected, my choice of words might be a moot point, but if I still had any chance at all, I had to take it.

When I got back to the hotel, it was nearly eleven, and I thought they must be back by then since Tate had to work in the morning. I swung by his room, unsure if I would actually knock or not, but when I got there, the 'do not disturb' sign hung from his door, and my stomach twisted uncomfortably.

Hopefully that didn't mean what I thought it might.

In the morning, I was in the staff room ahead of Tate for a change, sipping on my coffee as I waited anxiously for him to appear. When he finally did, he wore his usual casual smile as he nodded at me before helping himself to breakfast. From his body language, I had no idea how things might have gone.

"Where are you working today?" he asked me as he sat down. "I'm in reservations."

"Catering," I answered bluntly, waiting for him to move on to what I really wanted to talk about.

"Ah, that was one of my favourite days," he reminisced, taking a big bite of his eggs. "I got to try everything they made. One of the chefs had a soft spot for me."

There was nothing in the world I wanted to talk about less than catering at that moment. "That's because you're a shameless flirt."

He laughed, giving me a shrug. "When it means free food, you bet." Another forkful went into his mouth as he looked out the window. "It snowed a bit last night. It looks pretty."

The weather? Seriously? He had to be messing with me on purpose. At least he had mentioned the previous evening, though, which gave me an opening. "Yeah, I went out for a walk in it. Were you outside too?"

Tate smirked at me from behind his coffee cup as he looked back in my direction. "Are you trying to ask me how my date went?"

"I'm trying very hard not to," I grumbled. "But you're leaving me no choice."

That made him laugh. He certainly seemed to be in a good mood. "Well, if you really want to know, the date was great. Liv's just as fun and sweet as I thought she was, and I haven't had a night in private like that in... well, ever, maybe."

My stomach lurched as I remembered the 'do not disturb' sign on his door. I didn't want to ask, but I had to. "You slept with her?"

For a long moment he just looked at me, his face and eyes completely blank, betraying nothing, until finally, he burst out laughing.

"What's so funny?" I muttered, my stomach still in knots while I waited for him to answer the damn question. It would be one thing if he said they'd gone to The Playground and had sex in front of the crowd. I still wouldn't love it, since I knew he was interested in more than that from her, but I would understand it.

But if they had really spent the night together, alone in his room, that meant things were a lot more serious than I had let myself believe.

"The look on your face is what's funny," Tate said, still chuckling. "You just turned a shade of green I'm not sure I've ever seen on you before."

"I'm glad you're amused, at least." I pushed my chair back, getting to my feet. I was going to need a few minutes to process things before I went to work for the day. All the plans I'd made the night before, all my agonizing, seemed to be for nothing after all.

"Wait, sit down," Tate protested, gesturing to my chair. "I'm just messing with you. Sit down, Noah."

Warily, I lowered myself back into my seat. "Messing with me how?"

"Nothing happened between me and Liv. I spent the night in my room jacking off to crappy Austrian porn, that was the kind of night I had. I just wanted to see your reaction if you thought we slept together."

Was he telling me the truth? I scanned his face, looking for any hint of sarcasm, but he seemed sincere. "Why would you do that?"

"Because you've had your head up your ass when it comes to her for way too long. How long have you been in love with her?"

Love? I wasn't even sure I knew what that felt like, but I tried to answer him honestly, following my mom's advice. "Our relationship is complicated. We've known each other forever. She's just always been there, but I didn't know she thought of me that way until last year, and then when she walked in on me at our house, I thought that was it. So to find her here this week, to find out that she's interested in the same things I am, it's overwhelming. I don't know how I feel, exactly, but I know I want to find out."

He nodded at me thoughtfully, looking completely unsurprised by my unprecedented declaration. "She told me a story last night about you guys in a maze somewhere in England, and how you found her when she was lost and let her win."

I'd forgotten about that, but as soon as he mentioned it, the memories came rushing back: Olivia's tear-stained face when I'd finally found her, her embarrassment that I'd caught her crying and the warm feeling I got when I made her laugh again and watched her celebrating her victory. Jackson and my dad had both teased me about losing to her, but I never told anyone the truth. Her happiness meant more to me than my pride.

Was that what love was?

Tate wasn't finished yet. "As your best friend, I'd be slacking off if I didn't tell you to get off your ass and tell her what you just told me. She's still interested in you too, Noah, even if she doesn't want to admit it. But if you don't do something about it soon, someone else is going to see just what a catch she is, just like I did, and the next time, you might not be so lucky."

He was absolutely right. I had pretty much come to the same conclusion the night before, and armed with my mom's words of wisdom, I planned to do my very fucking best.

I spoke the words as soon as they entered my head, making my decision on the spot. "I'm going to ask her out tonight, and if it goes well, I'll tell her then."

Chapter Sixteen

A FIRST DATE

~Olivia~

Tate's words kept me up half the night: *It's because of Noah, isn't it?*

The more I tossed and turned, the more truth I saw in what he said. For so long, I had compared every man I met, every guy who ever wanted to go out with me, to the image of Noah I kept in my heart, and always found them lacking. I had saved myself for him for so long without even consciously realizing I was doing it.

Even after what happened the previous Christmas, when I thought I had given up on the idea of him for good, he was still there in the back of mind. In bed with the man I'd dated for months, I thought of Noah.

Being there in Vienna was because of him too. If I hadn't walked in on him a year earlier, I might never have figured out what my kink was or taken the time to explore it. I might have spent the rest of my life vaguely unsatisfied with my sex life but never really knowing why.

No matter which corner of my life I looked into, Noah was there, either in person or in the shadow that his presence cast. Could I ever completely leave him behind?

Did I even want to?

The other thing Tate said haunted me too: when I asserted that Noah wasn't interested in me the same way Tate was, he disagreed. Had

Noah actually said something to him, or was Tate just projecting his own feelings onto his friend? I didn't know, and it had me alternating between hope and hopelessness as I tried to figure it out.

Eventually, I had to come to the conclusion that the only one who truly knew what Noah thought was Noah himself, and lying there trying to guess what he wanted wouldn't do me any good. At last, I managed to fall asleep out of sheer mental exhaustion.

A knock on my bedroom door woke me up in the morning, and I groaned, not ready to leave my bed yet. This would have to be the one morning Tessa decided to wake up early.

"Can I have another half an hour?" I called out, pulling the covers tighter around myself.

"Only if you want your breakfast to go cold," an amused-sounding voice replied. It definitely didn't belong to Tessa, but still sounded deeply familiar.

"Noah?"

The word came out as a squeak as I quickly tried to clear my throat, sitting up and rubbing my bleary eyes. What was he doing there?

"I'm coming in, so make sure you're decent," he warned, giving me only two seconds before the door opened.

Him seeing me in my pajamas didn't worry me, since he had seen me naked just a couple of days earlier. The bedhead and lack of makeup were far more worrying.

Noah, however, seemed unphased by my appearance as he came into the room, pulling a room service cart behind him. Rather than wearing his usual suit, he was dressed in the neat, pressed, grey pinstripe uniform of the hotel's wait staff. The smell of the fresh waffles and fruit made my stomach grumble almost immediately.

"Sounds like I'm just in time," he teased. "I didn't expect to find you still in bed though, Liv. I wasn't sure you even knew how to sleep in."

He brought a cup of coffee over to me in bed, which I accepted gratefully. "Thank you. I didn't order breakfast, though."

"I know. It's my treat." He gave me a warm smile as he took a step back.

The first sip of the strong, black coffee helped to clear my thoughts as I tried to figure out what was going on. He was obviously working, but that still didn't really explain why he'd come to my room. "Did you bring Tessa breakfast too?"

"I tried to," he said, glancing back out in the living room of the suite. "She told me to fuck off and leave it in the kitchen."

That sounded about right, and I had to laugh. "Sorry about that."

He shrugged, not looking bothered about it at all. "She says what she means. I appreciate that."

That was one of my favourite things about Tessa too. "I'm sure she'll be grateful for the breakfast once she's awake."

"Well, I can't stick around that long. I've got to get back to work, but these are for you."

From the tray, he picked up a single long-stemmed red rose and a folded piece of paper with my name handwritten on it, passing them over to me.

"What's all this?" He'd never given me flowers before. Maybe my dad had sent it?

His next words took me even more by surprise. "Just a few instructions for our date tonight," he explained as he headed back towards the door.

"Our date?" Apparently, I'd missed something. "When did you ask me on a date?"

My confusion only made him smile. "Just now. You don't have plans, do you?"

"No, but..."

"Good. I'll see you back here at seven, then. Have a good day."

With that, he headed out the door, leaving me completely bewildered. What on earth had brought that on?

Still trying to figure things out, I unfolded the note, but it didn't offer very much additional information. It simply said he would come to pick me up at seven and that I should dress warmly.

Once Tessa got up, we headed out to enjoy our day in the city. In one way, it seemed impossible to believe we'd been in Vienna for a week already, but on the other hand, so much had happened since we arrived, I could barely believe it had *only* been a week. I hardly felt like the same person who stepped off the plane a week earlier.

That day, in the bright December sunshine, we visited the Hofburg Palace in the centre of the city and the Spanish riding school where the Lipizzaner stallions danced to classical music, awing us with their strength, agility and balance.

"Wouldn't it be nice if men were as easy to train as those horses?" Tessa pondered as we headed back out into the city after the performance.

"I don't think training them is easy at all," I protested. "It must take years."

"I suppose, but at least once they've got it, they've got it. You don't have to worry about them changing their minds."

Her date the night before hadn't been quite the success she'd hoped for either. Apparently, the business that her date was in town to conduct hadn't gone well during the day, making him moody and irritable during dinner. It killed off any attraction Tessa had been feeling towards him, so when he invited her back to his room afterwards, she declined.

"We don't need any men to have fun," she declared to me that morning when we were first catching up. "We can have a good time on our own tonight, right?"

The timing could hardly be worse to tell her what had happened before she got up. "Actually, I've already got plans with Noah. I'm sorry."

She had every right to be mad at me for ditching her, but her eyes lit up instead. "He actually asked you out, finally?"

"Well, he kind of told me we were going out, actually," I said, telling her about the breakfast and the rose and the note. "I don't know what it means."

"Really?" The look she gave me was distinctly unimpressed. "He asks you out the night after his friend takes you out, and you don't know why? You're not that dense, Liv. Obviously, he's finally realizing what he's been missing all this time."

No matter how much I wanted that to be true, things were never just that simple when it came to Noah. I wasn't going to let myself get carried away until I knew exactly what he had in mind.

By seven o'clock, my stomach was in knots. I wore an outfit very similar to the one I'd worn at Isabel's farm the year before, with skinny jeans and a Christmas sweater beneath my white coat, hat and boots. Would he remember that, or had it all made much more of an impression on me than it had on him?

At last, the knock at my door came, and I went to open it, my heart pounding. To my surprise, Tate stood on the other side. "Oh. Hi," I managed to say.

A smirk spread across his face. "I don't think anyone has ever been so disappointed to see me before."

My cheeks flamed red when I realized he was entirely right. I could hardly have sounded less enthusiastic. "I'm sorry. Hi, Tate. How are you?"

"I'm fine," he assured me, smiling to let me know he was teasing. "I'm here to chill with Tessa for the night."

"Oh." I hadn't realized they'd arranged that, but I was glad to hear it. At least she wouldn't have to spend the night on her own. "Noah told you we're going out?"

"He did," Tate confirmed. "He also sends his apologies..."

My stomach lurched so hard, I thought I might be sick, but thankfully, Tate wasn't finished yet.

"... for not coming to get you himself. He asked me to pass on the message that he's waiting for you downstairs."

Taking a deep breath, I tried to get my heart rate back under control. Nothing had even happened yet and I was already wound up so tight, a stray word could make me snap. "Okay, thanks. Have a good night, guys."

After waving goodbye to my two friends, I made my way down to the lobby. Though I couldn't see Noah there either, there *was* a hotel employee, holding another single red rose like the one Noah had brought to my room that morning. "Good evening, ma'am," the man greeted me politely. "This is for you. Please, go outside."

He handed me the rose before going back to his work and, more confused than ever, I made my way out the front door of the hotel, where I had to blink several times to ensure my eyes weren't playing tricks on me.

Another rose in his hand, Noah sat in the back of a horse-drawn carriage in his elegant black winter coat, looking for all the world like this was how he spent every evening. His green eyes sparkled as he watched me approach, clearly enjoying my complete befuddlement.

"What the hell are you up to, Noah Stamer?" I asked once the carriage driver had helped me into the carriage.

"Something I should have done a long time ago, Olivia Hanmer," he replied, looking me straight in the eye with a teasing smirk as he said my full name back to me. "And I promise, this will be a night you'll never forget."

~Noah~

I had never taken anyone on a real date before. It had never been necessary since I'd never been looking for anything more than friendship or a hook-up, and never both at the same time. It felt a bit like flying blind, but I'd seen enough movies and picked up enough things from the people around me that I thought I had a pretty good idea what to do.

The carriage had been inspired by two things: first, I had seen them going around the city during my time there and thought it might be something Olivia would enjoy, and second, I remembered Olivia's mom mentioning a carriage ride when we went to Central Park years ago. I couldn't remember why we were there, just our moms and us kids. Perhaps our dads were out of town on a business trip.

"The very first time I came to the park, your dad took me in one of those," Holly told Olivia as we passed the carriages lined up, waiting for customers. "Every time I see them, I always remember that."

"I want to go!" the young Olivia replied, but Holly shook her head.

"Not today. And besides, doing it with your dad was what made it special. Maybe when you're older, someone will make it a special memory for you too."

It wasn't Central Park, but as Olivia sat next to me, watching the grand buildings of the Ringstrasse go by, I hoped it might be the kind of special memory her mom had been talking about.

"Check out that building," I said, pointing to an office tower just outside the historic city centre that had half a Christmas tree lit up down one side.

Olivia's blue eyes sparkled in the reflected lights, the look of delight on her face making every second I'd spent planning the outing worthwhile. "That's amazing. My dad would love that."

"I know. I remembered you guys always went to look at the lights, so I thought you'd enjoy seeing some of the ones here."

Though she seemed reluctant to look away from the impressive view, she turned to look at me instead. "This is really sweet, Noah."

"Don't sound so surprised," I teased her. "I *am* capable of kindness sometimes."

"I know you are. I just... didn't expect this."

I could hardly blame her for that, but the happiness in her eyes made me want to do things for her more often. As Tate's words came back to me, I repeated them, turning them on myself. "You should always expect to be treated well, Liv. Anyone who doesn't recognize what you deserve is an idiot."

The driver turned off the ring road and headed towards the Belvedere Palace, another beautiful historic building in Vienna's centre. Unlike the first palace we went to together, this one hadn't belonged to the royal family, but it didn't make it any less impressive. Even better, there was a Christmas market set up in the stunning gardens. The carriage took us right up to the entrance and I helped Liv down before leading her through the garden gate and towards the market stalls.

We grabbed some food as we wandered around the market, talking about Christmases of the past. "Did you know my parents' first date was at a Christmas market?" I asked her as we walked around the lake to see the view of all the lights and the palace reflecting in the water.

Olivia gave a sarcastic laugh. "I might have heard the story once or twice. Every time we go to the Winter Wonderland in Hyde Park, my dad has to bring it up, like we've never heard it before. He says he knew that first night that your parents would end up together and that he and my mom were meant for each other too."

"Do you believe him?" I was genuinely curious about how much of a romantic she was. Did she believe in destiny and all of that?

"I believe he wanted it to be true," she replied thoughtfully. "But I also think it took time for their relationship to grow. Things didn't always go smoothly and my mom didn't make it easy for him. If he had given up, it might not have worked out. So, although there might have been an element of love at first sight, there was a lot of determination too."

"Is that where you get your stubborn streak from, then?"

She turned to me, ready to protest, until she realized I was teasing her and her eyes narrowed playfully instead. "You're one to talk. You were so sure about what 'kind of girl' I was that you never gave me a chance to prove otherwise."

She had me there. "In my defense, Liv, there aren't many women like you."

Her brow furrowed as she tried to figure out what I meant by that. "Like what?"

"Perfect for someone like me."

Her lips parted in surprise and it took all my self-control not to kiss her right then and there. That wasn't my plan, though; we still had more to see and talk about.

"Come on, we're going to be late."

Grabbing her hand, I pulled her back to the carriage that was still waiting for us outside the gates.

Once we were back in the city centre, we got out again to walk through some of the pedestrianized streets, illuminated with even more lights. Giant, glittering chandeliers were suspended in the street above us, elegant and classy to fit in with the beautiful buildings that lined either side of the pavement. Like many streets in the historic centre, the one we walked down led to Stephansdom, the city's oldest and most impressive cathedral, where a line of people was waiting to get in. I took Olivia straight to the door and gave our names, and we were quickly ushered inside the huge vaulted interior to a private little area in the church's nave, decorated with lights and greenery to separate us from the rest of the audience. The interior wasn't a lot warmer inside than outside, but the candles gave the space a cheery glow anyway.

"What is all this?" Olivia asked as she looked around at the stage set up in front of us and the wine and cheese on the little table next to our seats.

"It's a Christmas concert." This had been on my mom's list of things to do in the city, and though I never would have gone on my own, bringing Olivia sounded like fun. Dozens of memories flitted across my mind: Olivia singing carols with her dad, at her school Christmas concerts, and on sleigh rides at Isabel's farm.

"I got that," she replied with a laugh. "I just meant: why couldn't we sit with everyone else?"

I gave her a smirk that I knew she'd recognize as a joke. "Because I'm not like everyone else."

Her eyes twinkled with amusement as I poured her a glass of wine. "No, you certainly aren't."

We compared our favourite Christmas songs and what we hoped might be performed that night while we enjoyed our drinks and snacks, and once the concert began, we sat down next to each other, my arm around the back of her chair.

The music was as beautiful as the setting, a small choir supported by a string quartet and a piano, their voices echoing through the vast church interior and soaring up into the vaulted ceiling, the whole scene lit only by candlelight. It began to feel almost like a dream as Olivia's head rested on my shoulder.

At some point, her hand found its way to my thigh. I wasn't even sure when it got there, I just looked down and saw it resting there, looking completely natural and comfortable. I did notice when it began to move a little higher though, since my whole body began to heat up in response.

"Are you trying to distract me from the concert?" I murmured to her, curling my arm around her more so I could stroke the side of her face.

"I'm just trying to remind you that we're on a date," she teased me. "I don't imagine Noah Stamer goes on many dates that aren't a little dirty."

Her hand moved across to my other leg, brushing against my groin as it went, and I had to stifle a groan.

"I don't know exactly how kinky you think I am, but I don't usually get it on in a church."

She giggled before she could stop herself, and one of the singers glanced over in our direction.

"They can see us," I reminded her, but that was the wrong thing to say. Her eyes sparkled mischievously as she turned to face me.

"I thought that's what you liked."

"When the person watching has consented," I specified, though I knew she already knew that. She was just trying to rile me. "Nobody came here to watch us, Liv."

"Then maybe we should go somewhere that people do want to watch."

That time, her hand pressed down against my rapidly-hardening dick, and I couldn't entirely stop my groan. Though I did have more plans for the night, it looked like they might have to wait for another day. I still wanted to talk to her before we got too carried away. "Are you ready to leave now?"

She nodded mutely, getting to her feet as I did the same, and we made our way back out of the church as quietly as possible. "Is there a problem, sir?" one of the attendants at the door asked me, since I'd paid quite a lot for that space and we were leaving before the show was even half over.

"Not at all. Everything was wonderful." With Liv's hand in mind, I led her back to the carriage and whispered instructions to the driver. Less than ten minutes later, we pulled back up to the hotel and Olivia looked up at it in surprise before turning to me.

"I thought we were going to The Playground."

"Not tonight. I need to talk to you, Liv. I had reservations at a rooftop bar for us to do that, but I think maybe it's safer to do it here."

"Safer?" She repeated the word in confusion.

"If you're going to keep turning me on like that, I don't need to be arrested for public indecency."

That made her laugh and blush at the same time as I helped her down from the carriage. Giving the driver a big tip, I brought her back up to my room where we could talk in private, since Tate and Tessa were presumably still in Olivia's suite.

There were so many things I wanted to say to her, but a confession seemed the best way to begin, especially given we'd just been to church.

"You said that you didn't think I went on many dates that weren't dirty," I reminded her as we both took off our coats and boots and had a seat on the couch in my room. That was the first time I'd seen her without her coat on that night, and her sweet Christmas sweater and jeans immediately took me back to the previous Christmas and how tempting I'd found her then. Who could have imagined a year later we'd be together on the other side of the world? "Well, the truth is, I don't go on dates. Ever. This was my first one."

She examined my face carefully, trying to tell if I was lying, but I never lied to her, and I never would. "Why?"

"Because I never saw the point. I didn't need to date to have sex, and I wasn't looking for anything else."

Olivia shook her head. "No, I mean: why did you ask me out tonight then?"

That was exactly what I wanted to talk to her about, but now that the moment had arrived, my mouth had gone dry and all the words I'd prepared seemed to have disappeared. If I were to make my declaration and she were to tell me that she only wanted to have fun, like I had done to her last year, it would crush me.

How had she been brave enough to do what she did then? I never fully appreciated how courageous she'd been until that moment.

Trying to summon that same courage, I told her the truth. "I asked you out because seeing you here, and getting to know the kinky side of you while also reconnecting with the Liv I always liked has been incredible. I never imagined that you and I would share this kink. It didn't seem possible. That's why I turned you down last year: because I simply couldn't see a way to have what I wanted without hurting you. I pushed you away for your own sake, not because I didn't want you."

She nodded slowly. "I understand that, but now that we do know, we can enjoy it together. That's why I thought we would go to the club tonight."

I still wasn't making myself clear, apparently. "I do want to play with you at the club, and I hope that we will, but it's not *all* I want."

She licked her lips, like her mouth felt dry too. Maybe the air in the hotel was simply on the dry side. That would explain a lot. "What *do* you want, then?"

That was the question, wasn't it? And since she asked me so bluntly, I had to answer her the same way.

"I want all of you. I want you to be mine, Liv. I think I always have, I just didn't let myself feel it because I was afraid you'd reject me for who I am. But now that I know you won't, I think... I think deep down, it's always been you."

Chapter Seventeen

In Private

~Olivia~

A dozen different feelings rose up inside me as Noah said the words I'd always wanted to hear. I had spent so long imagining them, so many nights picturing the moment when he would truly see me and know what I had always known: we would never suit anyone else quite as well as we suited each other.

The whole night, the carriage and the roses, the Christmas market and the lights, the carols and the church, everything had been amazing, but none of it came close to hearing those words come out of his mouth.

In fact, the reality of finally hearing them was so perfect that, for a moment, I couldn't believe it had actually happened.

"Does this have something to do with Tate?" I asked, trying to understand what had inspired such a massive turnaround.

Noah's lips pursed in what almost looked like disappointment. "Yes and no. Seeing him appreciate just how amazing you are helped me to realize exactly what I'd be missing if I let you slip away, but this isn't something that just happened, Liv. I've always cared for you, I just didn't really know that's what I felt. You know how he told you that I never talked to him about you? My silence wasn't because I didn't think about you or because you weren't important to me. I didn't mention you because I didn't want to share you. You were so special to me that I wanted to keep you to myself. If that makes me an idiot, then I guess I'm an idiot."

My head spun more with every word until I couldn't sit still any longer. Adrenaline buzzed through me as I got to my feet, pacing across Noah's room while I tried to make sense of everything. "You really had feelings for me before all of this? Feelings that weren't just physical?"

Noah nodded, his green eyes watching me closely as I moved about the room, his handsome face looking tense as he tried to convince me he was telling the truth. "You don't know how many times I thought how great it would be if I could find a girl just like you who was into the same kind of stuff I am. I just never thought that girl could actually be *you*. I never thought I'd be that lucky."

I wanted that to be true so badly, but if he really felt that way, how had he never said *anything* about it before?

On the other hand, why would he lie to me? I'd already made it pretty clear I'd have sex with him regardless. What was he really after?

"Prove it," I demanded bluntly, and Noah's eyebrows raised.

"How?"

That was a good question. He wasn't going to have a signed and dated note from before all of this happened that said 'I like Olivia'.

However, no sooner was the question out of his mouth than a light sparked in his eyes. "Wait. I might have something."

Springing out of his seat, he went over to his laptop on the hotel desk while I followed behind him curiously. In less than a minute, he'd pulled up a spreadsheet and turned it to face me.

"What's this?" I asked curiously, bending down to take a closer look at it.

Noah cleared his throat. "We call it our fuckit list. Mine and Tate's. It details all the sexual stuff we want to try before we settle down."

I looked up at him to see if he was joking, but he simply smiled down at me sheepishly.

"Tate's the one who wanted to write it all down, but look: here's what I want to show you."

He scrolled down the list, too fast for me to make out all the individual items, until he got to number 53.

"Fuck the first girl you ever wanted to go out with," I read out loud before looking up at him again, still feeling confused. "I don't get it."

Noah pointed to the screen, to the column next to the item that had a checkmark in it. "Tate checked this off almost two years ago. He went back to his hometown and tracked the girl down, but my column is still blank. I haven't done it yet, because that girl is you."

The evidence was hardly conclusive, and the whole list idea was a little weird in the first place, but the fact that he had thought of it so quickly did seem to indicate there might be some truth behind it.

Noah closed the laptop lid again and sat down on the edge of the desk, facing me. "I knew pretty early on that there was something different about me, something that was going to make a traditional relationship difficult. Still, whenever I imagined being with someone in a meaningful way, the woman I pictured was always someone like you. Someone who works hard for what she wants, who never backs down from a challenge, who throws herself into everything she does, who's beautiful and smart and funny and so fucking perfect, it's not even funny. The only thing missing for me was the kink, and unfortunately, that was a dealbreaker. I always held back because I didn't want to lead you on. Hurting you is the last thing I'd ever want to do, but now that I know we share that too, there's nothing to stop me from saying what I should have said years ago."

That might have been the most words I'd ever heard Noah put together at one time. He wasn't usually one for big speeches, but every word he'd said was sincere and earnest and *perfect*. "What should you have said?"

He didn't waste any more words. "I want you, Liv. And I think you might still want me too, even after the way I behaved last year. Please tell me I haven't fucked it up beyond repair. Please tell me I'm not too late."

"What are you suggesting?" My voice began to tremble as I started to let myself believe this might really be happening. I'd been keeping my defenses up, not wanting to get hurt again, but they were weakening with every word from his lips.

He leaned in closer so his face was just a few inches from mine. "I'm suggesting that we keep dating, like we did tonight. I'm suggesting that when we get back home, we tell everyone that we're together. And most of all, I'm suggesting that we cross number 53 off that list right now."

A shiver of excitement ran through me as my whole body instantly came alive. How did he manage to do that with just a few words?

"Now?" I repeated, glancing over at the bed. "Here? Alone?"

From what Tate had told me and my own research on the matter, I understood that for people like us, being intimate in private meant something completely different from intimacy in public. At the club, in front of the crowd, there were no emotions involved. There in his room was an entirely different matter.

Noah got to his feet, his eyes still locked on me as his hands went to my hips, pulling me against his body, making his stiff cock impossible to miss.

"Now," he confirmed, answering my questions in the order I'd asked them as he placed a light kiss on my cheek. "Here." Another kiss, on my neck. "Alone."

At last, his lips went to mine, connecting with heat and desire and need, like all the years of pent-up wanting were released at once in an explosion that engulfed us both. I clung onto him for dear life, kissing him back just as hard, afraid that if I let up for even a moment, he might disappear.

He wasn't going anywhere, though. His arms swept my legs from beneath me as he carried me the few feet to his bed. The distance was hardly worth the effort, but I loved the gesture anyway. Being in his arms felt so right.

After setting me down on the edge of the bed, Noah pulled my sweater over my head as my fingers fumbled with his pants. There was no slow, drawn-out undressing. We'd both seen each other naked before and we were both eager to get back to that state as soon as possible. When I finally got his cock out, finding him hard and ready, I couldn't stop myself from taking it into my mouth. The taste of him was familiar, since I *had* done it before even though I didn't know it at the time, but somehow, the experience still felt new and exciting too. I'd never touched him that way intentionally before, where we both knew exactly what was happening.

Noah groaned above me as he pulled his own shirt off. "Liv, if you keep doing that, this is going to be over in about two seconds. Your mouth is incredible, but that's not where I want to be right now."

Looking up at him, his expression seemed almost tender, and the dampness between my legs was a good sign I wanted him somewhere else too, so I reluctantly let him go as I quickly removed my pants and underwear and Noah got rid of the rest of his clothing too. For a moment, we stared at each other, savouring the moment of anticipation, but only for a moment. Soon, his hands went under my arms, lifting me further onto the bed as he kissed me, his body covering mine while my arms wrapped around him.

"You're so beautiful," he murmured into my ear before kissing his way down my neck, his hips grinding into me. "You don't know how much I've wanted you."

I let out a choked laugh. "It can't be half as much as I wanted you."

He grinned as his face appeared above me again. "You always have to win, don't you?"

"Usually," I agreed breathlessly. "But maybe this time, we both can."

Lust darkened his eyes as his head dropped down again, finding my breasts that time. As he sucked one firm nipple into his mouth, his hand went between my legs, making him groan again as he felt just how wet I was. "Fuck, Liv. I can't wait, I need to be inside you."

"I need that too." I pulled his head back up so I could kiss him again. "Please, Noah."

My legs spread wider as he lined his ready cock up against me, but just as I thought he would enter me, he paused. "Shit. I need a condom."

"Do you?" My question was sincere. I didn't know what his rules and limits were, but for me, I didn't need one. At the club, yes, but not there in his room.

The question took him by surprise and curiosity filled his eyes as he looked down at me, the ceiling light backlighting him so that he almost seemed to be glowing. "I've never not used one."

That didn't really surprise me. Noah obviously took his responsibility seriously, and just like he hadn't wanted to lead me on, he wouldn't have wanted any kind of accidental pregnancy. However, I wasn't worried about that. "I'm okay without it, but it's up to you."

He knew immediately what I meant, that I took my birth control as seriously as I did everything else, and I could see the desire within him battling with his usual rules. For a few seconds, I honestly wasn't sure which way he would go, or what made the decision for him, but a moment later, he pushed into me just as he was, and all other thoughts vanished from my head.

"Oh, God, Noah."

He felt incredible as he filled me, satisfying that aching longing within me just as well as I'd always imagined he would.

"Fuck, Liv," he groaned back, his eyes closed as he exhaled in pleasure. "You really are perfect, inside and out."

"That's not usually what that phrase means," I couldn't help pointing out, and he laughed as his eyes opened, sparkling down at me.

"It's what it means now."

He quickly found a rhythm that worked for us both, keeping the pleasure steady while also drawing it out. Clearly, he didn't want it to end too quickly and I didn't either. I had never felt so complete.

With each thrust, the heartache of the past faded a little more. Each kiss made up for a day apart. Every stroke of his hands, working my body to perfection, proved to me that what he had said was true.

He wanted me, and I wanted him. I always had.

It was always him.

And when his fingers began to move against my clit, his thrusts growing harder and more urgent, I gave myself over to the pleasure of it entirely. It didn't matter to me that no one else was watching. *Noah* was watching, and that was all I cared about. That was what I had always wanted.

I called out his name one more time as my pleasure peaked, and I felt him shudder within me too, reaching his own climax. As we both fought to catch our breath, one thing was completely certain to me: nothing in the world was ever going to be the same.

~Noah~

That was... something different.

I'd had sex many, many times before. I honestly had no idea how many times. There was a list, for crying out loud, and it only captured a small portion of the things I'd tried.

But what just happened with Olivia... that wasn't on the list. That was something I'd never experienced before.

Though my cock was hard for her before we even started, there was still a part of me that was afraid my arousal wasn't going to last. I worried that once we got into it, I wouldn't be able to get off, or even keep it up long enough to get *her* off. To try to combat that, I looked straight into Olivia's eyes, remembering the way she'd looked at me when she watched me at The Playground the other night. The same desire and passion I'd seen in her gaze remained, feeling even more intense close up, and that helped a lot. In fact, it really fucking turned me on.

So what if there wasn't anyone else watching? *She* was still watching me. I was performing for her if not for anyone else, and somehow, that made it okay.

Once I began moving inside her, feeling the warmth of her body around me, watching the pleasure I was giving her, I relaxed even more. I was still turned on, maybe even just as much as I had been watching her at the club. Rather than watching someone else giving her pleasure, I gave it to her myself, but I still got to see her enjoy herself either way, and it still felt just as gratifying.

When I came inside her, fully inside her without even the condom to separate us, I finally understood what it must be like for the rest of the world, for the people who didn't need the crowd like I did.

It really could be pretty damn good, at least when Olivia was involved.

As I looked down at her in the aftermath of her own orgasm, our bodies still joined together, I whispered the first words that came into my head. "It looks like we *can* both win after all."

She laughed as her hands ran across my back one more time, her cheeks flushed and her hair spread out beneath her. "Fair enough. You've convinced me. We'll call it a tie."

Giving her one more kiss, I pulled out of her and lay down on the bed next to her, staring up at the ceiling, my body weak but my mind energized. For a long moment, we were both quiet, absorbing everything that had just happened, until I finally broke the silence.

"I don't really know what happens now," I admitted.

Olivia rolled over, her body curling into mine. "You mean with us?"

I didn't know that either, but I'd meant something else. "No, I mean, literally right now. Usually, after I have sex with someone, I say thank you, see if they need anything, and we go our separate ways."

Her body tensed beside me, just a little, but enough that I noticed it. "Do you want me to go?"

Fuck, that came out wrong. "No, not at all. That's what I'm trying to say. I want you to stay, but I don't know what I'm supposed to do now. I've never spent the whole night with someone."

The tension released from her shoulders as her hand came up to my chest, her fingers tracing light patterns across it. "That's not true. We've had plenty of sleepovers before. Do you remember that Christmas we went skiing in the mountains?"

Of course I remembered. "I had to sleep in the same room as you and Eve and Noelle and I was terrified of what you were going to do to me while I was asleep."

Her laugh sounded a little too mischievous. "We did talk about putting makeup on you while you were sleeping, but you kept waking up every time we got too close."

"Thank God," I muttered, making her laugh again.

"It's funny," she mused, her hand still dancing across my chest. "At the time, I thought our parents were just taking turns looking after us so that we could all hang out together, but now, I realize they were probably just getting rid of us so they could have some nights to themselves."

"Probably," I agreed. I hadn't given it much thought before either, but it definitely sounded like something my dad would do.

"Do you think they would have been quite so eager to put us together if they knew we'd end up in bed together like this a few years later?"

That brought Jackson's warning back to me and I decided to finally tell her about it. "Did you know your dad threatened to cut off my balls if I messed with you?"

Olivia immediately raised her head so she could look at me, her eyes wide with surprise. "Seriously? When did that happen?"

"At your high school graduation. He caught me staring at you and made his position pretty clear. How much do you think I need to really worry about that?"

The question made her smile, but another emotion flashed across her eyes too. "You were really thinking about me like that back then?"

I reached over to cup her face. "I told you, Liv: always."

That time when our lips met, the kiss was filled with far less urgency but a lot more tenderness.

We lay there together, talking and laughing until her eyes began to droop. "I didn't sleep well last night," she admitted sleepily, so once we both got ready for bed, we crawled back in together, still naked as I held her against me while her breathing evened out, and I soon followed, feeling warm and content.

When I woke in the early morning light, I couldn't remember what my dreams had been, but they must have been good since I was sporting some impressive morning wood. Or perhaps that was thanks to the woman next to me, still asleep in my arms. The feel of her and the smell of her, and the memory of everything that had happened the night before all combined to make me even harder, and as I rubbed myself against her, pulling her even closer to me, Olivia sighed in contentment.

That was about all the encouragement I needed, though I couldn't be sure she was fully awake yet. Groaning as my hand made contact with my hard dick, I pressed it down between her thighs, rubbing myself back and forth against her centre as my hand slid up her side, following the curve of her waist over to her stomach and up to her breast.

"Noah."

The soft murmur of my name made the blood rush to my dick even faster as I continued to move between her legs, teasing her as she began to wake up. Her exposed neck was too tempting to resist, so I didn't even try. I kissed her there, sucking on the tender, sensitive skin as my fingers found her hardening nipple, pinching it lightly.

"What time is it?" Olivia asked, letting me know that she'd fully woken up.

"Too early to get out of bed," I replied, reaching down once more to angle myself just where I needed to be. She couldn't have any doubt of my intentions, and when she opened her legs a little, wiggling her ass back against me, she made it clear she wanted it too. I pushed into her, relishing how tight she felt around me in that position, and groaned once more. "Fuck, Liv."

Held in front of me, there was not much she could do while I teased her, using long, languid strokes as my hips rolled against her ass, my fingers playing with her breasts and her clit.

"Just imagine us doing this up on that stage," I whispered into her ear as she writhed against me. "All those eyes on you while I fuck you just like this."

A whimper escaped her lips as she came, the thought of the crowd just as much of a turn on for her as for me. But as soon as her shivers subsided, to my surprise, she pulled away from me and, with determination in her eyes, rolled me over and pushed me down onto my back, climbing on top of me.

"I'd rather they watch us like this," she told me as she lowered herself onto my rock-hard dick.

I had no problem with that. Watching her as she rode me, her beautiful, lithe body bouncing on top of me, her lips parted in pleasure, I knew I'd be the envy of every man in that room.

"I'm so close, Liv."

She knew exactly why I told her and she quickly hopped off me, finishing me off with her hand so that I spurted all over her, the evidence of my pleasure painted across the beautiful canvas of her body.

That was what the crowd came to see, and once again, it didn't seem to matter that there wasn't actually any crowd there to see it. We could share in the fantasy together.

She was still stroking me lightly when my alarm went off and I groaned for a different reason entirely. "Fuck. I have to work today."

Olivia giggled as she got to her feet. "You better come and shower then."

We showered together, my fingers finding their way between her legs again until she came once more. Afterwards, still wrapped in my robe, she sat down at my desk while I began to put on my suit for the day.

"What else is on this list of yours?" she asked, opening my laptop. The screen was locked, but I walked over and used my fingerprint to unlock it. I had nothing to hide from her, which was the very best part of being with Olivia. She already knew everything about me and she accepted it all.

"Take a look if you like. We've almost checked everything off."

She started at the top as I buttoned up my shirt and grabbed my suit jacket. Tate teased me about my suits, but the importance of a good suit was another thing my dad had taught me. In business, first impressions were key.

Getting the kind of second chance that Olivia had given me was incredibly rare.

"You haven't done number 27 yet," she pointed out as she made her way down the list.

"No, we haven't," I confirmed. "That's one of the pitfalls of the club scene, I suppose. You don't come across many women who are inexperienced in any way, so we haven't found anyone who's interested but also hasn't done it before."

She hummed thoughtfully as she continued to look at the list. "Well, I've never done that."

I supposed that wasn't too surprising considering she'd only really been with one guy before that week, but something in the way she said it made me pause. "Is it something you'd want to try?"

"It might be," she said, turning to look at me with an expression both eager and open. "If you were there with me, I think I might enjoy it."

My dick twitched once again within my pants, which wasn't helpful since I needed to get to work. She'd taken me by surprise once again, but I loved that she wanted to continue to experiment.

"Would you want to do it with Tate?" I asked, trying to work out exactly what she was thinking.

"Would it bother you if I did?"

That was a good question. I'd never had a problem sharing with Tate before, except when it came to Olivia. But my jealousy was only over her affection, of the times like the one we were having right then, sitting around and talking, and the warm look in her eyes as she watched me. In the context of the club, when it came to our kink, I only wanted her to enjoy herself, no matter what that looked like. When I let myself imagine what it would be like to check that item off the list with both Tate and Liv, jealousy didn't really factor into it.

"As long as you don't have any feelings for him, it would be fine with me," I told her honestly.

Olivia got to her feet and came over to me, standing toe-to-toe with me as she looked me in the eye. "All my feelings are tied up in you, Noah. They always have been."

Always. The word filled me with warmth and satisfaction as I leaned forward to kiss her softly.

"In that case, it doesn't bother me at all. I'll let him know you're interested, and we can get a room at The Playground tonight. I need to go now, are you okay if I leave you here?"

Olivia nodded. "I'm fine. Have a good day, and I'll see you later."

She kissed me once more before going back to the desk and I headed out the door with a smile on my face.

That might have just been the best night of my life.

Chapter Eighteen

Number 27

~Olivia~

I had to shake my head as I continued to look through Noah's 'fuckit' list. I knew he was kinky, obviously, and I had done enough research before coming to Vienna that I didn't think there was much that could still shock me, but a few of the items managed to do it anyway, especially when I saw that they were already completed.

But more than the shock, the whole thing excited me too. Noah fully embraced every part of his sexuality, and that inspired me, not to mention how sexy I found it. With him as my guide and now my boyfriend too, anything seemed possible.

Tessa would be as fascinated by the list as I was, but I'd never remember all of it. There were a few things I needed to Google too. With my fingers hovering over the mousepad, I chewed my lip in indecision. Would Noah be upset if I sent myself a copy of it? He'd shown it to me readily enough, so it didn't seem like he was trying to hide it, and I wouldn't share it with anyone else other than letting Tessa take a look. She already knew all about his kinks anyway.

Making up my mind, I hit forward on it and started to type in my email address. To my surprise, the address was already in his contacts and popped up as an option as soon as I started typing 'Hanmer'. So did my dad's address, which was even more surprising. I'd never thought about Noah emailing my dad before, but when I thought about it, there was no reason he wouldn't. I emailed his mom sometimes.

What were our parents going to think when we let them know that we were seeing each other? The threat from my dad that Noah told me about had me giggling all over again when my phone buzzed with a text.

I just went to knock on your door and you're not there! Hope you are somewhere safe and sexy. Let me know!

Sending Tessa a message had been the last thing on my mind the night before, but if she was already up, I should get back to my own room. I quickly hit 'send' on the list and closed Noah's computer to lock it before putting my clothes back on and heading upstairs to our suite.

My friend sat in the living room of the suite when I entered, wearing her robe and sipping on a cup of coffee. "Same clothes as last night, I see," she pointed out, raising her eyebrows at me conspiratorially. "You didn't just get up early this morning."

"No, I didn't," I admitted, flopping down onto the couch across from her with a happy sigh. "I was with Noah all night. It really happened, Tessa. He wants us to be together."

Tessa squealed in excitement, knowing just how much that meant to me. "I knew it! Took him long enough, but at least he got there. And? Was it worth all the build-up?"

"It was incredible," I admitted truthfully, to more squealing from her side. "I still can't quite believe it."

"Tell. Me. *Everything.*"

I started at the beginning, as she requested and told her all about the sweet, romantic date he'd planned, our flirting in the church, and the conversation we'd had back in his room. As I expected, when I got to him telling me about the list as a way of proving that he'd always had feelings for me, Tessa's eyes lit up.

"What else is on this list?"

The curious twinkle in her eyes made me laugh. "We'll get to that, I promise."

I told her the rest first, about how he wanted to tell our families about us and about how we slept together in private, with no one else around.

She whistled, sounding suitably impressed. "That's a big deal, right?"

"It is," I confirmed. "I don't think he's ever done it before. Or at least, not for a very long time."

"You were his first!"

The idea made both of us laugh. Noah was so far from being a virgin, he wasn't even on the same map, but maybe in some ways, especially emotional ones, Tessa had a point. I was going to be his first girlfriend, the first person he introduced to his parents as someone he was interested in. There were a lot of firsts for us to experience together, even if the more obvious ones were already taken.

"And speaking of firsts..." I said, using the perfect segue Tessa provided. "I think I'm going to try something new with Noah and Tate at The Playground tonight."

At the mention of Tate, Tessa's brows furrowed. "You're going to do something sexual with Tate? After everything that just happened?"

"If he wants to," I clarified. "Noah still has to ask him, but yeah, if he agrees to it. It's something on their list, something they wanted to do together."

Tessa still looked confused. "But won't that be weird? I mean, he's your new boyfriend's best friend."

"And they do stuff like this together all the time. There's nothing emotional about it. In the club, in the spotlight, we leave everything else behind. We're just our bodies, without any of the other stuff attached. If we all enjoy it, I don't see a problem with it."

Tessa shook her head as she gave me a sheepish smile. "I just don't get it, but I guess if it works for you guys, more power to you."

That was the whole point, wasn't it? My kink wasn't her kink, but that was okay.

"What did you and Tate do last night?" I asked, realizing that the conversation so far had been entirely about me.

Tessa, however, wasn't going to be so easily distracted. "No way! You can't tell me something like that and not tell me what you're going to do tonight."

I had definitely left her hanging, though not intentionally. "Well, I was looking through Noah's list and I saw one thing they hadn't done yet. They wanted to find an anal virgin who was willing to try double penetration."

Tessa's eyes went wide and for a moment, I thought I had actually left her speechless. That would be a first.

Finally, she blinked slowly, the wheels turning in her head. "And you actually want to do that? In front of a crowd?"

"A small crowd," I quantified. "But yeah, I think I do. I know that with Noah there, if we start and I'm uncomfortable with it, he'll have no problem changing course or just stopping the scene. It feels safe, and if I can help them check off something they've been trying to do for a while, all the better. It can be a milestone for all of us."

Trying anal in front of a crowd had been one of my limits before we arrived in Vienna, but that was before I knew Noah would be involved. I trusted him enough that I knew he'd do everything he could to make it good for me.

"This list sounds fucking insane," Tessa pointed out, making me laugh again.

"I knew you'd think so," I told her, pulling out my phone. "That's why I took a copy so we could look at it together."

She squealed once more in excitement before coming over to sit next to me as I went into my emails, but when I got to my inbox, I had no emails from Noah, and my smile faded.

"That's weird. I thought I sent it, but maybe his computer wasn't connected to wi-fi or something."

Tessa groaned, leaning back against the couch dramatically. "You are such a tease."

That honestly hadn't been my intention, so I told her some of the things I could remember from the list before we got ready for our day.

Another brisk and sunny day waited for us, and we spent the afternoon visiting the Central Cemetery. One of the largest cemeteries in the world, as well as being home to the tombs of many of the famous composers we'd been learning about during our stay, it made a peaceful place for a long walk, and we spent more time there than we intended to, caught up in our conversation and the beauty of our surroundings.

Tessa and Tate had simply hung out in our suite the night before, watching TV and talking. "I think we could be really good friends," she told me. "He's a lot of fun. It's such a shame about the kink."

The shame was that their kinks didn't line up, but neither of them should have to change who they were for the other. Hopefully, they would both meet someone who fit their lives in every way, just like Noah and I did for each other. We were still young. There was still plenty of time, and plenty of new people to meet.

Tessa agreed to come to The Playground with us that night, mostly because she admitted she was curious about seeing me get 'double stuffed', as she called it. It surprised me that she wanted to watch, but I had no problem with it as long as she would be comfortable.

We met up with Noah and Tate for dinner first, though with my excitement building about the night ahead, I didn't have much of an appetite. "Did you talk to Tate about tonight?" I asked Noah quietly when we had a moment to ourselves.

He nodded, his eyes gleaming with anticipation just as mine must have been. "He's on board."

Tate himself congratulated me on my new relationship status with Noah, giving me a warm hug. "I'd really like for us to be friends, Liv."

"I would love that too," I assured him. He couldn't be taking the turn of events any better. All in all, everything had worked out as well as it possibly could.

As we walked into the Plaza at the club that night, Tessa and I in our lingerie and the men in their suits, with Noah holding my hand in a clear declaration of our new relationship, it truly felt like there were no limits on what we might do.

~Noah~

The whole day, it felt like I was walking on air. I had never really understood how much of a difference it could make to be in an actual relationship. It always seemed like a chore, something I needed to do eventually but which would definitely be less fun than what I was currently doing. But walking into The Playground with Olivia next to me, knowing that we were there to have fun together but that at the end of the night, she'd be sleeping next to me back at the hotel and would be the first thing I got to see in the morning, it actually made the whole thing even better.

Tate had been surprised when I approached him that morning with Olivia's suggestion for the evening. "You really want me involved?"

"We've been waiting to check this item off the list forever," I reminded him. "I wouldn't do it without you. Just because Liv and I are going to be seeing each other doesn't mean that anything between you and me has to change."

The relief in his eyes told me that he had been worried that it might. "In that case, I'd be honoured."

He also couldn't quite believe I'd shown her the list in the first place, but I shrugged that off too. "You already said it yourself: she's totally open to everything, and I don't want to hide anything from her. If it's going to work with us being in the scene while being in a relationship, we need to be honest with each other. I need to know I can trust her, and vice versa."

Tate nodded. "I get it. I still think you're the luckiest bastard in the world, but meeting Liv has given me hope. There *are* women like her out there; I just need to find one for myself."

As far as I was concerned, no one compared to Olivia, but saying that to him wouldn't be particularly helpful so I tried to be supportive instead. "You've obviously got a good eye, so I wouldn't worry too much. It'll happen."

The rest of the day was uneventful, other than a rather cryptic text from my dad just a couple of hours before we went to the club.

If that was a butt dial, it was an epic one.

Having no idea what he was talking about, I checked the outgoing calls and messages on my phone but I couldn't see anything that I'd sent. Confused, I sent him back a question mark, but he hadn't replied again.

I'd banished my confusion to the back of my mind by the time the four of us made our way to the bar in the Plaza and ordered some drinks to be brought to the room we'd booked for the night. The other supplies I'd requested were already there: condoms, a couple of toys, a couple of props, and a lot of lube.

Our cocktail pitchers arrived soon afterwards and we all sat down together to loosen up a little before the night kicked off properly.

"Are you still sure about this?" I asked Olivia softly while Tate and Tessa were arguing about the merits of homemade porn. "You know you can change your mind at any time, right? I won't be upset."

"I know," she assured me. "And yes, I'm still sure. I want to experience this with you, but I can't promise I won't feel differently once we start."

That was totally understandable. "Just say the word at any time, and we'll end it. I mean it. This is about you enjoying yourself, first and foremost."

Once our glasses were empty, I went out into the lobby to find our audience. Olivia had told me she wanted a small group, just three or four people besides Tessa. It didn't take long until I spotted a familiar face.

"Hey," I greeted him, walking up to the two men who were talking to a couple of women. "Great show the other day. Derek, right?"

The man who had sex with Olivia the other day nodded. "Hey. What's up?"

"My girlfriend wants to try something new, so I'm looking for some extra eyes who won't mind if it's a little awkward."

I'd never called Olivia my girlfriend out loud before, but fuck, it sounded right.

Derek grinned at his friend before looking back at me. "Sure. We love awkward. None of us is perfect the first time out."

That was just the attitude I wanted. "Great. Drinks are on me."

They came back with me to the room and got settled while Tate poured everyone some drinks and I explained what we were about to do.

"We might change course part way through if she doesn't like it," I warned them all. "But no matter what, you're going to get a show."

That seemed to satisfy them as they sat back, drinks in hand, and I turned to Olivia.

"You're on, Liv."

~Olivia~

Noah could hardly be more supportive as he explained the proposed scene. I was glad to see Derek again too, since I knew he understood limits and wouldn't be disappointed if things didn't go as planned either.

Hopefully, it *would* all go to plan. My body was already primed, anticipation and adrenaline rushing through me as Tate sat beside me on the bed, when Noah turned to me and invited me to get started.

Over our drinks earlier, we'd come up with the scenario we wanted to use for the scene, which wasn't far off the truth, really: Noah and I would play a couple and Tate would be his best friend who had always admired my ass. For Tate's birthday, Noah would offer to let him fuck it while he watched, and then he would join in.

With that in mind, I started us off by standing up and going over to Noah, giving him a deep kiss until Tate cleared his throat behind us.

"Oh, hey," Noah said, stepping completely into character. "I didn't hear you come in. Happy birthday."

"Thanks." Though he spoke to Noah, Tate's eyes were on me, scanning my body intently. As usual for the club, I only wore my bra and panties. It wouldn't take long to take them off. "You said you had a present for me?"

Noah nodded in confirmation. "I do, and I think you're going to like it. Why don't you show him, Belle?"

We were still using my fake name in front of the others, and I liked having that persona to step into. It helped me get into character as I spun around and showed off the little bow Noah had put on the back of my panties.

Murmurs of appreciation rippled through our audience as Tate inhaled loudly, looking between my ass and Noah. "Are you serious?"

"I know you've always admired it, and I've never touched it myself. It's brand new, and all for you."

Tate's groan was echoed by someone in the audience, and I looked out to see the people there starting to touch themselves and each other. They were clearly getting as turned on as I was, which was quite a lot. As Tate reached over to unwrap his present, my panties were already damp, sticking to me as he pulled them down.

"I hope you like it," I teased him, wiggling my ass in his face as he bent down to remove my panties entirely.

Tate's hands ran across my ass as he swore under his breath. "Fuck, Belle. I can't wait to stretch you out. You're going to feel so good on my dick."

His dirty words sent another shot of excitement through me, especially as I looked over to see Noah watching me with a proud smile.

My fantasy from the other day, having Noah right beside me as someone else fucked me, was about to come true, and I reached out to him. "You'll stay with me, right?"

"Of course," he promised, taking my hand. "I'll be right here the whole time."

Tate removed my bra next, leaving me naked in front of the small crowd as he and Noah both took their clothes off too. Both of them were equally as ready as I was, their cocks already standing hard and proud. Tate grabbed the lube from the table as he instructed me to get up on the bed on all fours, while Noah sat in front of me, his face level with mine as he leaned in and kissed me.

"You look incredible," he told me quietly, for my ears only.

Tate started by fingering my pussy, playing with my clit from behind as Noah and I continued to kiss. It gave me a bit of the friction I was craving, though I still wanted more. The chill of the lube startled me as Tate spread it over my back hole, slathering it on generously before he pressed a finger into me slowly as his other hand continued to work my pussy.

"It's so fucking tight on just my finger," he groaned, partly to me and partly to the crowd. "There definitely hasn't been anyone back here before."

Having his finger up my ass was a strange sensation, I had to admit, but not necessarily unpleasant, especially as he continued to tease my clit and Noah's tongue tangled with mine, helping to distract and arouse me.

Tate took his time, continuing to praise my tightness and willingness as he worked his finger in and out and gradually added a second one.

When I whimpered at the uncomfortable fullness, Tate immediately stopped.

"Just breathe through it, Liv," Noah encouraged me, whispering into my ear. "Let yourself adjust for a second, but if you want to stop, we can."

Following his advice, I took several deep breaths, getting used to the feeling until it seemed more manageable. "Okay," I told him with a nod. "Keep going."

Once Tate's fingers were fully inside, he separated them, pushing outwards gently to stretch me even more.

"You're doing fucking amazing, Belle," he told me. "I can't wait to get my dick in there, but first, I'm going to make you feel just as good."

His fingers left my ass, and a moment later I felt something else there, hard and cold.

"He's going to put a plug in," Noah explained to me, again whispering so no one else would hear. "To keep you used to the feeling while you come."

I nodded as Tate pressed the lubed-up toy into me. Again, the sensation was uncomfortable for a second, but I was so turned on, I didn't really care, and after a moment or two, my body began to adjust. With that taken care of, Tate turned his full attention to the rest of me. As he played with my clit, his fingers fucked me more insistently while Noah kissed me again, reaching down to caress my breasts as well. Combined with the plug, my senses were under complete assault, every part of me engaged and alive as the other people in the room watched. Every person in the room was entirely focused on me, and when I came, the small crowd applauded in appreciation.

Tate disappeared from behind me as my body came down from its high and Noah looked over my shoulder so he could keep me updated. "He's getting a condom," he explained. "Are you ready?"

I nodded in determination. I felt amazing, and I wanted Tate and Noah right there with me. I wanted us all to feel that good, all of us sharing in the pleasure together.

It felt strangely empty when Tate pulled the plug out, but it only lasted for a second before the head of his cock pressed against me. "Relax for me, Belle," he said, rubbing my ass once again. "I'm coming in."

Noah's mouth went to my neck, kissing and sucking me as his hands ran through my hair, and Tate began to push into me, very slowly.

"You're in control now," Tate's voice said from behind me. "Push back when you're ready for more. Let's see how deep you can take me."

Noah lifted his head to look in my eyes. "You can do this, Belle," he said, loud enough for everyone to hear. "Show him what you've got."

My eyes locked on Noah's, I pushed back, impaling myself further on Tate's cock. His wasn't as wide as Noah's, which was part of the reason I'd chosen Tate for this task, but it *was* long, so getting it all in was going to take a while. The other reason I'd chosen this arrangement was that I wanted to be able to watch Noah as it happened.

There was a bit of back and forth as I pushed back and changed my mind. Noah and Tate were both patient with me as the crowd called out their encouragement in a supportive way, and finally, when I felt I truly couldn't stretch any further, he was all the way in.

"How do you feel?" Noah asked, watching me carefully for any signs of discomfort. There was concern in his eyes, but pride too.

"Weird," I admitted. "But it's not bad."

"Are you ready for me too?"

That was what we were doing all of it for, wasn't it? I nodded and he kissed me once more, hard and possessively, before getting to his feet. With him guiding me, we got turned around so that Tate lay on the bed with me on top of him, my back to him and his cock still in my ass. Noah put on his own condom since we were at the club, and when he came back to the bed, he went down on me first, licking at my clit to get me worked up again.

It didn't take much. With the crowd watching, all clearly enjoying themselves, I was ready to give them what they were there for. Even Tessa had Derek's friend's hand down her panties. It looked like she was having a good time too.

"Okay, Belle, let's see if you can handle us both."

Still standing, Noah lined himself up with my empty pussy before leaning down over me, capturing one of my nipples in his mouth.

As he pressed into me, I cried out loudly. "Oh, fuck!"

Noah immediately stilled. "No? Or yes?"

He would stop right there if I wanted him to, but that wasn't what I wanted at all. I hadn't realized it was possible to feel quite so full, or so completely fulfilled. With everyone watching me, I had everything I could ever need. "Yes," I gasped. "More."

Both men moved slowly until I got used to it, Tate beneath me, running his hands across my body and kissing my shoulder and neck, and Noah above me, sucking on my breasts as he thrust into me.

"You're taking us both so well," he praised me, loud enough for every-one to hear. "We both love to be inside you, and everyone else loves to watch you. You're a goddess, Liv, a fucking sex goddess."

He used my real name, but at that moment, I didn't care. I *felt* like a goddess, worshipped by two god-like bodies using me for their own pleasure as I used them for mine.

Both men began to thrust harder as I loosened up even more, and my next orgasm came hard and fast, almost without warning.

"God, I love the way you feel when you come," Noah panted above me, not slowing his pace. He was getting close too.

So was Tate, grunting beneath me. "Come once more for us, baby. Come while we're both coming inside you."

Noah reached down to rub my clit as their words and the feel of their cocks drove me higher once more. As the world exploded around me, they were right there with me, all three of us in a realm of pleasure and satisfaction unlike anything I'd ever known.

When the room finally came back into focus, Noah's face was the first thing I saw, smiling down at me in utter adoration. "That was perfect. You're perfect."

I didn't know if that was true, but one thing I knew for sure: we were definitely perfect for each other.

~Noah~

Once our performance had ended, our little crowd erupted in rapturous applause. Olivia smiled at them all, looking comfortable and confident about everything that just happened, and I couldn't have been more impressed with her or proud of her. She was a dream come true, in every way.

Before the others left, I pulled Derek aside to ask how much longer he was in town.

"I'm heading home on Sunday for Christmas," he told me. "Why?"

"We're going to be doing something on the main stage Saturday night. Would you be interested in taking part?"

He glanced over at Olivia, who was sitting next to Tate on the bed while they laughed about something. "Of course. You've got yourself a good one there."

Didn't I know it.

The other man with them invited Tessa to spend some more time with them and she decided to go, so we agreed to meet back in that room once she'd finished. Tate asked if we needed anything, but when I told him we were fine, he left too, leaving me and Olivia alone. While she used the restroom to clean up, I got her some food and water, and a warm robe to wrap up in.

"You really were incredible," I praised her once she'd finished eating and we both climbed under the covers of the bed where I held her tight against me. "I think we should take it easy the rest of tonight. You might need some time to recover, mentally and physically."

Olivia nodded, snuggling into me in a way that felt like heaven. "That was pretty intense, but amazing. I'm glad I got to do it with you."

"Me too." I had a feeling I was going to need a whole new list of things I wanted to do with her.

Wrapped in each other's arms, we talked about her plans for the rest of the week and then she asked about my plans. "What are you doing for Christmas?"

"Nothing," I admitted. "Tate and I are here until the first week of January, and then we'll head back home for our last semester."

"Do you have any time off over Christmas?" Though the question sounded innocent, I knew Olivia better than that. She obviously had something in mind.

"I've got Christmas Day, and I could probably get a little more if I really wanted to. Why?"

She shrugged in a way that was meant to be casual, but actually meant she was really invested in the answer. I'd seen her do it too many times to be fooled. "London's not that far. You could come with me if you want, for a couple of days, and have Christmas with my family."

Accepting her offer was tempting, mostly because I wanted as much time with her as I could have, but the prospect felt a little daunting too. Although I had spent Christmas with the Hanmers before, I'd never done it without my own family, and certainly never while I was sleeping with their daughter. "You think your parents would be okay with that? I don't want to create any drama at Christmas."

"We're going to tell them about us right away anyway, aren't we?"

The note of doubt in her voice made me pull her tighter. Did she really think I hadn't meant what I'd said? "Of course we are. I just thought we'd wait until I got home, but you know your family better than I do. If you think they'll be happy to see me, then I'd love to spend Christmas with you, Liv."

"They love you," she assured me. "They'll be surprised, but in a good way."

Remembering Jackson's threat against me, I could only hope that was true. However, he had only threatened me if I was going to play with her, if I wasn't serious, and that couldn't be further from the truth. I was dead serious when it came to being with Olivia.

"If you're sure, then I'd love to. I'll talk to the hotel manager tomorrow."

A beautiful, radiant smile spread across Olivia's face, telling me just how much it meant to her. "Great. I'll let my parents know too."

We continued to talk and relax until Tate and Tessa returned, both having enjoyed their nights in different ways, and we all went back to the hotel together. Without either of us saying out loud what our plan was, Olivia came back to my room with me and spent the night beside me. It just felt right. Being there without her would feel wrong.

The rest of the week went by quickly. I had to work most days, and any time not spent working was spent with Olivia. We did a few more Christmas markets in the evenings, the four of us, but I wanted some time alone with her as well, so I asked her if we could spend the day alone together on Friday when I had the day off but Tate didn't.

"We'll go to The Playground in the evening," I promised, knowing she wouldn't want to miss the buzzing weekend night. "But will you trust me to plan the rest of the day?"

Luckily for me, Tessa already had plans with Derek's friend, whose name was Ken, apparently. Along with spending time together at the club, they had exchanged numbers outside of it too. He wanted to spend the day with her before they left the city on Sunday, so it worked out perfectly for all of us.

Olivia texted her parents to tell them that she and I had run into each other and that she'd invited me to London for Christmas. She didn't tell them about us dating; that was news which was better delivered in person.

"And they're okay with it?" I asked when she told me she'd been in touch.

She nodded, though I couldn't help noticing the hint of hesitation in her response. "Yeah. The reply was a little short, but they must just be busy with all the last-minute Christmas prep."

Speaking of last-minute plans, I got an unexpected text from my mom, telling me that they'd heard I was going to London so they were planning to come over for a week as well. Originally, they were going to have a quiet Christmas at home, just them and Eve, so I wasn't sure what changed their mind, but in the end, I was pleased about it. We could tell both sets of parents about me and Olivia at the same time, since whatever we told one pair would end up being shared with the other immediately anyway. They had very few secrets between them, if any.

Finally, Friday came and after having breakfast with Tessa and Tate, Olivia and I headed out on our own.

"Where are we going?" Olivia asked as we stepped out of the hotel and into a waiting taxi. "You sure like your surprises."

"I do," I had to agree. "But I'm pretty sure you'll like this one."

The taxi took us to the train station, and Olivia looked around curiously. "We're going to another city?"

"We're going to another *country*," I corrected her. The best thing about Europe was the ease of travelling from place to place, and in just over an hour, we arrived in Bratislava, the capital of Slovakia.

I had hired a driver for the day, someone who could show us around and translate when necessary, but would leave us alone when we wanted some privacy too. We visited the markets in the Main Square and Hviezdoslav's square, climbed up the steps of the old town hall for the amazing view and went up the hill to the castle. We ate a bit of almost everything at the markets, potato pancakes with different fillings, rolls with roast chicken, and strudels and trdelník for dessert.

There was never a lull in the conversation, never an awkward moment. Things between us were as easy as they had always been, with the added bonus that I got to pull her beneath the mistletoe at the photo booth and kiss her too.

It really was an almost perfect day, and as Olivia rested against me on the train back to Vienna, the thought of a lifetime of days like that with her, and nights like the one we were about to have, made me appreciate my good fortune all over again. I couldn't think of anything better.

That night at The Playground, we took it easy, watching some of the performances on the main stage while we touched each other. There was another glory hole event going on, and Olivia insisted I sign up, saying that she wanted to watch me. I could hardly refuse that request.

Once again, I had no idea who was on the other side of the curtain, but it really didn't matter. With Olivia watching me through the window, enjoying herself just as much as I was, I was only thinking about her anyway.

We were saving our real energy for our own big stage performance the next night. I had come up with a scene that I knew the crowd would love, and I hoped Olivia would love it too. The staff at The Playground had helped me source the costumes I wanted. They didn't even bat an eye. I supposed they must have heard every possible request in the world before.

When I took her to see the costumes at the end of the night, in preparation for the next day, Olivia's first reaction was to laugh, but I didn't miss the spark of excitement in her eyes either. Picking up the wig, she placed it on her head, bright blonde with ringlets which made her look more like the girl I remembered from our childhoods.

"Let me guess," she said, glancing over at the other three costumes. "Goldilocks and the Three Bears?"

Close, but I had made one important amendment. "Our version has a slightly different title."

"Which is?"

I grinned at her in anticipation. "Goldilocks and the Three Cocks."

Chapter Nineteen

THE SHOW

~Olivia~

Though I tried to stay in the moment and enjoy our last days in Vienna, my mind couldn't stop wandering as Tessa, Tate and I wandered through room after room of incredible art and design at the Kunsthistorisches Museum. Noah had to work since he'd had the previous day off, but Tate was free so he'd offered to join us. I was glad he'd come, partly because I enjoyed his company, but mostly because he and Tessa could keep each other entertained while I was distracted by all the thoughts spinning around my head.

That night's upcoming performance sat at the top of my list. Every time I thought about it, excitement, anticipation, lust and nerves all danced together in my stomach, forming a perfect storm. Though I'd performed several times in front of an audience, and even taken part briefly in Derek's stage performance the previous weekend, what Noah had planned for that night would be on a different level. We'd be doing a full performance, in front of a *much* larger crowd than any we'd had in the private rooms, and the whole thing would be centred entirely on me.

The fact that Noah had chosen a theme where I was the star made me feel incredibly special. He had no doubt that other people would find me sexy, and he fully trusted that I could separate my feelings from what would happen on stage. There was no jealousy on his part, only pride that other people wanted me and would take pleasure in being with me. I truly appreciated that, since he had no reason to be jealous. He was the only one I had any interest in going home with afterwards.

Besides our plans for that night, our trip to London kept coming up in my thoughts too. I had messaged both my parents to tell them that I'd invited Noah to join us, and though my mom's response felt fairly typical for her, my dad's was uncharacteristically clipped and tense, even over email. Was he upset with me about something? Had something happened that he hadn't told me about? I wanted to know, but I also didn't want anything negative to intrude on my blissful escape from reality, so I didn't push him on it or follow up. We would have lots of time to talk when I got to London and we could sort it all out then. If something had happened that I really needed to know about, he would have said something.

Noah's reactions whenever I mentioned the trip made it clear that he really did feel a little nervous about it, which I supposed made sense. He'd never been anyone's boyfriend before, and it *would* change the dynamics of our family get-togethers, but I felt confident it would be a change for the better. I had imagined Noah and I being together for years, and in every one of those imaginings, our parents had been thrilled with it. I couldn't see why that wouldn't be the case in real life too.

"What are you thinking about, Liv?" Tate's voice pierced through my musings as I stood in front of a painting without seeing it, my mind far away. "You've been staring at that picture of a woman making out with a cloud for ages."

I blinked in surprise as the painting in front of me came into focus, and I realized that was pretty much exactly what I was looking at. *Jupiter and Io*, the information card said, which didn't really explain anything. Why *was* the naked woman kissing a cloud? I needed to brush up on my mythology.

"I'm thinking about tonight," I answered honestly as we moved on. "I'm excited, but a little nervous too."

"I don't think you'd be human if you weren't nervous," Tate replied with a laugh. "But you're going to be amazing. As soon as we're up there, you're going to love it."

I had a feeling he was right. I just needed to stop fixating on it.

"I still don't get it," Tessa said, shaking her head as we entered the next room. "How can you guys know you're going to fuck each other later, when you're not seeing each other, and not find that weird?"

"Tessa!" I glanced around to make sure we hadn't been overheard, but luckily, everyone else seemed caught up in their own conversations.

"It's like acting," Tate explained, not at all bothered by Tessa's bluntness. "Actors kiss each other on film all the time, even if they hate each other. This is just going a step further, and Liv and I definitely don't hate each other, do we?"

He gave me a warm smile, different from the way he'd smiled at me before our date and before Noah and I got together. Then, there had been interest and attraction, but that afternoon, his smile merely felt friendly.

"We definitely don't, and for tonight, I'm really glad to know I can trust all the men involved. It would be weirder with a stranger, at least for such a big crowd."

"Are you coming to watch?" Tate asked Tessa, and she nodded, which didn't surprise me. She and I had already talked about it earlier.

"Ken's going to be there to watch Derek, so we said we'd watch together and then he's got a private room for us afterwards. *Completely* private."

Tessa had told me over breakfast how much fun she was having with Ken. He had come to Vienna to go to The Playground with Derek, who was a veteran of the scene, but Ken wasn't a natural exhibitionist. He liked to watch, but he preferred his own encounters in private, which suited Tessa perfectly. They'd spent the night together at our hotel the night before.

Unfortunately, he and Derek were flying home to Australia the next day, so it seemed that would be the end of their encounter. They'd exchanged numbers but Tessa was realistic about the whole thing. "If it ends up just being this week, that's fine. If we keep in touch and something else happens, even better."

It made me really happy that she had ended up with a good experience out of our trip too, though I knew I had definitely gotten the better deal in the end.

Finally, the time came to head back to the hotel to meet Noah after his shift, and after we had dinner, which Noah insisted I eat even though I wasn't particularly hungry, we made our way back to The Playground for the big night.

The costumes Noah had arranged were ridiculous yet sexy at the same time. My Goldilocks outfit consisted of the blonde wig I'd tried on the previous night and a dress unlike any I'd seen before. The top of it came up *beneath* my breasts, leaving them completely exposed, and the skirt was frilly and girly and *short*. Of course, I wore nothing beneath it. Thankfully, Noah had also arranged for a silky robe for me to wear over top of it while we moved about the club, saving the big reveal for once we got on stage.

The 'bear' costumes for the men were hardly less revealing. They had pants that looked like shaggy, furry bear legs, which opened in the front to get their cocks out when the time came. There were also two furry sleeves for their arms that tied together across their chests, but otherwise, their upper halves were the other kind of bare, leaving their chests and abs on full display. The look was finished off with headbands with little bear ears on them, which were kind of adorable. The overall impression was somehow really sweet and *really* sexy at the same time. Noah and Tate drew a lot of looks as we walked together through the Plaza, and when we found Derek in the lobby outside the stage, he was already dressed in his costume too.

Looking around at the three kind, handsome, virile and utterly desirable men, I really couldn't believe my luck. This was going to be a night I would never forget.

~Noah~

Olivia looked just as incredible as I imagined she would in that costume. There wasn't a man in the club who wasn't going to get hard at the sight of her. She was a star, *my* star, and I couldn't wait for her to prove it to herself and to everyone else there.

Waiting for our turn to be called onstage, I quickly reviewed the plotline of our performance with the others. There was no script, we were just going to wing it, but we needed to know when to make our entrances, as it were.

Tessa and Derek's friend went inside to get seated, and when a member of staff came to tell us they were ready for us, I turned to Olivia. "It's not too late to change your mind. If you don't want to go, we don't have to."

To my relief and my great pride, she shook her head firmly. "I want to. I'm ready."

Side-by-side, we walked into a completely packed room, the rows of seats filled and the air buzzing with excitement. Adrenaline pumped through my veins at the idea of all those people watching us, and from the way Olivia's eyes gleamed, I knew she felt it too.

"Good luck, everyone," I told them as we took our places at the bottom of the stage. "Have fun."

Olivia headed up first. The stage had been set up with a bed and some chairs, and a little wood stove, to look like the bears' house from the fairy tale. Olivia walked up onto the stage, still in her robe, and took a look around.

"It's raining so hard out in the woods today," she announced to the crowd. "I got so wet on my way here."

Not everyone in the crowd spoke English, but those who did hooted and hollered in appreciation at her opening.

Olivia looked around the stage curiously. "I'm so glad I came across this house, but it doesn't look like anyone's home. I guess I'll just make myself comfortable then."

What that, she took off the robe, revealing her very skimpy 'dress' underneath, and the applause from the crowd got even louder. Watching them watching her had me hard already, and I was sure Derek and Tate were just the same.

"It's a little bit chilly," she said, rubbing her arms, which pushed her breasts together, the nipples already hard beneath the gaze of the crowd. "Maybe I can start a fire."

Totally in character, she went over to the stove and bent over to look at it, letting the crowd see that she wasn't wearing anything underneath her skirt, and they shouted and cheered once more. The audience was hanging on her every word and movement, every eye in the room on her.

That was Derek's cue, so I gave him a nod and the tall Australian lumbered up the stairs in his bear costume to more applause from the crowd. The excitement in the room was palpable, everyone eager to see exactly how things were going to play out.

"What are you doing in my house?" he growled, and Olivia jumped up in surprise, spinning around to face him. Her eyes scanned his body with intent, her head moving up and down dramatically for the benefit of the people in the back.

"I'm so sorry, Mr...?"

"Grumpy Bear," he answered, keeping in character as he folded his arms across his chest. "Who the fuck are you?"

Olivia twirled one of the ringlets in her wig as she gave him an innocent smile. "I'm Goldilocks, Mr Grumpy. I just wanted to get out of the rain. I'm all wet."

The crowd reacted once more, perfectly anticipating where this was going.

"Are you?" Derek's tone was still angry, but also a little intrigued. "I better check for myself."

He walked over to her and reached up her skirt, lifting it as he swiped his hand between her legs, then brought it up to his mouth, licking his fingers as the crowd cheered.

A smile crossed the grumpy Derek's face. "Well, you were right about that. Lucky for you, I think I can help."

He bent her over again, her hands on the stove, just as she had been when he walked in, as he pulled out his ready dick from his pants and a condom from his pocket. There were murmurs of excitement as he rolled it on.

"Let's see just how wet you can get now," he said as he thrust into her from behind.

If I hadn't already been hard, that would have done it, as it clearly did for the audience. Olivia moaned as he fucked her, hard and fast for a couple of minutes, before he groaned in a fake orgasm, as planned.

When he pulled out of her, he slapped her lightly on the ass. "There you go."

Olivia stood up, adjusted her skirt, and addressed the crowd conspiratorially from behind her hand. "There *he* goes, he means. A little too fast."

Laughter and applause met her remark, as Tate walked up on stage next.

"What's going on here?" His attitude was goofy and smiley, the opposite of Derek's. "Were you having fun without me, Grumpy?"

"She's all yours now," Derek replied, taking a seat on the chair, his dick still out. "Goldie, this is Funtime Bear."

Olivia gave Tate an appreciative look of his own. "You guys must have a really good home gym."

The crowd laughed again, which quickly turned into moans of appreciation as Tate sat down on the other chair and pulled Olivia down onto his waiting, covered dick. She rode him like an expert, and I was afraid she was actually going to make him come, he seemed to be enjoying himself so much. But after a few minutes, she looked at the wristband on her arm as if it was a watch and looked out at the crowd again.

"This one is too slow."

More laughter greeted her as I walked up on the stage too. "You guys aren't having an orgy without me, are you?"

Olivia hopped off of Tate and came over to me, her eyes bright with excitement. "Hi, I'm Goldilocks."

"Horny Bear," I introduced myself.

She tried not to laugh even as the crowd did. "You sound like you might be just my speed, Horny."

"I think the problem, little girl, is that one bear will never satisfy you. You need all three, all at once."

A roar of approval swelled through the room as we all got ourselves into position. I rolled on a condom of my own before laying down on the bed in the centre of the room. Olivia climbed on top of me, taking me inside her as she smiled down at me. "You feel amazing, Noah," she whispered, just for me. "Just right."

I grinned up at her as Tate approached from behind, having covered himself with lube. He went in with his fingers first again, and I could feel him pressing into her, rubbing against my dick that was already inside her through her internal walls. And once his dick was inside too, Derek got up on the bed above me, removing his condom as Olivia took him into her mouth.

There were no more words, no more lines as we all fucked my beautiful girl together, filling her to bursting. The crowd went quiet too other than low sighs and moans and groans which mingled with our own, creating one continuous soundtrack of sex and pleasure throughout the room.

Olivia came with all of us inside her, her body shuddering and shattering beneath the combined force of all three of us. My hands caressed her, supporting her through it, but no one was stopping yet, not until we all reached our end.

Tate was the first to break, a few minutes later. "I'm close, guys," he breathed, and I looked up at Derek who nodded down at me. He could go too, and so could I.

Gently, we disengaged ourselves from Olivia, bringing her to the front of the stage and putting her on her knees while we surrounded her. Tate and I yanked off our condoms and all three of us stroked ourselves until we came on her, one by one, until she was covered with the evidence of just how much she turned us all on.

The applause was deafening, several in the crowd on their feet as Olivia stood up and took a well-deserved bow.

I'd arranged a private room for us where I took her afterwards, just me and her, and we showered together, cleaning each other up. With that taken care of, I took her to the bed in the small room. There, we had sex again, just the two of us, without the condom that time, the memory of the performance still fresh in our minds. When I came inside her, I felt so invincible that I couldn't imagine how anything in the world could ever bring me down again.

Chapter Twenty

CHRISTMAS EVE

~Olivia~

Lying in bed in the private room with Noah felt so comfortable that I could have happily gone to sleep right there. After everything that had happened, I almost couldn't believe how relaxed I felt, but Noah had made it the perfect experience. He ensured I was prepared beforehand, supported throughout, and cared for afterwards. His own comedown, if he had one, was secondary to my wellbeing, and I knew without him having to tell me that it would be that way for as long as we were together.

It had taken him a long time to give himself to me fully, but now that he had, he was all in. I never did anything halfway, and neither did Noah Stamer.

But while The Playground was for many things, sleeping wasn't one of them, so when the time came that we had agreed to meet Tessa and Tate back out in the Plaza, I reluctantly got up.

"Do you want me to carry you, Liv?" Noah offered, and I had to smile. He really would if I asked him to, but I wasn't quite that worn out.

"No, I'm okay. Let's go back to the hotel."

We found the others having one last drink in the Plaza with Derek and Ken. Tessa and Ken said their goodbyes and Derek gave me a warm hug. "I had a great time playing with you, Liv."

I looked up in surprise as he said my real name, and he laughed, pointing to Tessa.

"She couldn't keep your aliases straight."

Tessa gave me a sheepish shrug, but I couldn't really say I was surprised. She had struggled with it from the beginning.

Noah and Derek shook hands too. "If you guys are ever in Australia, let me know," Derek said. "Though it's not quite this level, we do have some fun places. I could show you around."

"We will," Noah promised before pointing to a small signet ring that Derek wore on his pinky finger. "What's that for? I've seen a few people here wearing them."

Derek held out his hand to show us the ring properly. "It's kind of a secret symbol to let people know this is your kink, a way for us to identify each other in public. I bought it here at The Playground."

I didn't need to ask Noah if he was going to get one too. He obviously intended to, and the idea gave me a little thrill too: a public yet secret declaration of exactly who we were. Who knew what new adventures it might lead to?

The night must have taken more out of me than I realized because by the time I woke up in Noah's bed, the late morning sun already streamed through the window. Noah had left for work hours earlier, leaving me a sweet note to tell me so.

The rest of our time in Vienna passed in a blur. We made one last trip to The Playground on Monday evening, our last night there, but we didn't participate in anything. Topping Saturday's performance would have been difficult, but I had a feeling that given the time, Noah would come up with something, and I couldn't wait to find out what it would be. Our future together was wide open, and that thrilled me.

On the morning of the 24th, Tessa and I said our goodbyes to Tate. Noah had invited him to come to London with us, but he declined, saying he had to work. "Not all of us are the boss' son who can ask for extra days off whenever we feel like it," he teased Noah.

Noah accepted that, but he told me afterwards that as long as they'd known each other, Tate always turned him down when he was invited to spend Christmas with him. "I think it's a hard time of year for him and he'd rather deal with it alone."

Imagining the happy, confident Tate I had gotten to know over the past two weeks as a guy with hidden demons wasn't easy, but I supposed we all had our secrets. Hopefully, it wouldn't be too long before he met someone he trusted enough to help him tame them.

Noah and I said goodbye to Tessa at the airport as she boarded her flight back to New York to spend Christmas with her family. "Thanks for inviting me on this trip, Liv," she said, giving me a tight hug. "It was definitely an experience."

"That's one word for it," I agreed, squeezing her back. "Thank you for not judging me, Tessa."

"Oh, I still think all this shit is weird as fuck," she said with a laugh. "But it obviously makes you happy, so I'm happy for you."

That was the sign of a true friend. I told her I'd see her back at college in January, and Noah and I waved as she went through her check-in.

Finally, Noah and I got on our own flight, heading for London and the family Christmas that awaited us there. When I had booked the flight, I got a regular economy seat, but Noah had us both upgraded to business class.

"Is this really necessary for such a short flight?" I teased him once we were settled in our seats. "Or are you just incapable of mingling with the commoners?"

He smirked back at me. "Hey, this is already slumming it. Normally, I use my dad's private plane."

When I shook my head at him, Noah took hold of my hand.

"This is one of the best things about being with you, Liv. The kink is great, don't get me wrong, but I also love that you don't care about my money. I think that's another reason why I haven't really dated before.

At the clubs, no one knows who I am, they treat me just like any other guy there, but the women that I meet at college or through friends, they all know my position as well as my name. It's hard to find someone who doesn't look at me with dollar signs in their eyes, but you never have. That's part of the reason that our friendship was so special to me, and why it hurt so much when I thought I'd lost it."

That was a pretty big declaration from Noah, and I'd had no idea he felt that way. Most of the time, I honestly forgot just how rich he was. To me, he was simply the boy I grew up with who became the sexy, irresistible man sitting across from me. His bank account didn't matter to me at all.

However, I noticed that while he said he loved that I didn't care about the money, he still hadn't actually said he loved *me*.

On my side, I had no doubts. I loved him, fully and completely. Part of me always had. But though Noah had promised we would be together, love was a word he hadn't said yet, and I didn't want to put him on the spot by declaring how I felt. I didn't want him to feel like he had to say it back if he wasn't ready.

The flight didn't take long, and soon, we were landing at Heathrow and getting in the car that Noah had arranged for us. My dad had offered to come and pick us up, but Noah insisted that Jackson making the trip would be a waste of his time. The car would take us to the hotel where our families were staying, the flagship Stamer hotel in central London that had been indirectly responsible for our parents meeting in the first place. My dad and Cole had come to London to work on plans for the building but weren't happy with the proposals they'd received, and that was when they met my mom and Gemma, who were just getting started in hotel design.

I'd heard the story many times, every time we stayed there, but I never got tired of it. I loved their love stories, and as Noah and I walked into the lobby, hand-in-hand, part of me hoped that someday, we might take our own kids to the hotel in Vienna and tell them about our story too.

I might just leave out a few of the details about The Playground, but I suspected our parents probably left a few things out of their stories too.

As Noah picked up our keys from reception, I had to shake my head at myself. I was definitely getting ahead of myself, thinking about kids and our future life together. First, we still had to let our families know we were dating.

When we got to the door of my parents' suite, where we'd been told everyone would be waiting to greet us, Noah let go of my hand, and I looked over at him questioningly.

"Let's say hello to everyone first," he suggested. "Then, we can tell them."

I didn't see why we couldn't walk hand-in-hand into the room and announce it that way, but if he didn't feel comfortable with that, I wouldn't push him. He took my bag from me as I knocked on the door, and Gemma was the one who answered.

"Happy Christmas!" She swept me up in a big hug before releasing me and embracing her son instead, who endured her attention with good humour.

A chorus of greetings rang out as we were quickly surrounded. I wished Noelle and Eve a happy birthday as well as a merry Christmas, and as soon as I got the words out, another voice cut in, warm and cheerful as always.

"Merry Christmas, Livy. I'm so happy to see you." My dad pulled me into a big bear hug, lifting me off my feet as he spun me around, just like he used to when I was a little girl. When he put me down, he scanned me over quickly, as if he was checking I was still in one piece. "It's going to take a little while to get used to the new hair."

He had seen my new darker hair in pictures, but that was his first time seeing it in person. "Do you like it?"

"Well, you know I'm partial to blondes." He grinned over at my mom, who rolled her eyes as she came up to hug me too. "But you look beautiful either way, honey."

"How was your trip?" my mom asked. "Was it what you hoped for?"

"Even better." I couldn't help glancing back at Noah, who was talking quietly with his dad. His face seemed to have gone paler than usual as they whispered back and forth, and my brow furrowed. What was that about? Trying not to worry, I looked back at my parents. "Did you know Noah was going to be in Vienna?"

My mom and dad exchanged glances that also seemed slightly cautious. "We did," my mom told me. "But we didn't want you to feel obligated to spend time together if you didn't want to. The two of you didn't seem like you were on the best of terms lately. How did you run into each other?"

"It happened literally as soon as we arrived. He was working in the reception of the hotel when we got there to check in."

"And things are okay between the two of you?" my dad asked, his lips tightening as he looked over at Noah, who still seemed a little uneasy.

"They're really good." He couldn't have given me a much better opening than that, so I didn't see the point in putting off the announcement any longer. "Actually, I've got something to tell you all."

I said it loud enough that everyone could hear, and they all turned to look at me as I gestured for Noah to join me.

He swallowed nervously and for a moment, I thought he might actually refuse, though I couldn't imagine why. Finally, he did come over, though he didn't touch me. He leaned over and whispered in my ear instead. "This might not be the best time, Liv."

What did that mean? He kept saying that, and I was starting to feel like he didn't really want to tell people at all. "Well, I have to say something now," I whispered back. "They're all waiting."

He looked out at the group of people watching us with a grimace. "I think I should talk to your dad first."

What century were we in? He didn't need my dad's permission to date me.

"Don't be a drama queen," Noelle called out. "Tell us already. Are you pregnant?"

"Noelle!" My mom shushed her before turning back to me with concern in her eyes. "You're not, are you?"

"Of course not!" Why was that the first thought they jumped to? At least on the plus side, what I actually had to say would sound even better after Noelle got them worried. I gave Noah a reassuring smile. "It'll be fine, don't worry."

"Livy?" My dad's eyes moved between me and Noah warily. "What's going on?"

I took Noah's hand, which wasn't all that easy when he stood so stiffly beside me, and smiled at everyone. "It's nothing bad. In fact, it's great news. Noah and I are seeing each other now."

I wasn't sure exactly what I expected, but it definitely wasn't for all the adults in the room to immediately look over at my dad, whose face went nearly as pale as Noah's had a moment ago.

"Jackson…" my mom said, putting her hand on his arm, but he pushed it off, which wasn't like him at all.

"Noelle and Eve, could you please go watch some TV in the other room for a few minutes?" My dad's voice was calm but cold, not really sounding like him either.

My sister shrugged and did as she was asked, and Eve followed, but not before giving me a smile. "Congratulations, I guess. I mean, he's my brother and it's kinda gross, but if it's what you want, then congratulations."

"Thanks, Eve." I smiled back at her as the two of them went into one of the bedrooms and closed the door behind them. Even after the door was closed, nobody spoke, and it started to annoy me, so I addressed our parents all at once. "What's the problem?"

Once again, everyone looked at my dad, and finally, he answered me, though he kept his eyes locked on Noah instead of me. "The problem is that he doesn't deserve you. You have no idea what he's really like."

"What?" I looked over at Noah, who did his best to hold my dad's gaze despite his obvious discomfort. "I know exactly who he is. Noah has never lied to me."

"Are you sure about that?" My dad's voice was growing warmer, but the warmth came from anger rather than affection. "Has he told you about his list?"

His list? For a moment, I stared at him blankly, until finally realization washed over me, cold and strong, knocking all the wind out of me.

The list. The list that I never got. My dad's email address in Noah's computer, and my distraction when Tessa texted me.

My stomach lurched as it hit me all at once. *Oh, God.* I sent my dad Noah's list. And it would have come from Noah's email address, so he thought Noah had sent it, and Noah would have had no idea.

This was a complete disaster. My dad had obviously already made up his mind about Noah, and what would Noah think when he realized the whole thing was all my fault?

How on earth could I explain any of this to any of them?

~Noah~

I couldn't imagine a way this could be going much worse. After my mom let me go and I gave Eve a quick hug, my dad pulled me to the side. "I know you've been busy with work and everything so I haven't pushed you, but now that you're here, you're going to need to talk to Jackson about that list you sent him."

My eyebrows drew together in confusion as I glanced over at Olivia's dad, who was still giving her a huge hug. "Jackson? What list? I didn't send him anything."

My dad gave me an incredulous look. "Playing dumb won't help, Noah. I assumed you sent it in error, which is why I sent you that text. Didn't you check your sent messages?"

"I did, but there wasn't anything there." I still didn't have a clue what he was talking about. "What does he think I sent him?"

Though his expression was still serious, I didn't miss the way his lips twitched. "I believe you titled it your 'fuckit' list?"

What? It felt like all the blood in my body stopped in its place, leaving me cold and numb. "That's... that's not possible."

My mind raced as I tried to figure out what happened. I would never send that list to anyone, but somehow, it must have been sent, since there was no way my dad would know about it otherwise. I didn't even have a copy of it myself, it lived on a server where Tate put it and shared the link with me.

Tate? I zeroed in on my friend in my mind, looking for a suspect. Did *he* send it to Jackson? Why would he? I thought he was happy for me and Olivia, but had he actually tried to mess with us? It didn't make much sense, but neither did any of the other possibilities I tried to come up with.

"I don't know how it happened, but it definitely did," my dad told me. "You owe him a few drinks to get over the shock he got when he opened it up."

I still didn't understand. "And it came from *my* email?"

My dad nodded, which pretty much eliminated the idea of Tate sending it. He didn't have access to my emails. No one should. "Jackson called me into his office to ask if the list was some kind of joke."

Hope rose inside me for just a second. "What did you say?"

His critical look killed that hope off immediately. "I told him I didn't know anything about it, and that he should ask you himself. But I assume it's no joke, and I can only say that having it all in writing is a stupid idea, Noah."

I knew that. I had thought so from the start. *Fuck.* This was really bad. Now Olivia's dad thought I was some kind of sexual deviant, which, though it might be true, was hardly the image of me I wanted him to have, especially when Olivia was eager to tell everyone that we were seeing each other.

In fact, she seemed determined to do so right at that moment, unfortunately. Before I could answer my dad, Olivia announced to the room that she had something to tell everyone and beckoned me over to join her.

My stomach felt like lead as I walked over to her and whispered to her that I should talk to her dad first. I wasn't sure what I would say, but I should say *something* before he found out that I was dating his daughter. I really did want to keep my balls.

But Olivia announced it anyway, despite my objections, and Jackson reacted exactly as I would have expected him to, knowing what I knew. He said I didn't deserve her, and he was right: I didn't deserve the Olivia that he knew, the one I thought had known, the sweet and innocent perfect daughter she seemed to be to the rest of the world.

But the Olivia I had gotten to know in Vienna, the deeply kinky one, the one who accepted me just as I was, I definitely deserved her, and she deserved me too. We were made for each other.

How could I explain that to her dad without exposing her too? Embracing her kink was one thing; having her parents find out about it was another thing entirely, and I didn't want to be the one to out her if she didn't want them to know.

Though I still didn't understand how the list could have been sent to him in the first place, clearly it had, and all I could do was take responsibility for it.

"I can imagine that list was a surprise to you, Jackson." I kept my tone as non-confrontational as I could as I looked him straight in the eye. "I didn't mean to send it to you. I only found out just now from my dad that you received it, or I would have called earlier to discuss it with you."

He looked at my dad for confirmation, and received it in the form of a curt nod.

"I figured you didn't mean to send it to me," Jackson told me, his face tight. "The fact that you did bothers me less than the fact that it exists at all. It's your life, you can do what you want with it, so I wasn't going to bring it up. Your personal life was none of my business when you were just my friend's son, but when you tell me that you're dating my daughter? That's when it becomes my business."

"It's still not your business, Dad." Olivia squeezed my hand as she responded to her father, letting me know she had my back and had no intention of backing down.

"I'm sorry, Livy, but I disagree. What that list shows me is a complete disregard for women. Anyone who could make a list like that is someone who views women as a means to an end, who's interested in nothing but his own enjoyment. " He turned back to me with a look that could only be classified as disgust. "Did you even know the names of half the women you used to check things off this list?"

"That's not fair," Olivia protested, but I shook my head at her.

"It's okay, Liv. Let him finish." I didn't like hearing it either, but he obviously needed to get it off his chest, and I wanted to know exactly what he thought of me. That would be important if we were going to find a way to move past this.

Jackson took a deep breath, clearly trying to measure his words too. "I understand that you're both adults and I can't stop you from doing whatever you want to do, but I'm also not going to pretend to be happy about this. Olivia is one of the most precious people in the world to me, and she deserves a man who will cherish and respect her. Any man who would write that list can't truly understand what those words mean."

He choked up as he finished speaking and turned away from us while Holly put her arm around him. I glanced over at my dad, looking for advice or a little help, but he merely raised his eyebrows at me. That simple gesture told me he wasn't going to fight my battles for me, that he believed I could defend myself, so I would have to try to do so.

"I think we can all agree the list was a bad idea," I began, trying to lighten the mood a little, but the words fell flat. Jackson didn't acknowledge them at all, so I kept talking. "I'm not going to make any excuses for it. A stupid joke between my friend and I got out of hand, sitting around one night coming up with the craziest things we could think of. Have I done the things checked off on that list? Yes. Did I know the names of everyone I did them with? No."

Olivia shot me a desperate look and I could practically hear her in my head though she hadn't spoken a word. *This isn't helping, Noah!*

I forged ahead anyway. "For a long time, I thought there was something wrong with me. Sex wasn't exciting. Relationships didn't appeal to me. There's a reason I've never had a girlfriend before, and it's because I didn't think I would ever find anyone who could accept all the different parts of me, the good and the bad, the vanilla and the kink."

Jackson winced as I said the word, but he did look back over at me at least, giving me the chance to speak just as I had let him have his say.

"Last Christmas, Liv told me she was interested in a relationship with me, and I turned her down because I thought she deserved someone like you described: someone who would put her on a pedestal and cherish and respect her for who she was. Someone not like me."

Jackson looked over at Olivia in surprise as I continued speaking. Obviously, she had never told him anything about the previous year, but neither did she contradict me. She simply leaned into me, giving me her full support.

"However, something magical happened in Vienna. Liv got to know the real me, the full me, and she still liked me anyway. I got to know the real her too. You asked if she's seen the list? She has. I don't want to hide anything from her. I want her to know everything about me because I *do* respect her. I *do* cherish her. And more than that, I love her."

The words were out of my mouth before I could stop them, and Olivia looked up at me, her eyes wide. That wasn't exactly the way I had intended to tell her; hell, I wasn't even sure if I had fully realized it until that moment, but once the words were out there, I couldn't deny it.

Of course I loved her. I'd be a fool not to, and I was done with being an idiot. If nothing else, that was one lesson I'd taken on board from the last two weeks.

"What Liv and I do in private is our own business, but if you're worried that I'm going to hurt her or treat her badly, then I promise, Jackson, you have nothing to worry about. It's the last thing I want to do. I love her, and I want to be with her, and I hope you can accept that because I'm not giving her up, not for you and not for anything in the world."

While Jackson processed that, his lips tight together as he thought it over, I glanced over at my own parents. My dad had his usual smirk back on as he gave me a nod, while my mom had her hands over her mouth with tears in her eyes. It looked like she finally knew exactly what I'd called her to talk about the week before.

When I looked back, Holly gave me a small smile too before turning back to Jackson whose expression was still a little pained, but maybe slightly less than it had been.

"Livy?" He looked over at Olivia who was still standing next to me, still holding my hand. "Is this really what you want?"

She nodded at him firmly, tears in her eyes too. "I love him too, Dad. And about the list..."

I tried to interrupt, worried she was going to say something she might regret later, but she shook her head at me. She had always been stubborn, and I loved that about her. If she had something to say, I couldn't stop her.

But when the words came out, they were a total surprise to me. "I'm the one who sent it to you, by mistake. I didn't know I did it until just now."

"What?" That question came from nearly everyone in the room at the same time.

Olivia turned to me with an apologetic look. "I'm so sorry, Noah. I meant to send it to myself, but I got distracted and I must have hit my dad's email address instead."

Stunned silence filled the room for a beat, and then another, and then... my dad started to laugh.

Everyone looked over at him in surprise. My dad laughing was not a common occurrence. When he did, a chuckle or a bit of a smirk was usually all that we'd get, but this was much more than that. He was full-on laughing, his face bright with amusement.

My mom began to laugh too, and so did Holly, unable to keep from joining in. Jackson just looked at them all in disbelief, until my dad spoke to him. "Come on, Jackson, that's funny. Looks like your little Olivia has definitely grown up."

The girl in question next to me blushed as her dad looked over at us once more, but at last, his lips twitched too. "I suppose it *is* a little funny."

With relief flooding my body, I laughed too, and Olivia looked up at me in surprise and a bit of disbelief. "You're not mad at me?"

"Oh, we're definitely going to have a talk about how email works later, Liv, not to mention private documents. But right now? You just said you love me. How mad could I be?"

Her look of concern melted away as she looked around the room, at everyone closest to us, all sharing a laugh at our expense, and finally, she began to laugh too.

That was my breaking point. She looked so beautiful, so joyous as she realized everything was going to be okay, that I had to kiss her. I couldn't help it.

It didn't matter that our parents were there to see it. They were going to have to get used to it, because I intended to kiss her many, many more times for a long time to come.

Let them watch.

Chapter Twenty-One

New Year's Eve

One week later

~Olivia~

Every time a car drove up to the front door of the hotel, I perked up, hoping to see the face I was waiting for, but each time, I was disappointed.

"Seriously, Liv!" Noelle complained next to me as I sank back into my seat for the fiftieth time. "He'll be here soon. Calm down."

I shot her a dirty look. "That's easy for you to say. When you're in love, you'll feel differently. I guarantee it."

After a wonderful Christmas with our families, Noah had to return to Vienna on the 26th to get back to work, but he promised to come back and spend New Year's Eve in London with me before I flew home with my parents. We already had plans to see each other when we got back to the United States too, but he said it wouldn't feel right if we didn't see in the New Year together, and I couldn't agree more. This was going to be *our* year, our first year together and hopefully the first of many to come. I wanted to kiss him at midnight and I wanted him in my bed afterwards too.

Things were still a tiny bit awkward between my dad and Noah, but not nearly as bad as they might have been, and I felt sure that with time, it would all blow over entirely. When he saw the way Noah treated me over Christmas, he seemed to relax a little, and the more time we all spent together, the better it would get.

Gemma was delighted for us both, and Cole also gave me a warm welcome to my new role as his son's girlfriend. "We might need to rethink you working at Stamer Hotels, though. I can say from personal experience that working with your spouse can be a little distracting."

Over my head, he and Gemma shared a rather heated smile.

My mom also cornered me one night in the hotel after Noah had gone back to Vienna. "I don't need any details. I just want to make sure that whatever you two are doing, you're being smart and safe about it."

"We are," I promised, trying not to blush at the idea of my mom ever finding out exactly what Noah and I had done together.

"And it's definitely what you want? I don't agree with everything your dad said, but that's one thing we're in total agreement on: you deserve someone who makes you happy, Liv."

On that point, I could tell her the full truth: "No one in the world could make me happier."

"Then I'm thrilled for you both." She gave me a hug as she chuckled. "Noah Stamer, huh? Who would have thought?"

I would have. I always had.

At last, another taxi pulled up and Noah appeared from the back, looking just as handsome as ever. In fact, he somehow looked even better now that I knew for sure he was mine. His eyes lit up as I came out the hotel's front door, and as he wrapped his arms around me, I inhaled his familiar scent and immediately felt whole again.

"Have you had fun without me, Liv?" he murmured as he kissed the top of my head.

"Not nearly as much fun as I have with you," I teased him, pressing my hips against him, feeling him already starting to get a little hard.

"Let's wait for that until there's no chance of your dad interrupting us," he told me wryly. "The last thing I need is Jackson walking in on us."

He took a step back and finally gave me a proper look, his eyes softening as he did. In preparation for our night out, I had braided tinsel into my hair, just like I did at Isabel's house the previous Christmas on the night I tried to seduce him. I hadn't known if he would remember, but from the look on his face, it seemed pretty clear he did.

"It's going to be torture to wait until we get back, but at least tonight, I won't have to resist the temptation. I'll drop my bag off upstairs and we can head out."

We had a full evening planned. Gemma had heard about a café in Greenwich from some of her London clients called Tables & Fables. They had an open mic night where authors did readings from upcoming books, so we'd decided to check that out, and afterwards, we'd be heading into the centre of the city for the New Year's fireworks. Cole had booked us a capsule on the London Eye to see the fireworks from a bird's eye view, the kind of thing that only the super-rich could pull off, but none of that mattered to me. I would have been just as happy to stand in the crowd along the Southbank, jostling for position with all the other happy revellers. As long as I spent the night with Noah, it would be perfect.

The little café bustled with life as we all walked in, the air filled with excitement and mouth-watering smells. My stomach began to rumble almost immediately. Thankfully, Gemma had already reserved us a table or there wouldn't have been anywhere to sit at all. It looked like mostly locals and regulars, everyone seemed to know each other and there was some kind of celebration going on in one corner of the room. The whole atmosphere was full of hope and happiness, perfect to celebrate the New Year.

Noah and I offered to go up to the counter and place the order for our whole group and a handsome older man served us, offering an apology before we even said anything.

"Welcome to Tables & Fables. My name's Jonty and I don't usually work here: it's my wife's café but she's swamped tonight so I'm helping out. I therefore apologize straight off in case I get anything or everything wrong."

Noah and I both laughed and assured him we could be flexible. After placing the order, which Jonty reviewed with us twice just to make sure he'd got it right, he handed over the card machine for Noah to pay, and that was when I noticed the small ring on his pinky finger, a perfect match for the one on Noah's hand, the one he had bought on our last night at The Playground.

Noah obviously noticed it too. "Is your wife someone you met in the scene?" he asked curiously, flashing his own ring so Jonty would know what he meant.

Jonty gave us an even warmer smile than before. "It's not how we met, but we're both involved. What about you two?"

Noah gave me a quick affectionate look before replying. "We've known each other forever but we're just beginning to explore that side of things together. I don't know anyone who's married and still doing it, so that's inspiring to hear."

Jonty nodded, leaning forward to us across the counter, happy to talk with us about this even though he obviously had other customers waiting. "For a while, we tried to turn that part of ourselves off, but it didn't work. We still loved each other but there wasn't that same excitement. Now that we've embraced it again, things are better than ever."

"And there's never any kind of jealousy or problems because of it?" I asked curiously. Although Noah and I hadn't experienced that yet, I could understand how it might happen over time.

However, Jonty shook his head firmly. "As long as you've got a solid foundation of love, respect and communication, there's no reason for jealousy. It's bringing us both pleasure, no matter who else is involved, and at the end of the day, it's always the two of us."

That was exactly what I wanted to hear, and Noah and I smiled at each other once more, even more hopeful for our own future than we had been before.

"Jonty, there's going to be a queue out the door if you don't get moving," a new voice cut in. It belonged to a beautiful woman with long, blonde hair who came up to Jonty with a teasing smile. "Did you break the card machine again?"

"Not this time," he replied with a laugh. "I was just having a quick chat with these young American customers who were curious about our London lifestyle."

He gestured to Noah's ring and the woman immediately understood what he meant.

"This is my wife, Billie," Jonty introduced us and we all said hello.

"I'd love to stay and chat," she told us. "But as you can see, we're chock-a-block in here tonight! I will say, though, that if I was ten years younger, I'd be all over you."

We all laughed as Noah took the compliment in stride. "Maybe another time. I'm game."

Billie raised her eyebrows in amusement. "I didn't mean you."

Her eyes moved to me, and my cheeks flushed as everyone laughed again, heat spreading through my body at the suggestion. That was something I hadn't tried yet, but maybe in the future, I would. I still had a ways to go to learn exactly what my likes and limits were.

We returned to the table and our families, and as we watched Billie and Jonty laughing and teasing each other while they continued to serve the café's customers, Noah put his arm around me. Other people made it work, being committed to each other and still embracing their kink, so there was no reason we couldn't too.

We all enjoyed the food, the readings and the atmosphere, and the café was only getting busier as we made our way out of it. Next up was the London Eye where more food and some champagne waited for us. Noah got caught up in a conversation about Stamer Hotels with both of our dads, so I wandered over to the other side of the capsule, looking out on the sparkling city below us.

"I never appreciated how beautiful London is when I was growing up here," my mom said, coming up beside me with her own glass of champagne. "It wasn't until your dad and I lived here together that I really fell in love with the city."

I could understand that. Having the right person with you made all the difference. "Is it your favourite city?"

She shook her head without hesitation. "No. I love it, but New York will always be my favourite, since it's where I learned what love really is. I suspect Vienna might be the same for you."

She was probably right, and I smiled wistfully as the memories played across my mind: the Christmas markets, the museums, the palaces, the cathedrals and the carriage ride, and, of course, The Playground. "It was the trip of a lifetime. I'll never forget it."

As if he had somehow heard my thoughts, Noah appeared behind me, wrapping his arms around me, not caring who was watching. "Neither will I."

My mom smiled at us both before going back to my dad and giving us some privacy.

"It's almost midnight, Liv," Noah said, still standing behind me, his body pressed to my back, his scent and his strength enveloping me. "Do you have any resolutions for the new year?"

"Just one," I told him.

"Which is?"

I grinned, though he couldn't see me. "To love you, and your kink, just as much as I can."

His grip tightened as his lips pressed against my temple. "How did you know exactly what I was going to say?"

My dad started out the countdown, counting down from ten as we all joined in, and when we got to one, I twisted around to face Noah and kissed him at the exact moment the new year began. Fireworks began to go off all around us, but I didn't pay them any attention. What we had right us was all the fireworks I could ever need.

~~THE END~~

Acknowledgement

The characters of Billie and Jonty as well as the Tables and Fables café in Chapter 21 are from the novel *Festive Flings* by Emma-Lee Johnson and are used here with the author's permission

IF YOU ENJOYED THIS...

The romance continues in the next book in the series, Gingerbread Gamble, focusing on Olivia's sister, Noelle. Turn the page for a preview from the first chapter!

GINGERBREAD GAMBLE

~**Noelle**~

The thumping bass of the music vibrated through my body as I peered through the crowd at the party, searching for the familiar red hair of my best friend, Eve. Wafts of beer and pizza and a dozen different perfumes and colognes all mingled together in the air as a trickle of sweat dripped down the back of my neck.

My red-and-white sweater dress seemed perfect for a December party when I put it on earlier that night, but the heat pumping out full-blast combined with the press of bodies filling every available inch of space made the small off-campus house feel like a sauna. The hair I'd spent an hour straightening beforehand had kinked into a frizzy mess and my makeup had probably started to run. Heat was not my friend.

"Have you seen Eve?" I asked a group of girls I recognized from one of the classes we had together. They all shook their heads, barely sparing me a glance as I thanked them and moved on in frustration. I'd been looking for fifteen minutes already. Where could she have gone?

When she told me twenty minutes earlier that she needed to use the restroom, I thought she'd be a couple of minutes at most. To pass the time, I made my way to the kitchen to get another drink, and there at the counter, I bumped into Corey Davison.

My mom told me that every girl has one dream guy in college, the unattainable ideal they lust after, and Corey had been mine from day one. We were in the same economics class in our freshman year and I fell hard for him, as did half the other girls in the class. Standing six foot three with dark hair, blue eyes and a jaw you could cut glass with, he could have easily been a model if hockey didn't take up so much of his time. Gorgeous and funny, he ticked every box I had for my perfect man. Over the years, we moved in a lot of the same circles and my crush only got worse with the passing of time, though I couldn't be sure he even knew my name.

But that night, when he saw me at the kitchen counter by myself, he came over to say hi, proving that he did know I existed after all. "I don't usually see you without Eve at your side," he greeted me with a charming grin that made my knees weak in a way that had nothing to do with the alcohol. "I thought you two might be surgically attached somehow."

That exaggeration had some basis in truth. Eve and I had been born on the same day, to parents who were best friends with each other. We grew up as best friends too, and even now that we were in college, we still spent a lot of time together. I hadn't realized Corey even noticed me enough to make that connection, and it flattered me that he had been paying attention.

"She's just gone to the restroom," I told him honestly, trying to keep my voice from wobbling with nerves. Part of me still couldn't believe he had approached me at all. "She'll be back soon."

"Not too soon, I hope." Still wearing that same grin, he leaned closer to me and for a brief, heart-stopping moment, I thought he might actually kiss me. Could the moment I'd been waiting more than three years for actually be about to happen? It would have been out of the blue, sure, but I wouldn't have complained.

Unfortunately, my imagination had gone a step too far. He simply reached around me to grab another beer from the counter, his strong arm brushing against me before, with a wink, he left the room and I exhaled in both pleasure and disappointment.

It might not have been much, but that conversation counted as one of the longest I'd ever had with him one-on-one. I couldn't wait to tell Eve that I'd actually flirted with my dream guy, even if calling it flirting might have been a stretch.

Not that Eve knew the identity of my mystery crush. She knew that I liked *someone*, but I had kept his name a secret even from her, too afraid that somehow word would get back to him and he would find the idea ludicrous. Though Eve naturally had some curiosity about the object of my desires, she respected my privacy enough not to push me on it. We hardly had any secrets from each other, so she understood that if I kept one, it meant I really didn't want to tell her.

However, after fifteen minutes of searching for my friend, all the excitement of what I wanted to tell her in the first place had faded, replaced with simple worry. Eve never just disappeared without giving me a heads-up. Something felt wrong.

"Hey, Noelle. Have you seen Eve?"

At first, I thought the question was in jest, that someone had heard me asking around for Eve and decided to make fun of me, but when I turned around and saw where the question came from, that thought quickly disappeared. My arch-nemesis, Aaron Speelman, stood behind me, and I would place money on the fact that he had no sense of humour at all.

While 'arch-nemesis' might have sounded a bit dramatic, it fit nonetheless. Aaron and I always seemed to be going head-to-head against each other: for top marks in our classes, on the debate team, and even in the election for student body president, which I had won by the narrowest of margins earlier that fall. When he 'congratulated' me, he made it clear why he thought I'd won.

"If Eve didn't personally campaign on your behalf with all the sports teams, it wouldn't have even been close."

"You're one to talk when Corey went to all the sororities to put in a good word for you," I argued back. Aaron and Corey were best friends just as Eve and I were; not only in the sense of being friends, but in the way that Corey and Eve were the extroverted, popular counterparts to the quieter Aaron and me.

Exactly what Corey liked about Aaron, however, I had yet to figure out.

Unlike his god-like friend, Aaron was closer to my own height, his brown hair messy and his glasses slightly bent no matter how many times he straightened them. That evening, he wore a plain button-up shirt that had come untucked from his pants, like he had started to tuck it in but lost interest half-way. Aaron always looked like he had just fallen out of bed, but not in a sexy way. I might not be as naturally beautiful as Eve, or my sister, Olivia, for that matter, but at least I made an effort. Aaron didn't seem to care at all.

"I don't know where Eve is," I answered Aaron's question. "I'm trying to find her myself."

His brow furrowed, making his glasses slide down his nose, and he pushed them back up again. "Where have you looked?"

I told him where I'd checked, which encompassed the entire ground floor and the backyard. Even though the temperature had dipped below freezing, a few people were drinking outside, but Eve hadn't been one of them.

"You haven't looked upstairs?" he asked, and I shook my head.

"It's just bedrooms up there, isn't it?"

He gave me a look that made it clear how foolish he considered that response. "That's exactly why you should be checking there."

He headed for the stairs before I could say anything else, so I hurried after him. "Wait, what are you going to do?"

"Make sure she's not in trouble," he muttered. My eyes were level with his ass as I followed him up the stairs, and I couldn't help noticing it actually filled out his Chinos rather well. I had never looked at it before, for obvious reasons.

Without any hint of embarrassment, Aaron threw open one door after another, surprising couples in various states of undress. As soon as he saw they weren't Eve, he gave a short apology, closed the door, and moved onto the next one.

Soon, only one door remained, and as we moved towards it, it opened on its own from the other side. Eve walked out a second later, stepping almost straight into Aaron who, by that time, stood right in front of her.

"Oh! Hello." She gave him a curious look before spotting me over his shoulder and flashing me an apologetic smile. "Sorry, Noelle, I should have sent you a message. I got distracted."

"Apparently." Although I felt relieved nothing bad had happened, her behaviour surprised me. Hooking up with a random guy at a party wasn't usually Eve's style. Rich, beautiful and confident, she could have any guy she wanted, and she almost always made them work for it. Though she was no virgin, a quickie in someone else's bedroom didn't usually fall within the Eve Stamer playbook.

Before I could figure out what any of it meant, the guy she'd been in the room with appeared in the doorway behind her, and my heart dropped down to my feet.

"Did we keep you waiting?" Corey asked with a laugh, double checking that he'd done his fly up before he put his arm around Eve and walked past Aaron and I down the hall, looking incredibly pleased with himself. "Have fun, kids."

Eve gave me a smile too, letting Corey lead her along. "See you downstairs."

Oh, God, no. Feeling suddenly dizzy, I leaned back against the wall, my head swimming not just from the heat but from the thumping of my heart and the churning of my stomach. Corey and Eve? Out of every guy in the world, why did it have to be him? In a stunned stupor, I watched as Corey's hand moved down Eve's back, palming her ass before they headed down the stairs together.

Even in my disappointment and heartache, I couldn't blame her for a second. She had no idea how I felt since I had never told her, and who wouldn't jump at the chance to be with Corey? I certainly would have.

The situation left me so dumbfounded that it took me a moment to realize what Corey had meant by his comment about keeping us waiting: he thought Aaron and I wanted to use the bedroom ourselves. Self-consciously, I glanced over at Aaron, taking a step further away from him while Aaron scowled at his friend's retreating back.

"Fuck," was all he said before heading into the bedroom and slamming the door behind him, leaving me in the empty hallway while moans and grunts drifted through the other closed doors and the party carried on downstairs.

Though I'd grown used to being the runner-up in so many ways, as I stood there with my back against the wall, my heart breaking inside my too-warm dress and not even my best friend to confide in, I had never felt quite so insignificant.

~**Aaron**~

Standing above my best friend as he slept, his arms thrown wide across the bed and his mouth open as he snored loudly, I couldn't help thinking how easy it would be to cover his stupid, good-looking face with a pillow and put an end to his suffering.

Or maybe just my suffering. To be fair, he seemed perfectly content. He'd probably never suffered a day in his life. The state of his room, filled with dirty laundry and takeout food containers that the maid hadn't cleaned up yet, seemed to support that theory.

With a sigh, I pushed my uncharacteristically dark thoughts out of my head. Killing him would be a step too far. Cutting his dick off would suffice, but I didn't do that either. Giving his shoulder a hard shove, I simply woke him up instead. "Get up, Corey. It's almost nine, we have to get to the airport."

He groaned, rolled over and covered his eyes with his arm. "Fuck off, Aaron."

Not satisfied with that response, I grabbed hold of his covers, pulled them off, and immediately regretted it. "For fuck's sake. You can't sleep with some clothes on?"

"The ladies don't complain," he replied, turning back to me with a grin, not bothered in the least by his exposure. "Neither does your mom."

"So original. You're such a child." I threw the covers back at him. "You've got twenty minutes before we need to leave. I'm going without you if you're not ready."

He ruined my dramatic exit by calling out after me: "No, you're not. You won't leave me behind and you know it."

Just because he was right didn't mean I had to tell him so. We both knew I would have never been invited on this trip if not for my friendship with Corey. The wealthiest, most popular students in our senior year were spending the next ten days together in a massive house in the faux-alpine town of Leavenworth, Washington. Though I didn't qualify as either rich or popular, my status as Corey's best friend got me in by default.

The destination had taken me by surprise when Corey told me where we were going. Wouldn't the Caribbean be a lot more fun, not to mention warmer, I wondered? But when he explained that Eve Stamer chose it because of her love for all things Christmas, that changed things. If Eve liked something, I could learn to like it too.

Besides, Corey said we wouldn't be spending our time going on sleigh rides or baking cookies anyway. Twenty horny college students on a big break together before our final term and graduation would lead to all kinds of adult fun, and he promised me it would be the perfect time to hook up with any of the girls. I only had interest in one of them, though, which I told him shortly before he slept with her himself three days before.

"It just happened," was his only explanation when I confronted him about his hook-up with Eve the following day. "I can't explain it. We've never really been attracted to each other before, but last night, it just clicked."

I had a pretty good idea what made it 'click' for him: the moment when I admitted to him just how much I liked her. Listening to me talk about all of Eve's good qualities, he suddenly paid a lot more attention to her than ever before. Seeing me getting ready to make my move, he swooped in first. He wanted her because I did, and whatever Corey wanted, he got. It never occurred to him that it would be otherwise.

"It's not just a one-night stand," he added, which only made it worse. "I think she might be the real deal."

And now, instead of using this trip to try to make my move with Eve, I would have to sit back and watch the two of them together instead. Given the situation, I had considered not going at all, but the devil on my shoulder pointed out that Corey might easily do something to screw it up, especially with a lot of alcohol involved and other pretty women around. That thought convinced me to suck it up and go ahead anyway. If he screwed up bad enough, Eve might need some support. I'd seen him break plenty of hearts before, and I would rather not see Eve be next on that list.

Ten minutes after I told him we needed to leave, Corey hauled his ass downstairs and out to my waiting car. I'd left it running because of the cold December weather, silently counting up the cost of the gas I was wasting. "You're late," I told him tersely when he pulled the passenger door closed.

"Which is why you planned for us to get to the airport an hour early anyway," he pointed out, completely accurately. "We're fine, bro. Chill."

That could be Corey's motto in life, but it didn't work for me. While Corey coasted through life, relying on his charm and good looks to get him through, I had no such assets. I worked hard for everything I had, relying on my intelligence to do the heavy lifting. People might not like me the way they liked Corey, but they had to respect me. I planned everything in advance, leaving nothing to chance. How the two of us ended up as best friends remained a mystery to everyone, including us. He drove me crazy, but he also pulled me out of myself, making me take risks I never would have otherwise.

Risks like this trip, for one. I had no control over anything for the next ten days, and that both terrified and exhilarated me. Anything might be possible, including a chance to really get to know Eve Stamer, so long as I could get her out of Corey's greedy grasp.

Despite Corey's tardiness, we were the first of the group at the airport, and he took a seat across from me in the waiting area once we were through the security checks, leaning back and placing a hat over his face. "Wake me up when someone interesting gets here."

My eyes rolled so hard that my glasses slipped down my nose. Seriously, what did I see in this jerk?

Thankfully, only a few minutes passed until the next people arrived, including the most interesting person I could think of: Eve Stamer herself. She'd pulled her red hair back in a messy bun above the cashmere turtleneck she wore over her skinny jeans and brown boots, looking like she'd just stepped off the pages of a magazine, as usual. My pulse immediately increased, as it did every time I laid eyes on her.

"I told you we were going to be too early," she complained, her gaze completely skipping over me as she looked around. "There's nobody else here."

"Aaron's here," another voice pointed out. I hadn't noticed Noelle until she spoke, but of course she would have been there. She and Eve were inseparable.

In contrast to Eve's casual elegance, Noelle always looked like she tried too hard. Though her brown hair naturally curled, she always tried to straighten it, making it frizzy instead. Her makeup looked too heavy for the time of day and she seemed uncomfortable in the clothes she'd chosen, pulling at the fabric over her stomach, just like she had in her sweater dress at the party the other day.

"I think that's Corey under the hat," Noelle added. Interest immediately sparked in Eve's eyes as she walked over and took the seat next to him, ignoring me entirely.

"Are you hiding from me?" she asked, poking him in the ribs.

"Why don't you come and hide with me?" He lifted his hat enough that he could pull her close for a kiss before putting the hat back in place, leaving the rest to our imaginations.

Unfortunately, I had a pretty damn good imagination.

Noelle looked just about as thrilled with the new situation between our friends as I did, grimacing as she took a seat across from them, leaving a few empty seats between us. "Hey, Aaron."

"Hey." Aside from arguing with each other in debate club or in the classes we had together or when we competed for student body president, Noelle and I had never really had a proper conversation. I knew nothing about her on a personal level and she knew nothing about me.

Luckily, the rest of the group started trickling in so our awkward small talk only lasted a few minutes. My relief over that was short-lived, though, as Corey pulled me to one side when we all stood up to board the plane. "Can you switch places with Eve for the flight?"

He couldn't be serious. "It's a five-hour flight, Corey. I don't want to sit next to someone I don't know."

"You know her," he assured me. "It's Nolie... whatever her name is. Eve's friend."

The self-centred bastard couldn't even remember the name of the girl he'd helped me campaign against, the one I'd complained about multiple times. When I raised my eyebrows in disbelief, he groaned.

"Come on, just watch a movie or whatever, you don't have to talk to her. I promise I'll make it worth your while. Any girl you want on this trip, I'll put in a good word for you."

The only girl I wanted, he'd already claimed for himself, but I gave in anyway, knowing he would wear me down until I did. I gave him the cold shoulder as we boarded the plane, jostling with all the other people travelling before the holidays, everyone carrying their winter coats along with their carry-on bags. By the time we reached them, Noelle and Eve were already getting settled in their seats.

"How about you come and sit next to me instead?" Corey asked Eve, giving her the smile that no girl seemed able to resist. "Aaron wants to sit with Nol... with your friend."

At least he skipped over mangling her name, but putting the blame on me for the seat switch was a stretch and he knew it. Noelle looked ready to protest, but she didn't have a chance; Eve had already gotten to her feet. "That sounds great. See you guys there!" she exclaimed as she headed a few rows back to sit next to Corey instead, taking all my hopes with her.

With a sigh, I dropped into Eve's abandoned seat. "Sorry," I apologized to Noelle. "I had no say in this either, so you don't have to pretend to be happy about it. You don't need to talk to me or anything."

"Yeah, thanks," she mumbled, shoving some earbuds in before turning to look out the window, intent on ignoring me already.

Five hours had never seemed so long.

~Noelle~

Eve and I rarely fought, but at that moment, things were tense between us. Ever since the party, she'd done nothing but gush about Corey and I couldn't take much more of it.

"You always said you didn't understand his appeal," I reminded her the morning after the party as we lounged around in our shared dorm room. Sitting cross-legged on my bed, I did my best to keep my voice level so as not to betray my level of investment in this conversation. "Every time another girl talked about him, you said you couldn't see the big deal."

That had been the other reason I never told Eve about my crush. Mostly, I wanted to avoid the crippling humiliation I would have suffered if Corey ever found out about it and didn't return my feelings, but also, I knew Eve wouldn't have approved. She would have told me I could do better, though where she got that idea from, I couldn't guess. Aside from Eve, the only people who had ever considered me a catch were my parents, and they didn't count. Everyone else saw me only as Eve's less attractive friend or the plainer of the two Hanmer girls.

"Oh, I still don't think he's anyone I could be serious with," she assured me. "The guy's all style and no substance, but right now, that's kind of what I want, you know? It's just a bit of fun. We're almost done with college, this is our last chance to just be young and stupid. In just a few months, we'll have real jobs and big decisions to make. Why not enjoy ourselves while we can? And I can assure you, I enjoyed it."

Hearing the details of exactly what happened between her and Corey might just have made me sick, so I jumped on the first part of what she'd said instead, about how this wouldn't be a serious relationship. "So, this is just a one-time thing?"

The idea of Eve and Corey together at all still stung, but I could have dealt with a drunken hookup at a party.

Unfortunately, Eve shook her head, a satisfied smile playing on her lips. "He's asked me to come over tonight, and we've got that trip coming up. It'd be fun to have someone to do couples things with."

My heart sank even further. Ever since the trip to Leavenworth had first been mentioned, I had imagined Corey and I together: ice skating hand-in-hand, going on the sleigh ride, having a snowball fight, kissing in front of the fire, making gingerbread together. It would be the perfect Christmas romance, and now, Eve would get to live out my dream with a guy that she didn't even really like that much.

If I told her how I felt, she would probably back off, but realistically, what claim did I have on him? He'd never given me any indication he might be interested in me, and for all I knew, he really liked Eve. What right did I have to interfere?

Over the next couple of days, I did my best to accept things the way they were, but Eve noticed my lack of enthusiasm anyway. When she asked me why I seemed upset and I tried to insist otherwise, that only made things worse. She informed me bluntly that she had been looking forward to this trip all term and wouldn't let me ruin it by pouting the whole time, so I should either tell her what was bothering me or get over it.

And now, she abandoned me on the plane, leaving me with Aaron freaking Speelman instead. Would it be too late to just get off the plane and stay home? Right now, that sounded preferable to being stuck with Corey's annoying best friend for the whole trip while *my* best friend made out with the guy I'd always wanted.

Aaron said I didn't have to talk to him, and I had no intention of it. Instead, I put my earbuds in and looked out the window at the grey December sky above the Newark runway, trying not to cry in frustration. Ten days of this I had to get through, ten days that I could have just been home with my family enjoying the Christmas season instead of feeling like the third wheel in a relationship that I would prefer to see crash and burn.

Aaron pulled out his laptop next to me as soon as the plane had levelled out in the air, and his typing only made me more irritated. He had actually brought along work to do on this trip, while I had purposefully left all mine behind, trying to focus on having a good time instead. Now, that seemed like a ridiculous pipe dream.

Another half hour passed in silence during which I glanced over at his screen every now and then. The paper he was working on had been assigned for a philosophy class we were both in, one that I had only begun making notes for. In spite of myself, I had to admit I found his argument rather compelling. It certainly beat the self-pitying thoughts in my head, and before long, I found myself caught up in it.

"You misused that phrase." I hadn't meant to speak the words out loud, but apparently, I did, since Aaron glanced over at me, his eyes narrowed behind his black, thick-framed glasses.

"Excuse me?"

Since I couldn't pretend I hadn't said it, I repeated myself, pointing at his screen. "Here, you said 'a priori' when you meant 'a posteriori'. Personally, I wouldn't use either though. It makes you sound pretentious."

"I don't remember asking for your opinion," he muttered under his breath, but he scrolled up and deleted the words anyway. "You've got nothing better to do than read over my shoulder?"

"Not really. Eve and I were planning on getting drunk on the flight so I didn't bring anything else to do."

His jaw tightened for no reason I could think of. "Well, you've got a call button on your seat. Don't let me stop you."

"It's not the same on my own," I pointed out. "Drinking by myself is just sad."

"So, if I have a glass of wine, you'll have one too and stop pouting?" His eyes were still on the computer screen rather than on me, but I could imagine the condescending look in them anyway. It didn't help that he'd used exactly the same word Eve had used to describe my behaviour.

"I'm not pouting. I'm stating a fact."

"No, you're pouting." He closed the laptop lid and turned to face me. I'd never been this close to him before, close enough to really see his eyes behind his glasses. They were actually a rather interesting shade of hazel, and for just a second, I wondered what he would look like without the glasses on. "Red or white?"

"What?" The question made no sense to me, and his jaw clenched again.

"Wine," he said slowly, as if speaking to a child. "You wanted a drink. Do you want red or white wine?"

"Oh. Red, please." I couldn't tell if something had upset him too or if he was always like this, but drinking with him sounded better than drinking on my own, so I answered him as graciously as possible.

He flagged down a flight attendant and ordered us both a drink, paying for it even though I tried to insist I could cover my own. He could be surprisingly firm when he wanted to be. "Cheers," he gritted through his teeth as he raised his glass.

I followed suit, draining my glass quickly in the hopes that the alcohol would help. Aaron's eyebrows raised as he watched me swallow it all down, but he kept his mouth shut.

In the silence that lingered afterwards, I spoke instead. "Why did you bring your laptop along?" I asked, pointing at the computer that still sat on his table. "We're supposed to be on vacation."

"Not every minute of the day will be filled," he replied in that calm, analytical way of his that always got under my skin. "I might as well be productive when there's nothing else to do."

"You could just, I don't know, talk to people." I shrugged as I raised my glass again, trying to get every last drop out.

"People like you who would rather ignore me?"

He had a point, but I pursed my lips at him anyway. "I wouldn't have ignored you if you'd chosen to sit next to me, but you're only here because you were forced into it, same as me."

He huffed into his glass, neither confirming nor denying that. When he'd finished his wine too, he held the glass up. "Another one?"

"Please." The more, the better.

Aaron got us both another drink, and another one after that. With each one, we talked a little more. We complained about people who were chronically late and the fact that no one had any kind of itinerary for this trip we were on. We laughed about the way our philosophy professor always accidentally stapled his sweater to the papers he brought to class, and we talked about the limited power of the student body government.

He actually could be somewhat interesting to talk to, at least with alcohol involved. Clearly, I started to feel far too comfortable, because when Eve walked past on her way to the restroom, giving us a wave as she went by without bothering to stop and say hi, my eyes narrowed after her and Aaron immediately noticed.

"Is something going on between you two? Are you fighting?"

I shook my head slowly. "We don't fight, exactly, but I can't say I'm thrilled about her and Corey together."

"You and me both," I thought he muttered under his breath, though the wine might have made me imagine it.

"What?"

He quickly shook his head. "Nothing. What's your problem with Eve and Corey? You think he's going to hurt her?"

I snorted in a very unladylike way. I had no concerns about that at all. If anyone ended up getting hurt, my money would be on Corey. "I just don't think it'll work out. They're not right for each other."

I tried to keep things vague but Aaron wouldn't be put off. He kept asking questions. "Because he's a player?"

I wouldn't use that word for him. He might date a lot, but it just meant he hadn't found the right girl yet. "He's perfect," I thought.

At least, I *thought* I thought it, but as Aaron's eyes grew wider behind his glasses, my heart began to race.

Oh, shit. Did I really just say that out loud? To Corey's best friend?

How in the world could I talk my way out of that?

MORE FROM THE AUTHOR

<u>Contemporary Romance – 18+</u>

Callahan Series
A Matter of Time
A Piece of Land
A Change of Heart
A Work of Art

Christmas in the City Series
Mistletoe Mistake
Candy Cane Challenge
Tinsel Temptation
Gingerbread Gamble
Stocking Standoff
Eggnog Experiment

Standalones
Leading Lady
A Set of Three
Charity Case
Hired Lover

<u>Contemporary Romance – New Adult/Clean</u>

It Figures duet
It Figures
Figuring It Out

<u>Historical Romance – 18+</u>

Lady in Waiting Series
Lady in Waiting
King in Training
Princess in Hiding

<u>Paranormal Romance – 18+</u>

Cold Lake Pack Series
The Curse and the Prophecy
The Spell and the Legacy
The Dream and the Destiny

Mismatched Mates Series
Mismatched Mates
Misguided Motives
Mistaken Meanings

Serena's Story
The Alpha's Second Chance
The Returned Mate
The Vampire's Consort

Sacrifice Series
Blood Donor
Life Giver

Paranormal Romance – New Adult/Clean

The Alpha's Prey

KEEP IN TOUCH

Daily updates from my works-in-progress, bonus chapters and more can be found on my Ream account, Chilli & Chocolate, along with Emma Lee-Johnson:
https://reamstories.com/chilliandchocolate

You can find and follow me on Facebook at:
facebook.com/melodytyden

Join the Facebook group Melody's Romance Corner for fun games, interaction with the author and exclusive news and excerpts.

You can also sign up to my newsletter at www.melodytyden.com for all the latest news.

www.ingramcontent.com/pod-product-compliance
Lightning Source LLC
Chambersburg PA
CBHW072052190726
48294CB00005B/1481